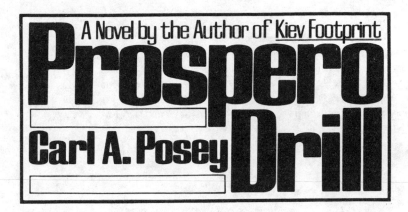

A Novel by the Author of <u>Kiev Footprint</u>

Prospero Drill

Carl A. Posey

Library of Congress Cataloging in Publication Data

Posey, Carl A.
    Prospero Drill.

    I. Title.
PS3566.067P7   1986   813'.54   85-25169
ISBN 0-312-65198-8

First U.S. Edition, 1985

First published in Great Britain by Robert Hale Ltd.

10 9 8 7 6 5 4 3 2 1

For my Father and my Son,
the other flying Carls.

...I have bedimm'd
The noontide sun, call'd forth the mutinous winds,
And 'twixt the green sea and the azur'd vault
Set roaring war; to the dread rattling thunder
Have I given fire, and rifted Jove's stout oak
With his own bolt; ...

Prospero, in *The Tempest*, V-I

Author's Note

Although I have great admiration for the men and women who fly and try to comprehend the hurricane, they make no appearance here. Beyond some fundamental scientific principles and historical fact, the people and events depicted here are fictional, and any resemblance to persons, living or dead, is purely coincidental.

I gratefully acknowledge the generous help of two high-time pilots – Fred Werley, of NOAA, for introducing me to the flight deck of a modern research aircraft: and Captain Bill Johnson, U.S. Navy (Ret.), for his valuable review and comment on the aviation in *Prospero Drill*.

My vision widens its grey fringe. I seem to
return, awakening in a shattered cage of
wind and noise. My right leg glistens with
moist red curds, but no pain troubles me.
The control wheel fidgets in the gentle grasp
of the automatic pilot. We fly a shallow turn,
circling, circling eternally ...

THE DRILL
Thursday
T + 2 h 23 m
Lat 23.8 N
Long 84.3 W

The windscreen tugs my eye with a spiderweb of cracks,
prismatic, beautiful with light in the trapezoidal metal frame.
Glass shards flake off the ruined windows and fly gleaming into
the shadowed roaring cavern behind me. My eye follows the
flying glass and comes to our flight engineer, lying where the
explosion threw him, a big man named Bruska, crumpled now,
his torn thorax revealing yellow fat, purple organs; he is still.
The blood on me is his. My throat palpitates with nausea. I
raise my line of sight to the horizon.

Three meters ahead of us the barber-striped gust probe
leads our airplane on its orbit, which holds us in the
cloudwalled cylinder of hurricane Dolly's eye. I watch the
churning, elongated clouds that winds have ragged into the
flat, hard wall of white between us and the tempest. Then,
weakened by the sight, I turn away.

Where is the copilot? Gone. The right hand side window is
edged with him, where pressure squeezed him out. Peterson.
The memory rims my sight with darkness ...

I occupy the pilot's seat on the left side of the ruined cockpit.
But the pilot stirs behind me. His damaged breathing rattles
down the intercom, fills all the headsets in the plane; Newman.
I look at him, find him grey, pressed against the small metal
table of the mission scientist's station, holding his chest shut
with both hands. But his eyes are open, clear with pain, and
stare into mine. "Call Bradenton," he says into his mike. Each
word cracks his broken chest, increases his leaks. I nod. I look
beyond the pilot, through the cockpit door. Sorel lies in the
aisle, watches me with empty eyes. Others move towards us,
slow as swimmers.

I think of Dolly, of what we have done, what the fly has done
inside the old woman who swallowed it. I guess she'll die. My
mind rejects alternative possibilities: the storm, somehow
deflected by our intercession, intensifies and spins south

eastward, ripping into Cuba, and, because of Prospero, forcing us toward that larger storm of fire and fallout; or the hurricane veers more to the north east, destroying the Keys before it howls into Miami and the coastal cities, to tear at the sandy foundations of all those condos and hotels.

Ah, God, I think. Ah, God. I am at the end of every tether now. Responsibility for all this stalks me like a large and hungry animal, for I know my motives for permitting what I might have stopped were small, possibly vicious, probably silly. No large insanities or fine national interests blinded me; so that I am left more accountable for the day's mistakes and consequences than Sorel, or those who used us so casually to fight their endless war.

I shake my head to clear it, and tell myself: In a plane awash with real blood, don't fret over what is figurative. Look where you are, think what you have to do ...

Reminded that my hands hold our future, that I will finally save us or feed us to our doom, my fingers tremble, my knees go weak. I try to remember whom I kill with the smallness of my aeronautical experience, and think of Rory – God, even my love lives or dies with me today. I try to remember who is here besides, and who is dead.

And, thinking of the dead, I think of Prospero.

"Prospero is dead. I'm sorry." Ted Grose told us this in his deep, thuggish New Jersey voice. The ugly words meant that our Prospero had been killed by enemies, killed by them again; and, because Grose was one of us, and because he was a gentleman, one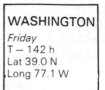

also heard, between the sounds, something like: I wanted it to go this year as much as you did, we fought the good fight, and still they killed Prospero. "I'm sorry," he repeated in a softer voice.

Sorel and I reacted in much the same way, both stricken into the silence such words of dying bring. For we had been prepared to tell them Prospero was ready, waiting only for an opportunity that met our guidelines, to brief them on the logistics of the experiment, the promising hints from simulations made of numbers, new increments of aircraft instrumentation – the details of a major experiment finally about to begin. Instead we had this word of Prospero's murder, a purely technical kind of death, perhaps, and yet one that would engender real death, reaping what was sown this August afternoon in Maryland. It makes me bitter and sad to recall it.

Grose was our agency's administrator, a meteorologist as we were, decent, middle sized, his only vanity a brunette wig which floated above the large wise forehead. Next to him sat Carney, our resident two-star admiral, ruddy and Irish-faced. He had eschewed his admiral's costume for a grey silk suit, and watched us with the pale neutral eyes of the military man among civilians, giving us his soft outsides, watching from a hardened interior. He deferred to Grose, who ranked him in the hierarchy of government; but, where Grose traveled economy class, our house admiral could always find one of those Navy jet bombers whose bomb-bay had been silkened for flag grade officers.

Pete Thompson, a grey-faced long-hair from Budget, was there, his angularities curled into a chair, his small bright eyes reading my dislike, across the polished table. So was Jonas, the science guy from the State Department, neat and clean and nearly faceless, no doubt a resident spook of some sort, dressed in the natty seersucker of diplomacy.

A small group, to do away with something the size and weight of Prospero; and unalike, their only common feature was that now, seeing our grief, they viewed us with mild apprehension, as though Sorel or I would leap across the huge conference table and grab them by their throats. But, there was more in the room than just the people. With them came the presence of State and Defense, those big federal departments that dwarfed our small, billion-a-year agency, departments that could totally lose track of budgets like ours down in the noise somewhere. And there was the White House …

"No one pretends this is a scientific decision," Jonas was saying in a voice that seemed to want to call us boys: Not to worry, boys. "It's purely a political problem, and it's got the attention of the White House. We've got these stories about hurricanes being seeded to dry up the Mexican west coast, or to suffocate the Cuban sugar harvest …"

"Crap," Sorel said, breaking silence.

"Of course it's crap, of course," Jonas exclaimed cheerfully, "but it's also part of the perceived reality down there. What you perceive, well, that's your life, Henry."

"Those stories ran years ago," Sorel muttered angrily. "Years ago. And now you're saying Prospero has to pay for them? Come on."

"It just took a while for them to percolate into what you'd call the inner consciousness of the White House, Henry. Now they have, at an ex*tremely* critical juncture …"

"Well, we all read the papers," Grose put in. "I don't think we need to go back through that here."

"Of course not," Jonas agreed, before racing on. "But all the papers care about right now is that the Soviet Union has injected these new planes into Cuba …"

"Stormbats," Carney put in lazily. He seemed merely to drone, but he could make a room, even one with Jonas in it, go quiet and attentive. "Nuclear capable, long-range, all-weather. *Very* high capability. *Very* provocative move. We tell the Soviet Union, Take them home. They tell us Stormbat's unarmed, instrumented for hurricane research. Horseshit, we reply diplomatically. But we can't prove they're armed or instrumented. Could be both. Could be true. The Russian navy operates in the world ocean. They need to know something about hurricanes. Maybe it's level. Maybe it's not; we assume not." He looked around the table, then withdrew himself once more into his drowsing, attentive silence.

"That's where we get closure," Jonas put in now, using the skewed vogue word for the linking of events. He picked up such terms like a blue suit hoarding lint, and we had laughed about the power such words had over him; now, in a way, we were paying for it. "Just by claiming to be into hurricane research, they raise the issue of Prospero and entrain the agency into a problem that should have proceeded at a very high level between the U.S. and Soviet Union. We're innocent bystanders, sure. But we're still victims."

"We often are," Sorel said bitterly.

"For small federal agencies, it's the equivalent of the human condition," budgetman Thompson put in.

Annoyed by any intelligence but his own, Jonas pressed on, "But we *are* entrained at this point in time, and we really can't escape it. Everyone sees the parallels with the missile crisis in '62. Everyone hears about the messages flying back and forth. But no one – and I mean, no one – is sure how close we are to a flashpoint. We have a new administration. The new man in Russia is an unknown quantity. Cuba is *always* a wild card. And what they claim to be hurricane research planes lie at the centre of these tensions. Do we add to this set of flammables an experiment that, in the perceived reality of Cuba, is a CIA plot to destroy the sugar crop? I don't think so. Neither does the – the, uh, White House."

At this reminder of Jonas's true connections, Grose looked at us unhappily, his characteristically sad eyes sadder. Here was a good man trying to keep himself and his agency in one piece against the uncertainties and intrigues that always enter office with a new administration, and heavy pressure from federal elephants like State and Defense. I felt as sorry for him as he seemed to feel for us. "I think we've been taken for a bit of a ride on this. But I don't see any chance of saving Prospero at this point. It's caught in too many other currents. We can't do much beyond watch it get swept away."

"You know, Ted," Sorel said in an even English voice, "this isn't the first fucking we've taken because of some failure of nerve in Washington. It looks to me as if we get raped every time we come through the neighbourhood. What would you have us do this time, tear everything down, turn the planes into Miami diners? What?"

Grose shook his head in gentle reprimand. "We don't need that, Henry. We *do* need research, we still need to expand our understanding of hurricanes. We can do that without seeding them. When you get a storm, you can still fly research missions into it. This isn't the end of the world, Henry."

"Only the end of the world is the end of the world, Ted."

The admiral stirred once more. "You know," he began with great deliberation, "it seems to me you might benefit by using the flying money remaining this hurricane season to hone your technique a bit. I mean, it would make a lot of sense for you to try a full-scale drill on the next one, if there *is* a next one, so that when you finally get your chance to seed, all the, uh, choreography will be in place." Later I would remember the long stare Sorel and Carney exchanged, and how the admiral looked as if he knew in a rough way, at least, what would follow. Of course he did. People like me tend to underestimate the craft and power and will of admirals and generals. Carney, somnolent as a warm bee, already had us locked up, already had inoculated this still-unformed Prospero rehearsal with latent death.

"God, what a lot of cock this is," Sorel told the room wearily. "I don't see much point in staying on." He stood up with the world on his shoulders, snapped shut his venerable leather case and said, "Goodbye, gentlemen." And, to me, "Come on, Jake."

He left the table, the administrator's great airy office, like a parachutist, seeming almost to leap out of the place on his athletic, long-legged stride, out and across the expanse of beige carpet before the well-dressed middle-aged secretaries grazing there could utter, "Goodbye, Dr Sorel," although they said it anyway, futilely, like people waving after a departing airplane.

I kept my seat, and more than kept it: I made myself heavy in the big, leathered library chair. Sorel's temperamental rushes were the contemptible part of him, but they swept my emotions like the gravitational field of a passing planet; there was always all that hell and chaos while he made his angry transit. Yes, but, in fact, he *was* the Jupiter in our little system, so that my own gravitational field caved in early during these encounters.

So for an embarrassing and interminable couple of minutes I stayed where I was, slowly gathering my papers. Grose gave me a tired, half-smiling shake of the head as reassurance, the others fidgeted away time in the brightly windowed office, giving Sorel, the residual aura of him, time to get out of sight, out of the building. It would spare their having to talk to him later, avoid a scene between senior people. No, that is too bitter by half, for Grose *had* tried for us. I was raw and hurt by the death of Prospero, and now it's difficult to remember anything but the little garden of death Carney and perhaps Jonas began to plant that afternoon. Finally, I rose, murmured goodbye and trotted after Sorel, hearing one of the secretaries fling after me, "Have a nice *flight*, Dr Warner."

I caught up with Sorel at the elevator and boarded with him. Suspended in the tiny cage with this tall, lithe man in his middle fifties – a man with the rosy face of a mean British boy, flushed with anger now, the mauve cheeks accentuated by the mop of straight white hair – I felt him worldlessly transmitting his mood: fucked again, fucked again. It was my mood too. We had lost the world; our world anyway.

The experiment called Prospero, we used to hear, was Sorel's whole life. Well, it had also become mine, and the central part of everybody's back in the Miami lab. Most of us came to it as converts from early skepticism, beginning with the idea that seeding a hurricane wouldn't produce much of anything in the way of an effect because, in simple terms, it was too big and we were too small. Then going over (and over, and *over*) data from the last real seeding – hurricane Debby, in 1969 – one began to believe that the observed reduction in maximum winds of about 30 percent after one of the seedings might have been more than just natural variability. We began to see, to believe in, a human signal in that faltering wind; after that the hook seated itself and we settled into the project – a complicated kind of aerial ballet within a hurricane in which we would, with relatively little seeding agent, try to turn the immense energies of the storm against it, causing it to expand, to slow, to weaken. We saw ourselves running a ten-million-dollar project that could produce a billion dollar's worth of saved life and property. Like pilgrims bent upon good works, we set out through science and technology to do it.

Conventional wisdom held that nobody but Henry Sorel could put such a project together, so thoroughly did it combine the ideas of science and technology, the public good, research aviation and other not quite congruent elements. Maybe so. Sorel had got the new planes, the big computer, the talented people, and he had kept Prospero together against the forces that tend to tear federal projects apart in an agency where ten million still means a lot of money. Sorel had kept husbanding and managing the thing. It was he who named it for Shakespeare's weather-changing magician in *The Tempest*, and got the mathematical models running and the theory into intelligible forms, so that, after five years of his leadership, we'd reached the point where we could go critical on Prospero, and really learn whether seeding a hurricane would weaken its winds, without producing some other, possibly more destructive effects.

That had been three years ago, and then, as today, the decision had gone against Prospero. Three years ago they'd taken a day and a half to reach the decision. Today the whole thing, from opening remarks to murderous conclusion, had run less than an hour. Next year they'd do it in a memo. "Next year they'll do it in a memo," I said to Sorel.

"Maybe to you, Jake. But not to me." The thin Midlands voice vibrated with his anger.

"Come on, Henry."

"Yes, come on, Henry. People've been saying that to me all afternoon. Maybe you can spare me it."

"Sure." I flushed. These moments spent on eggshells while Sorel cooled down were not my favorites. They reminded me I labored as an understudy to an older actor of undiminishing power and industry, a job that could kill (or, more likely, pickle) you with a particular kind of uncomfortable inactivity. One hated always to be deferring to the larger emotion.

The elevator jiggled to a landing and we went out through the grey tiled entrance hall and left the building, which had been new a decade ago but was beginning to come apart now.

"They'll have to recycle the whole suburb in another year or two," I said into our silence.

"I don't know. Maybe they'll rehabilitate the place with the ten million they just cut off me." He imitated a smile. "I'm not going to take anything out on you, Jake. But it left me feeling most shitty, to have them gut us again, and do it over some insanity in fucking Mexico, or fucking *Cuba*." He closed his eyes for a moment. Then, "Look, I can't do eight hours in your little plane today. The noise is terrible and the Martinis lack flavor. Drop me at National and go see your wife and child. And we can talk about our future, if we have one, Monday in Miami ...?"

"Okay." Then, to say something relevant, and because my deeper feelings are not much on display, I added, "You understand that I'm disappointed too."

"Oh, sure, I know that. That's why we needn't talk till Monday."

This was in August, a season that bakes out Washington and its suburbs, the jungly green going brown around the edges, the ochre cloud of smog above the metropolitan area more persistent, a deeper yellow, than in spring. Still, it made the blood rise to be out on the beltway with the Maryland hills and trees flashing by, the Potomac rushing over those big rocks out west of town, and the parkway along the Virginia side all big hardwood deciduous, the shining river slowing and broadening toward town. This stretch of parkway remained one of the places my mind went when the endless summer of Miami got me down.

I dropped Sorel at National Airport while we were still trapped in the sluggish eddy of traffic that drifts outside the main terminal. He hurried off, his white hair flying like an angry flag, and soon one of the automatic doors swallowed him. It left me feeling lonely. I could see back in a corner of my mood the big wingless bird of depression begin to stir, and tried to put a frame around it. This didn't get me out of the terminal traffic any sooner, but I felt less like somebody trying to turn over in a covered box. Ah, well, I knew the feeling. It wasn't all Sorel and Prospero. It had to do with visiting Lenore.

She lived in a Spanishy nest of condominiums called Pyrenees Village in one of the corporate freeforms that spread like living cells from the Potomac south. The white towers of the place formed an island of stucco in the sea of red and beige and white brick that covers this corner of Virginia. Between the stylishness of the Village and its distance from town, I'd always thought she had opted for nothing instead of something.

We started out together in a life that felt moderately uncomfortable for both of us, and had moved up a couple of times until we lived in one of those blond-brick and redwood Colonials on a tenth of an acre of Arlington. Back then I'd been at agency headquarters and Sorel still graced what we called the university sector, occasionally making rain for farmers, or trying to. When Lenore – Lennie, for we steered around the Edgar Allen Poe thing in her name – and I split up we cleared nearly sixty thousand dollars on the house, and we split that the way we had our life together: raggedly, down my side of the middle. She might give the same definition.

I guess we accomplished the break without too much bitterness, although amicable divorce is not something I understand, and the oppressed, headachy malaise that came to me just ahead of these infrequent visits may have flowed from hatred. But give Lennie her due. The marriage hadn't been bad for me, and I'd loved her, and my boy Charlie was everything to me; whereas she'd been quietly – almost quietly – suffocating. When Charlie got to school she went to work for an Arlington PR firm, and when it came time for me to go on to Miami and what later became Prospero, she couldn't turn loose of the life she'd made. Hell, you couldn't blame her. I didn't offer to quit the agency in deference to her career, either.

The consensus among our Washington friends must have been that we parted pals, mainly because our screaming had been kept between us, and probably because our marriage was already worn out when it exceeded its elastic limits. By the time we snapped apart I don't even think we cared much what happened with old Charlie, who normally haunts me enough that I can't think of him without a surge of grief. I don't mean he is gone, dead, or anything. I only mean he makes me sad and guilty that he has no home except the Spanishy nest in northern Virginia, and no dad except when he comes down to suffer through a month of the Miami summer with me. Maybe my feelings reflected a faint terror that caught me when, looking into his eyes, I saw a bottomless pit he urged me silently somehow to fill. At 9 he lives on the border between being a big kid and being a littlely – his hand still enters mine sometimes when we're walking, but it happens less and less.

I always stopped in on these Washington trips, and it was always a slap, to enter Lennie's world and find it so constantly unfamiliar. We had ground rules. I refused to call before dropping in. And I refused to follow her lead and call her place "Lennie and Charlie's." They weren't a couple and I wasn't going to make them one.

Lennie opened the door when I rang, swinging the big antiqued wooden slab past her so that she seemed to appear in what film people call an optical wipe, suddenly filling the frame, larger than life, and a powerful reminder that one had once had a beautiful wife.

"Jake," she said. Her voice had never quite grown up; a high school sound echoed in it perpetually. Her pale eyes held just a touch of humor, and she smiled her big white-toothed PR smile as though in a moment we'd be on the air.

I took her in; these visits brought sudden mnemonic shocks, remembering intimacies. She had lost a little weight, perhaps she looked a little hard (perhaps I wanted her to). That night her lovely-breasted body seemed almost to tremble inside its pale wrap of shimmering, insubstantial cloth, and carried a touch of tan; she wore her strawberry blonde hair long and niftily coiled across her elegant neck. Almost unable to swallow, I said, "Hi, Lennie," and crossed the threshold, crowding her a bit.

She spun around and took a few quicksteps on her dancer-sized legs so that she met me again entering the living-room. "Jake," she said, "there's someone I'd like you to meet."

Someone was a man about my age and nearly Sorel's height, handsome in a way you would find familiar if you read the vanished magazines. Dark hair. Rusty skin, going to shiny grey along the jaw where he could never quite cut away all the dark masculinity. I bit down on the jealous reflex such encounters always brought. He came over and stuck out a long, square Jon Whitcomb hand, which I shook while Lennie said, "Jake Warner, Tom Gordineer." While we murmured our wary glad-to-meet-yous, she added, "Tom's a pilot too."

"Mm," I replied, wondering what sort of pilot, but sensing that I was out of my aeronautical class. Reluctantly I asked him, "Where do you fly?"

He gave the expected animal grin. "Out at Patuxent."

"Ah," I responded. "Navy test pilot?" He nodded. I wondered what to say about my relatively slight experience, and opted for a kind of brag. "I own a Cessna 182," I said, wanting him to know that such a plane cost a hell of a lot of money, for a normal working stiff.

"That's a *very* nice machine," he said, and we warmed toward one another as pilots almost invariably will, transcending such details as whether one is sleeping with the other's ex-wife or one has merely the cube root of the other's flying expertise. "A *very nice* machine." Then we were off on the merits of the Cessna, chattering away like girls about how it will take off with full tanks and anything you can fit into the cabin, and how great it is on long hops over rough terrain, and what a fine short-takeoff, gravel-strip plane it is, and on, and on, becoming in an instant part of the band of brothers, as pilots call themselves.

Lennie couldn't stand it. "Since you're here together," she said in a glass-etching voice that stole our attention, "I can ask you, Jake, the favor I'd planned to call you about tonight anyway. Tom's flying down to Key West next week and he's asked me to come down with Charlie. As much as we want Charlie to be with us, I think it'd be better for the two of *you* to get together. I know Charlie's *counting* on seeing you, and you must be *dying* to see him."

"Good," I said. Recalled from aviation to remembered intimacies with this lovely, manipulative woman, I thought, I'll be glad to babysit while you shack up, old girl. But I said, "Let me know your plan. If there's a hurricane I'll get somebody to help out."

Gordineer looked interested. "Hurricane?"

"I'm at the hurricane lab in Miami. We fly the storms when we can." I gave him back his grin. "And sometimes when we can't."

"We may meet in one next week."

"I didn't know you-all trained that hard."

He ignored my nastiness, perhaps recognizing its sources.

Or perhaps, even then, he saw what our rendezvous in a hurricane would be like, what it would engender, and felt sorry for me. I don't know. "Ah, no," he said easily, cryptically, "we're testing some, uh," then, bumping against a security classification, "some, uh, all-weather gear. I guess we'd try it in a hurricane if we got a chance."

"Well, follow those rules of the road, stay clear of Cuba, and all that." Now I wonder if I really saw a shadow cross his magazine-quality face or whether it is something I've daubed in retrospectively. I guess what I believe is that the idea Admiral Carney hatched at mid-afternoon only provided a means of activating something already in place, like a bomb waiting for a fuze. But I don't know whether Gordineer knew then that we were it. And there is no way now to ask him.

But he laughed, and said, "Sure."

"Is Charlie around?" I asked Lennie then.

"Spending the weekend with friends."

"Must be something going around," I said.

Lennie assumed her stressed look, in which three horizontal lines deepened above worried green eyes. "Have a drink?"

I shook my head. "No, thanks. Look, I don't want to hold you two up. You go on. I'll let myself out after I've left a note for Charlie."

She glanced at her gold-wafer sandwich. "Maybe we should, Tom. The reservations are for eight-thirty, and we want ..."

"Fine." He didn't like my staying around, familiarly, in his lady's apartment. I didn't blame him.

"Nice meeting you," I said as they got her into a gauzy peach summer wrap. "See you another time, Lennie."

They reciprocated their goodbyes and went out.

For a moment I stood in the long, richly naugahyded, carpeted, wooded room, a room full of furniture I didn't recognize; we had really burned those bridges. Then I walked down the narrow hall to the room she'd saved for our Charlie. It seemed small and leftover. But that's unfair. She'd given Charlie exactly the room he wanted, in exactly the style. Handmade bunk beds and nicely carpentered drawers filled one wall, windows another. The rug was Navajo, the desk a blur of model airplane parts and drooling tubes of cement. One of the walls was cork, nearly covered with various

Charliecana. What he displayed was a gestalt for parents.

My stuff – satellite photographs of hurricanes, our new airplanes in flight, an Air Force Hurricane Hunter patch, an honest-to-God barograph trace of a hurricane brushing Antigua, and a bunch of other line-of-duty souvenirs like that, including a photograph of me on the flight deck behind Sam Newman, a good friend who flew for Prospero – still dominated the contributed quarter of the wall. But I was being stalked there, along with Charlie's loyalties. In a random pattern that encroached upon my stuff but did not displace or even quite surround it, you could see old Tom moving in. Color photographs of A-6 *Intruders* crowded my four-engine turboprop. An Annapolis pennant brushed my orange-and white Texas flag. There were photographs of Charlie seated in an A-6 cockpit, wearing a great golden, insect-eyed helmet, at the beach with his mother, capering with his new, big friend. And there was an enlargement showing the right hand side of the *Intruder* cockpit: rain streaked the windscreen, all was darkness and lightning and cloud; and there, on a dark grey rectangular display, floated the white ghost of a MIG 25, so detailed seen in infra-red that you could make out the cockpit and the man it held in the center of the target. Around the display a crowd of weapons controls stood ready to do the necessary. I felt the footsteps on my grave, and shivered. "Hate to have you after me, old sport," I told the pervasive spirit of Gordineer, to push the silence back.

I broke a small clearing on the top of Charlie's desk, and, with one of those large, steel-leaded school pencils that are never sharp, wrote:

Dear Charlie Whiskey
I was in town unexpectedly and dropped by, but your mom said you were spending the night with friends. Sorry I missed you this time, but it looks like we'll see each other next week in Miami. I hope so, anyway. Maybe we can fly over to Freeport. Or something. I'm really looking forward to having you around. I'll ...

I'd started to say, "I'll see you tomorrow." But, looking for another moment at his wall and seeing the adults circle him, trying his loyalties, I decided to finish:

... be flying south tomorrow. See you next week, son.
                          Love,
                          Daddy.

I left this awkward message where he might find it and more or less fled into the night. And, needing comfort, I turned the Avis compact back toward Washington National to check on N803CW, the present love of my life.

Eight zero three Charlie Whiskey, as she was known, was the Cessna Skylane I'd begun to buy with my portion of our real estate profits. The plane with white, vermilion and maroon trim, had been almost worth the divorce, and had been even a kind of mistress for me; or maybe a nurse. Her call letters were for Charlie – he'd been born August 3, CW were his initials. Among other things, the plane meant we had something persistent and important to share. I resolved to get a good air-to-air photograph of her to push back the evil forces on his cork wall.

That night I walked out on the asphalt ramp and gave the plane a pat and fiddled around, checking the tiedowns and whether all the switches were off, touching the thin metal shell of the fuselage with affection. Of course, you never get what you want when you approach a machine sentimentally, when your emotional wand tries to animate the inanimate. Zero Three Charlie Whiskey kept as close as a cowboy's horse on this night, a shining machine that flew, small and fragile-seeming on the apron at Washington National. I leaned against the Skylane and watched the strobes and beacons drop lovely and surreal from the darkness into the dotted rows of runway lights. The sky beyond the city's hazy dome of light looked clear – you could see planes a long way out, before their landing lights poked back the night. Less disappointment and fatigue and I'd have had headed for home then.

As it was I went back to the motel and had a couple of beers and a beef sandwich in the bar, and looked at the late news, where the weatherperson said tomorrow's weather would be more of the same, suggesting that an early start would get me home before the summer thunderstorms began building over the Florida hotplate. She said hurricane forecasters in Miami watched a disturbance located in the western Atlantic, and then went on to the local picture. When she ran the satellite loop I took a closer look at the smear of cloudiness and light rains over the Atlantic about a hundred nautical miles east of St Lucia. Just a wave of low pressure – a wild card in the tropical atmosphere.

Next morning the FAA briefer had very little weather for me along the line of flight. Some cumuli would develop into isolated thundershowers farther south, where summer had consolidated its power some weeks past, and the days ran along hot and humid, cooled only by occasional passing storms.

So it was a fine day to fly out of the city and over the surprising emptiness that still separates most American towns. I stayed at thirty-five hundred feet along the Piedmont, the low coils and bumps of the worn-down eastern mountains rising blue-grey off in the haze they wore even before there were mills and factories and cars. Four hours got me to Savannah, for lunch and fuel. Three more running fairly low a couple of miles off the beach got me into my neighborhood and I began listening to the automatic terminal information tape from Miami International. Then I went over to Miami approach control. They gave me a transponder code and vectored me to a left base for runway nine left, shuffling me in among the big guys. They turned me over to the tower, which admonished me to keep pedalling because I was number one to land ahead of an inbound heavy DC8. A 727 turned off the runway ahead of me, so I came almost to the threshold at cruising speed, then cut everything, put on full flaps and fluttered to earth well down the strip. As I changed to ground control frequency and turned back toward the general aviation terminal, the DC8 came in, a beaked black form riding a cloud of jet exhaust.

Taxiing back took me past the agency's hangar. Both of the new planes stood outside, big, pretty in their blue and black trim, with the mildly deformed look of research aircraft – a gust probe protruded from a streamlined pod on the right side of the nose, a bulge aft of the wing marked the position of the high-rate-of-fire 'gun' we used to deploy seeding flares, the wings dangled instruments and pods for external stores. It saddened me to see the new birds. They'd be doing errands for yet another year, growing old on cloud physics and boundary layer research missions – when they'd been born to kill a hurricane.

And it saddened me as well to think of my own bird as

something frail and puny. I suppose, underneath the labor of flying south, my mind had been worrying some aspect of my love for Charlie and my life without him, so that I felt suddenly bereft of my son, and empty. I am a little ashamed to say now that this was mainly the jealous reflex, remembering the photos of the world of Lennie's current boyfriend on Charlie's wall. Of course, one knows intellectually that what bonds fathers and sons is blood and affection and the long journey together through time. But at the less rational level I had wrapped all of these into what I thought was my largest offering of all – this little airplane that bore his initials. On this Saturday night at least, that offering seemed bogus and shallow against the open, friendly companionship of his new friend from the Navy ...

"Prospero, this is Navy. You okay?"

I look to port. The *Intruder* floats a little ahead of us, off our left wing. The warriors inside wear green and black suits that gleam, and golden helmets, and have green insect eyes. "Prospero, you okay?"

I reply. "Navy, we've got a problem." I hesitated, willing myself back to where we are. "Heavy damage on the flight deck. Copilot and engineer dead. And the pilot."

Sam Newman gurgles into the intercom, "Not dead."

"Pilot's badly hurt," I amend.

"Warner – is that you?" Navy wants to know.

"That's right." I think of Navy's name: Gordineer.

"You flying that aircraft, Jake?"

"It's on autopilot."

"Jesus," he replied, and for a moment gives his silent blessing. Then, "Okay, Jake, I'm going to move around your aircaft and see how bad off you are. Here we go now." The *Intruder* drifts ahead and descends slightly, then slows so that we fly past it overhead. A moment later it bobs back up on the right side of our plane and floats off that wing for a time. "Belly radome's pretty scratched up. Nose radome too. Don't see any fuel leaks or smoke, but you've got some damage out in your number three and four nacelles. Most of the damage looks to be around the cockpit, maybe a few meters back aft on the starboard side. We'll hang around long's we can."

"Roger," I say to the Navy plane. I think of our airplane, its body raked with jagged holes, its flight deck awash in blood and glass and bits of metal, whipped by the two-hundred-knot gale roaring through the shattered windscreen. Unfair, to be so much a virgin of an airplane, and to have such troubles, such wounds. Then I see Bruska's form back in the shadows. Newman's breath vibrates through the intercom like gravel in a drain. *Those* are wounds. The plane is a machine, opaque to pain. On the intercom I tell the crew, "This is Jake. Bruska's badly wounded. Dead, I think. Newman's – wounded. I'm in Newman's chair. Is Gino Saperelli on?"

"Right here, Jake," the steward's frightened tenor replies.

"We need to get Newman more comfortable. Can you take care of him?"

"Roger."

I call the electronics station. "Ed Mattson, how's power?"

"Fine, Jake. Got everything turned off we don't need to fly with. You okay?"

"I'm okay."

The intercom revives a little. Don Chesney, today's navigator, says, his voice shaking, "Want to go anywhere in particular, Jake?"

I peer out at the white cylinder of cloud in which we fly our circle. "I'm working on it."

"Ever land one of these before?"

"Nope, never have." I watch the control wheels move in response to the autopilot's mechanical demands. Maybe we will fly on endlessly, dead but restless; or fly until the huge tanks are sucked dry and we fall into the sea. I touch the wheel, reach down and move my fingers across the grey power console next to my bloodied leg. My fingers absorb something of the machine.

I call our communications man. "Ira Weld, you there?"

"Yeah, Jake." A fearful note floats in his voice; he sees the end of work, of family, of grandfatherness, everything. It occurs to me everyone aboard *should* be frightened.

"Ira, try to raise Prospero One."

"Roger."

Newman murmurs, "Good, Jake, good." I sense movement behind me, around the pilot. Saparelli has leaned Newman back and winds gauze pads around the broken chest as tightly as he can and have the pilot still breathe. Rory joins him, her deep blue eyes caverned with mourning and fatigue, but fearless; nothing has been broken in her after all. She has no time for me, but neatens the steward's work, then helps him with the ginger walking of Newman back to one of the bunks in back. The pilot's headset is off; his rattling breath no longer fills the intercom. Someone has covered Bruska with a poncho. He lies folded into a foetal position, his big grey hands and bloody feet poking from under the O.D. plastic.

"Prospero, Navy."

"Go ahead," I reply.

"We may have a, uh, problem. I'm going to move around in front of your plane so you can look us over, okay?"

"Okay," I say. The *Intruder* moves ahead of us and climbs slightly so that we can see its grey underbelly, the empty racks where its rockets had been; and, yes, there, something has split the right hand wing, a thin smoke of fuel flies toward us, over us, like a vapor trail. But I know the spume of spray dooms Gordineer and the unnamed, golden-hatted man beside him. "Navy, you've got a hole in your starboard wing, and losing fuel."

"Uh, Roger, thanks." The imperturbable voice returns from an airplane that is now just a canopied hearse; one listens for a trace of fear in it, the slightest hint that what must happen now is in some sense unfair – but nothing like that enters Gordineer's voice. "Don't know about the damage. We weren't hit. Bet it's structural, all that speed in Dolly. Pass that along, if you would, Prospero. I was, uh, hoping we just had a busted fuel light." A pause. The golden-headed figure's hands move about the nearby cockpit, stroking switches, preparing for terminal flight. Then, "Jake, we, uh, need to transfer some classified material from our computer to yours. Can you give my man here a frequency?"

Ira Weld comes on with a channel into our computer, and adds, "Navy, I'm putting out a Mayday for you." A faint background clicking mars our radio signal as the Navy plane begins its transmission – a transmission, one thinks, that tells of its last encounter with an enemy.

"Many thanks." Silence. "Sorry to leave you alone out here, old buddy, but, uh, we're gonna have to punch out."

"Tom ..."

"Not to worry." Then, "Sorry it was you, Jake. Tell Lenore – tell Charlie."

"Sure, sure."

"I wish ..." Silence. "Oh *shit!*" The first and only note of complaint, followed by the weary acquiescence pilots give to gravity. "Okay, there she goes. Okay. So long, Prospero."

The golden-headed figure in the *Intruder* waves a melancholy salute. I wave back. Then, with the beautiful relative motion of aircraft in flight, the Navy fighter drops away from us, an immensely heavy glider, veering toward the center of the eye. As they pass through ten thousand feet the hatch explodes away. A tiny figure rockets out of the right side of the cockpit, seconds later, the pilot follows. The dead *Intruder* continues its fall, and vanishes into the eyewall.

All of us know what they face, Gordineer and the weapons officer who shares this final flight with him. They will come down in the frothy swell of the eye, where winds and waves are light. They may escape the entangling parachute risers and disc of suffocating cloth. They may inflate and clamber into their tiny one-man rafts. But they are held within the circle of the hurricane's calm center; finally the storm must overtake them, finally they will die in the sea. I watch the parachutes drop down and down, until the scattered low clouds of the eye take them in. We do not see them again.

Then it is just us, droning above a choppy blue-grey ocean and thin, tortured clouds, carrying death and pain, and the potential for still greater death and pain, around and around the eye of our hurricane. I am tempted to rest my forehead on the yoke, to sleep, to cry, to tilt the big plane into the ocean, follow Gordineer to something known. I long for the grey land of faintness and fatigue where I had been an hour, a minute, a second before. Perhaps my spirit left my body. Perhaps that is the only way off this plane today.

But then, rousing, I think of Gordineer, his reflex to stay with us while fuel let him, to stay with us while his own opportunities diminished. I think of his quiet voice against the certainty of approaching death, and feel a start of deep affection for this man I'd hated and of regret that my Charlie must now be without such friends. And, as I did that night by my airplane in Miami, I remember the photos on my son's cork wall, of him in the A-6 cockpit, of him in his golden helmet, of him, happy, capering along some strand with his new man. Gordineer had said to me, speaking as one doomed brother to another, "See? There are worse things than being doomed," and passed his courage over like a relay baton. It helps me toward resolve, the long connection and coincidence that tie the lost flyer and my son and me together in the storm. I may still weep over present losses, and prospective ones. But Gordineer has shown the way to courage.

Sorel called the meeting for eight-thirty Monday morning, giving most of us time to get coffee and go upstairs to our long yellow-walled briefing room. The hurricane displays there constituted a short course in the recent history of our kind of

MIAMI

Monday
T – 73 h 30 m
Lat 25.5 N
Long 80.2 W

meteorology. You could see how poor the raw data products had been back in what I'd call our DC-6 period, and really how little we'd known about the big storms at a time when we'd begun to think we understood them rather well. The exhibits from hurricane flights in the new planes showed the state of the art: digital radar readouts in color, printed off the computer tapes, storms trapped in them like insects in amber, eternally. With our new instruments we had a level of detail that let us read within a few hundred meters where to probe, where to seed, where to take those crucial measurements that would tell us what seeding does ... It was in these new sets of hurricane data that the hypothesis underlying Prospero, what we called the seeding hypothesis, seemed to have been confirmed.

The last block of illustrations was labeled "PreProspero", which some grad student had graffitied into "PrePosterous." A blank area to its right read, "Prospero One". Until Friday, that would have been our first seeding mission, flown when the Atlantic hurricane season began to heat up after August. We would have counted down the end of the summer, waiting for the storm that met our complicated criteria of distance from a base, time to landfall, size, intensity; and then, with that optimum storm somewhere out east of the Antilles, we would have deployed to Puerto Rico, and begun a gruelling five-airplane sequence that kept a seeder in the storm continuously for about twelve hours, with three monitoring airplanes from the Air Force Hurricane Hunters squadron filling in the data gaps at various flight levels. But – no more. I shook my head sharply and went to one of the student chairs in the front corner of the room to sip my instant coffee.

Jim Westheimer and a couple of his senior people came in, and he nodded at me. I nodded back. "How was Washington?" he asked.

"Hot, humid, turning brown."

"They gut us again?"

"I don't want to spoil Henry's surpise."

"Some surprise." Westheimer's voice always carried a vague note of complaint, a suggestion that something was unfair; given the kind of man he was, perhaps something was. I always thought it derived in part from his being in charge of our hurricane modeling group, from spending too much time in that imaginary world and too little in the real world of the big storms. The term "modeling" of course evokes a bunch of people assembling model hurricanes out of wire, cotton, and plastic arrows. And of course that isn't what I mean. They made their storms out of mathematical equations. It sounds arcane until you remember the first time you had to plot a circle in algebra, and the first time you changed it to an ellipse simply by changing the value of the x or y. That descriptive property in mathematics becomes more and more elegant until you can express entire worlds that way, and move them in and out of time. Run through the simple, extremely nimble minds of a computer, these worlds crystallize out as arcade games, or predictions of human population in the year 3000, or scenarios for war, or models – sets of equations that simulate some aspect of reality. Mathematical models, or simulations, are what antivivisectionists want to substitute for monkeys, and, in fact, I always looked at our hurricane modeling as a kind of bloodless vivisection – we can run a hurricane with some of its water taken out, or with a warmer ocean under it, or, for Prospero, with a load of our silver iodide seeding agent in the rainbands, and see how it behaves, all without leaving the lab. But the penalty with models is that you're always working with a simplified shadow of the real thing.

I guess that Westheimer, young and sparsely made and thin-limbed, while married, a father and somebody's son, was a kind of numerical model of a man, in whom basic principles had been set in motion thirty-some years ago that simulated his version of humanity. He had no irregular surfaces, no wide range of greys, no interesting blemishes. He was exactly what he seemed: frail, dry as paper, a little spoiled; one felt he absorbed light, humor, life, and so one leaned away from him.

But his hurricane models were becoming the stuff of scientific legend. He'd used them to discover what some of the earlier efforts to modify hurricanes had done wrong – the errors in tempo and timing which had blocked progress until Prospero got going. And he'd pointed up some of the uncertainties of wrestling with something so violent and large. For example, we could "seed" one of his imaginary storms and get wind reductions of twenty to thirty percent in the eyewall, where a hurricane's winds are greatest; but, in a model run with more ice than water in the cloud tops near the eye, we often got no perceptible change. And, in model storms made to resemble rather small, tight 200-mile-an-hour hurricanes like 1969's Camille, our mathematical seeding sometimes seemed to cause the model storm to intensify. In fact, while the models contributed to the theory underlying Prospero and shaped the experiment, they were just guidance. The real proof would come in a hurricane, one made of real thunderheads and terrible winds and rain as dense as the ocean, not a jerry-rigged assortment of raging mathematical equations. I admired Westheimer's work and even understood it, but I didn't like the man. Perhaps there was some snobbery there. Oh, hell, of course there was. His career lived in our computer. Mine lived in the hurricane.

Others drifted in. Sol Murchison, who ran our airplane facility. Billie Chatham, who ran the Hurricane Center, "Dr Hurricane' to his numerous media pals, half preacher, half distinguished scientific uncle to us all. A couple of data management types came in, and some mid-level scientists – Dick Pettry, a small, square, ugly, young man with a curly brown beard and gentle eyes, more interested in means than ends, his dainty foot always reaching for that next rung. A squad of grad students I didn't know beyond an early-summer greeting, tall and lithe and definitely Florida, the men and women so pretty and vain you wondered about their scientific abilities until you saw them work around the clock in a steamy radar van out in the Everglades. Gary Himmell, a tall, swimmer-built black graduate student from Gainesville, entered, with pretty little Carla Hendrix in tow. She was beautiful in an old-fashioned kind of way, tended to freckle more than tan, wore a braid that, when unwoven, let her honey-colored hair fall to her narrow waist, eyes the yellow-brown of wolves', grand skin, great humor and the

integrity of a skyscraper. She and I only nodded now, for we'd
been lovers in those rough times when I was spinning and
reeling like a drunk from the divorce. She had expressed deep
feelings, gambled and lost in her little time with me. I could
barely look at her now, so vivid and eternally fresh was my
memory of causing her to act badly out of her pain; and of
being unable, being broken, to reciprocate the large
compliment of her affection. And she, remembering my gift of
pain, always flinched away from me now. In a world I find
hard hearted, she was not; she was a species, probably an
endangered one, of old-fashioned girl. That was why I didn't
like her being with Himmell, so much the boy to her woman,
and believed (if one can believe something like this without a
bunch of ego in it) that, as handsome and with it as he was, she
had gone to him to punish herself, and me. Today we did our
cool nod and looked away from one another, both saddened
by the contact.

And Rory Merchant. I signalled to her to sit by me, but she
tacked off toward the front of the room and took a chair near
the lectern. She and I shared the detailed running of Prospero
between us. I ranked her, but on days when we flew I ran the
mission director station on Sorel's plane, Prospero Two, and
Rory was chief scientist on her own plane, Prospero One. Her
interest went deeper than mine; when she talked about "my
science" she could have been talking about her love, or child,
or human spirit. I loved her anyway, without much in the way
of results.

Sorel arrived, long and moody as a stork, and seized the
lectern, shook it provisionally, found it wanting and went to a
nearby table, which he put one foot on, assuming what might
be called the relaxed professor position. In his best classroom
manner, he quieted the room with a sweep of his bright blue
boy's eyes, swung his glasses up into his white hair and began
to tell us how things were.

"As the late President Kennedy is said to have remarked on
hearing the bad news from the Bay of Pigs, 'Fucked again.'"
The room clanged with diffident laughter. "That's precisely
where our lab is as regards Project Prospero. As of last Friday,
Prospero is dead, according to our administrator, Dr Ted
Grose. It had nothing to do with me or you or the lab or with

science. It is just pure political crap. The White House is stampeding toward the canyon again on the current Cuban crisis, and they have lumped us into it because of *this* nasty little bugger." He unfolded and displayed a color page torn from *Aviation Week*. It showed a Russian fighter in an air show fly-by, a plane that looked like all Russian fighters – beefy, variable-sweep wing, twin vertical stabilizers aft, the fuselage swollen aft of the cockpit to accomodate two big engines. But this one also had the slightly skewed look of research planes: the nose radome was a bit bulbous, the wings sprouted with accessories, a long radome projected from the tip of each stabilizer. "Stormbat," Sorel continued. "The Soviet Union have put a squadron of these into Cuba, ostensibly for hurricane research. Our military say they're nuclear-capable, and have labeled the act as a provocative one. But the hurricane research business has drawn us into it. So we should put this little beggar up on our board – it's *really* cost us." He let the picture drift out of his hand, to be intercepted by one of the grad students and hurried off to the bulletin board in the rear of the room.

"What this all means to us," Sorel said now, "is we may never have the opportunity to test the theories we've brought so far into science these last few years. I expect we shall have to move into other areas of tropical meteorology and hurricane research, perhaps working on the prediction problem more. That would be you, Jim. And working less on research in the field. That would be you, Jake." We looked at each other for a moment; he had something to communicate in silence, but I couldn't read the signal. I nodded. "We're a small enough lab," Sorel went on, "That we don't have to get rid of people when we lose this kind of funding. What the loss of Prospero will mean, though, is we will probably have to re-form in a package that is more interesting and palatable to headquarters, with more research and less experimentation in it." He paused, studying the little band of people who lived virtually in the palm of his hand. "I think the lab will probably get a new director if Prospero is allowed to die. I guess that's all I have to say, unless there are questions."

Westheimer was first. "Can you tell us more about their rationale for deferring Prospero?"

"Deferring. I like your gentle choice of words, Jim. Such rationale as there was, beyond the Stormbat business they felt some of the problems hadn't been resolved. Those uncertainties have produced some real faint-heartedness at State, especially where Cuba is concerned. You remember the newspaper stories that the CIA tried cloud seeding to destroy the Cuban sugar crop, and how droll we found them at the time. Well, the Cubans believe the reports, and they're militantly opposed to any weather modification in the greater Caribbean area. With the Soviet involvement they're dealing from strength. So State is being extraordinarily timid, even for them.

"What troubles them on the scientific side – this issue does have a pinch of science in it – are some of the ambiguities which persist in your models – the effect of seeding on storm track and surge heights, for example. I believe we've sorted these problems out in our field work. But some of the old model runs still scare them, Jim. See what you've done?"

Everyone laughed but Westheimer. "Well, Henry, our models only simulated what's there," he said defensively.

Sorel bridled. "There are models and there are storms. This isn't the time to tell me we deserved to lose Prospero because of some greatly simplified on-off computer solution. I may make you fly a hurricane yet." Having bullied one of his people, he relaxed and looked around for more questions.

None came, so I intruded. "Henry, it might be worth noting that they didn't just whack off Prospero money."

"Good, Jake," he replied. "That's right. We still have the airplane hours budgeted that we had going into the hurricane season. One of the benefits of a quiet season."

"Carney suggested we try a full-scale drill if we get a storm," I said. "I think that's probably the best we can do this year, and recommend we go for it."

"We can't get the Air Force monitors in, though," Murchison lamented, characteristically mournful about the business of sending airplanes out into storms. He was a big dark man of infinite responsibility for his aircraft and crews, who scowled a lot and imitated maintenance officers at forward combat bases and liked cigars. But he understood the scientific requirements as well as and sometimes better than we did. "No way to get Air Force."

"We can run a mock seeding mission, though. It won't hurt to have our two planes maneuvering together in a storm. Adds polish." I turned to Chatham. "Any prospects for a drill?"

He grinned. "Too soon to call. We've been watching a disturbance that crossed into the Caribbean Saturday. Right now it's drifting about a hundred nautical miles south of Jamaica, and we get reports of lots of rain and electrical activity. It's still quite disorganized, but I'd say it has potential."

Sorel, who had gone quiet, revived. "Jake, let's focus on this one. If it matures I want us to mount a real honest-to-Christ dress rehearsal of a Prospero seed mission. Get set up to respond on a very short notice with a nominal ten-hour multiple seeding mission. Perhaps we'll go out in style."

Remembering him as he was on that Monday, one wonders how anyone could have anticipated the sudden activation of the crack that ran through Sorel, as imperceptibly as the San Andreas fault crosses some California streets, the sidewalk kinked slightly by the creeping earth, but not much sign beyond that. I think the mission was exactly what it seemed to him then, a rehearsal, a chance to learn a little more before they closed us down. He was all right on that Monday. Carney knew about the crack in Sorel, and I think he probably gambled on it, especially as our storm heated up and began to look like Camille. But, at this point, we didn't even have a hurricane, nothing that would touch Sorel on those wounds that will not heal. One heard in his voice, read in his face, nothing of obsessions. One had no hint how dirtied we would be before it ended.

I said, "Okay," then added to Chatham, "If that system's just in the Caribbean, let's say we're three days from first 'seeding' – so we're at about T, Tango, minus seventy-two hours, and counting. We'll update this as needed." To my surprise, the prospect of a mission excited me, lifted my depression over the death of Prospero. Yes, and it touched everyone in the room. We needed something so much that even this drill looked good. I hoped the tropical depression Chatham was monitoring would turn into a hurricane. Often they burbled along for a few days, then pooped out over the Atlantic. Sometimes they matured into hurricanes, idled all the way across the Atlantic and then deepened into something evil in the Caribbean. The possibilities were as broad as bridge hands, but less controllable. I made a note to check with Chatham later in the day to see what else they'd got from the satellite. "Murch," I told Murchison, "I'll need your current aircrew rosters to work up the mission."

"I'll get them over to you this afternoon."

"And, Jim," I went on, turning to Westheimer, "you'll need to begin matching this disturbance against your model, so we can go predictive as early as possible."

"Okay." He bristled, his spare curved body had an excited look; he drank some light and went into the hall.

No one had further questions, so we all got up and began that circular shuffle that moves small crowds out of little rooms. I shuffled up beside Rory Merchant. "Lunch?"

She turned her tanned, heart-shaped face toward me; I almost fell into the deep China-blue eyes. "Don't feel much like celebrating, Jake."

"Me, neither. But I sho God feel like being with you."

"We could talk about the mission."

"If there is one."

"Don't be downbeat. What're you going to call it?"

"Prospero Blank. Prospero Minus One."

"The Lesser Prospero."

"The Least Prospero."

"Prospero *est mort*."

"Prospero Drill."

"I like that," she said.

"Good." We split up then, with promises of lunch.

Lunch. I try to reconstruct my sense of time around vague rumblings within that remind me we have not eaten much today. The sun hangs above the western tier of Dolly's eye, hovering, as it seems to me we do in the calm center of the storm. The thin red

numbers on the digital clock dance away our seconds, our lives perhaps, coming up on 17.27 Greenwich time, 33 minutes to two in Key West, Miami – Cuba. The Cubans. God, it has been just over an hour …

I say to no one in particular on the intercom, "We've been here just over an hour …"

Saperelli, who wanders the plane like an electrical man, dragging thirty feet of headphone cable, sings back, "Time sure flies when you're having fun." Laughter on the intercom.

Ira Weld shatters this sense of suspension, releasing time once more. "Jake," he says on the intercom, "Prospero One's on mission VHF."

I reach down to the grey console and turn the frequency selector. It is my first alteration of the airplane; the touch is electric.

"Prospero One, this is Warner on Two."

"Gil Bradenton here, Jake." I feel some of my responsibility flow toward him. "What's your situation?"

I tell him.

"Jesus!"

"We've got casualties. Peterson's gone. Bruska's gone. Sam Newman's bad. Sorel …" I look at Sorel, who stares opaquely at me from where we have him wedged into the aisle. He is not dead. But it is all brain and heart; if he lives it will be in a glass tank of nourishing fluids. "Sorel got thrown against the overhead. He's bad."

"Plane on autopilot?"

"Affirmative."

"What's your heading?"

"We're flying a standard rate circle to the left."

"How's your airplane, Jake?" Bradenton asks, willing me to be more of a pilot.

"Navy walked around us. Didn't seem too bad. Cockpit's torn up, the windscreen's out on the right side. He didn't see any smoke or fuel.''

"What's your altitude?"

"Twelve thousand."

"What's your position, Jake, do you know?"

"Gil – we're in the eye."

Silence crowds in upon us. I sense Bradenton's yielding us up, shrugging away the wingless bomber falling in flames, the doomed unparachuted figures on the sky, the cartwheeling cross of fire dancing along the runways of Danang. Then he returns to us. "Okay, I understand you're in the eye. How's your radar?"

"Out."

"Aw, *shit!*" Another silence. He does not want us dying under his care. "Okay. Excuse the outburst. Usually we handle problems like yours in the simulator, Jake. How you holding up, anyway?"

"Okay."

"That's good. Now look. You sound a shade dull, okay? I want you to get up and move around. Don't leave the flight station – the autopilot might let go. But shake yourself some. Time you're back in your seat I'll be coming up behind you. We gotta get you current in that airplane, old buddy."

I unstrap and stand up. In the hatch behind me, Saperelli, goggles at my bloodied leg. I shake my head and indicate the plastic mound that is Bruska. "His," I yell into the gale. I am self-conscious to be in full view of the men whose airplane I have – seized. And which, I think now, is probably going to kill me later on this afternoon. And you, and you, and you. Their heads turn towards me as I look down the aisle, but they isolate me with their silence; if there is a charm they don't want to break it. If there is not – well ... I try to look contained, like royalty.

But I do have a secret source of confidence. Bradenton has made me his student, and himself my instructor. The instructor will take me in, absorb my errors like a Jesus soaking up my sins, get us safely through the hurricane, safely on the ground.

Far aft, Rory bends over Sam Newman, who has been doped and strapped into one of the folding cots just forward of the galley, his face grey and old beneath the tan. Perhaps sensing my great need for her, she leaves him to Saperelli, threads past

the still form of Sorel, and steps into the flight deck. I touch
her shoulder and she jumps. "Bradenton's coming," I say.

"That's good." Her voice is worn. The transfer of Newman
reddened her flight suit. "How do you feel?"

"I'm okay. How are you?"

"Okay."

"How is Henry?"

"Alive." I feel his glazed eyes staring forward. "Only alive."

"Jake, can you do it?"

"I'll tell you at dinner."

We lean toward one another for a moment, our spirits cleave
– then, conscious we are the only ones aboard the plane who
are not solitary, we bend back. I touch her cheek. "I hope to
God I don't hurt you today, old friend."

"You won't."

"Tell Newman Bradenton's coming." But I know he swims
behind the narcotic; if he hears he can give no sign. I hope his
chest has stopped leaking.

Rory turns away, hesitates for a moment, watching Sorel.
Then she seems to steel herself and walks back to Newman.

Superstitious, I follow Bradenton's orders to the letter: I
shake myself like a wet dog. Saperelli brings a thermos of
coffee and some paper towels. I drink the coffee, but too
quickly, burning my tongue. I use a paper towels to wipe the
larger chips of flesh off my right leg, careful to ignore their
source, and unable to: the act of removal saddens and sickens,
for it marks the end of Bruska, again.

When I look up Newman's seat remains vacant. I feel mild
surprise; apparently I have had my secret hope of another,
more experienced aviator aboard today, and my fear of it, too,
for I begin to warm to this. The act of flight, of controlling
such a machine, draws me, begins to separate me from fear.
My mind looks into the future, toward the hurricane, toward
the landing, and at last can almost see it happening. Until this
moment it has peered into the future only a minute or two at a
time. I touch the power levers without moving them. In the
middle of the grey panel tremble a multitude of engine
instruments, the glyphs of turbine civilization, unintelligible to
Piston Man. But the rest of the panel has soaked into
familiarity. I know where to look for airspeed and altitude and

heading and attitude. I adjust the seat until I'm comfortable
and plug my headset into the pilot's console so I can use the
wheel-mounted push-to-talk button to transmit without my
hand leaving the control wheel. Okay, I think. I'm a pilot. This
is my plane.

A figure looms behind me. I flinch from it, thinking it is
Death ... Then the reporter comes into bright light and the lips
form words that are lost to the wind and turbine scream, like
sounds uttered behind a waterfall. He plugs in his headset.
"Can I help?"

I shrug, shake my head.

Pointing to the chief scientist's station behind me, he asks,
"Can I use this chair?"

I nod.

We are bound, then. He plans to keep me company through
the eternity between this moment and the Next Step: the
hurricane, the landing. He helps me toward my bullfight, this
friend and enemy named Borg.

"It's Borg," Bella Moore said, making a face.
She was the big, middle-aged black woman I
shared with Rory, tough and smart and
maternal, a friend one somehow could not
touch because she emanated such large
social and structural integrities. She was

holding the phone like a baby when I got back to my office.
"It's Borg," she repeated, "on line five."

Steven Borg wrote science and environment for the *Herald*,
and strung for *Time*, and had done a kid reporter stint in
Vietnam for one of the university news services. I spent the
several seconds it took me to get to my own phone
second-guessing him. We acted cordial but mutually alien, in
the sense that we evolved very much from our own worlds and
not much from one another's. I thought he did a reasonable
job in his work, though, and probably he thought the same of
me. Our only bad moment had come a couple of years back
when I'd called to tell him a piece of his on weather
modification had been shit. I think what I'd disliked about it
was something snotty he had about science. Some science
writers feel they missed an avocation, not being scientists, and
write out of their longing and regret. Borg saw scientists as
merely playful, and while he understood difficult technical
subject matter better than most, he sometimes let that beam of
benign contempt illuminate his copy. I decided to be careful of
him today, and burbled, "Hey, Steve," insincerely into my
phone.

"Hi, Jake." A flat, gravelly Illinois voice tinged with ten
years or so in the south. It evoked the thin, rangy man, the
broad-mouthed triangular face, the expensive wrinkled suits –
but the man it evoked was also older than Borg, who seemed
middle thirties to me.

"What's up?" I asked.

"I hear Prospero got killed."

Jesus, not half an hour after our meeting and somebody had
whistled the press into our lives. I wondered whether it had
been one of our house reds (every lab has an ideologue
somewhere), or Sorel, or Rory, protecting "her science".
"Yeah, I heard that too," I said.

"Ha ha and ho ho. I guess you did. But, look, my editor

thinks we should do kind of a Prospero retrospective. Pull in the old material and how the project's changed over the years, the new players and the old, that kind of thing."

"Sounds fine." But he sounded insincere as hell, and I knew why: he hadn't mentioned the Stormbat crisis.

"He wants it before Prospero begins to decompose."

"So you need to start yesterday." My tone gave him a look at my lack of interest.

"No, hell no. Not till tomorrow or Wednesday. *Huge* intervals of time. Only thing is, I'd like to begin writing by the weekend. Tomorrow good?"

I'd been trying, while we talked, to stay ahead of him, to think through my alternatives, like the systematic man of science I was supposed to be. If he picked up our story and told it as it was, it might help turn things around; the White House hates ridicule, and nothing would make it seem sillier than to flinch away from a hurricane research project because of Soviet or Cuban sensibilities. On the other hand, it could also be told wrong, and bury Prospero still deeper. So I was trying to sort these out when I told Borg, "This isn't a good week for me. We've got a storm that might develop into something. We could be flying by Thursday or Friday. So I'm running around for a mission and I won't be able to put in much time for you. No one will."

"Don't need much. Why don't I come by your office first thing tomorrow, then get in half an hour with Sorel and maybe another half-hour out at the airport with a photographer?"

"I have to be at the airport at seven-thirty. Let's start there. Then we can come back to the lab and you can have Sorel."

"Great."

"See you at the field." Then, deciding to buy a little more time, deciding to bring him further into our lives in the hope of getting some benefit for Prospero, I added quickly, "Want a seat when we fly?"

"What's second prize, being buried alive?"

"Two missions."

"Christ. Sure. Put me down for a seat. Thanks, Jake."

"Welcome."

So the week became complicated early. In a way I resented Borg's intrusion into what I'd hoped would be a smooth curve of gradually increasing activity, one that had all of my attention. Now, with the conversation behind me, I wondered at inviting him in, at adding an element that could only erode the stability of our operation. Getting the lab and oneself up for any research mission required less waste motion than it looked like I would have, and mounting a Prospero flight, even a drill, was just that much worse. It bothered me because it's in the waste motion – the motion induced by distraction – that you forget something. You don't chat all the way down to a landing. Okay, and perhaps, even at this stage, a whiff of something rotting gave me an extra set of pre-mission jitters.

I called Murchison and told him I'd be out tomorrow morning early with Borg and a photographer, and asked him not to put the crew lists on the shuttle so I could pick them up out there. But he'd already sent them in to Sorel, he told me. Preoccupied with telling him Borg would fly if we had a seat, if we flew, I didn't challenge him on the procedural charge: crew lists came to me.

Then I rang Sorel, and got the aging, hard-voiced female named Rachel who guarded him, and who in her heart believed the lab was hers. I told her to clear half an hour on Sorel's calendar about nine-thirty Tuesday and she, after the usual sparring for the championship, grudgingly gave it to me, to give to Borg.

Murchison called back to ask how we were identifying the mission. "You calling it Last Patrol, or what?"

"Prospero Drill." When I'd hung up I pencilled the mission name across the top of a yellow legal-sized pad. I liked it. So would Sorel.

And then I pawed around in all the yellow call slips Bella had strewn across my desk during the meeting, and decided to try Pete Thompson, the fiscal scavenger from headquarters. "Sorry to be so long getting back, Pete," I lied. "This phone system's really something else."

"I know what you mean, Jake. Look, reason I called is we've got to know whether or not you're going to use those airplane hours this fiscal year or if we can have the money back for other objects. Since Prospero's dead ..."

"Sleeping."

"Yeah. That Prospero can *sleep*, man. Anyway, we thought

we could get some of the money back."

"No way, unless you just take it away from us. We've got a storm developing out in the Atlantic now and we're planning a drill if it matures and if it comes within range ..."

"You guys really employ those ifs, pal."

"Ifs is all headquarters left us, Pete. But – if we get a hurricane we're going to fly a full rehearsal. Morale is lower than whale shit down here now, so it's money well spent."

"You telling me we can't have the money?"

"I'm telling you you can't have it back unless we crap out for the rest of the hurricane season. Sorel'd go to God to protect this last mission."

"So what else is new?"

"Can't blame you for trying, Pete. After all, without you guys the veldt'd be littered with bodies."

"Funny. So long, Jake. If you don't get your storm we'll send down a paper sack you can fill with small, unmarked bills."

"Do that." We said goodbye through a thin film of frost. Dealing with Pete wore me down, always. The man spent his life circling the boundaries of projects like Prospero, waiting for something not to be consumed. Pete kept the agency from underspending, year in, year out. But toward the end of September, the last month of our fiscal year, he began to circle more and more swiftly as weak projects and delayed ones straggled from the federal herd.

Another *You were called by* ... slip said Moriarity in headquarters public affairs had called about Prospero and wanted to talk to me. I thought this one over awhile, then punched in the Maryland number. Moriarity's pretty, able lady came on and put me through to the Man, as he liked to call himself. "Yeah, Jake, thanks for calling back," he rumbled in a broadcaster's deep, uninformed baritone. He was one of those large, expanding men of about 50 who are so hearty and so insincere and so stupid about science as to be hard to take seriously. We've had good ones and bad ones, so I'm not just knocking PR types in government; in adversity they often have the only sense of humor for many miles around, and one with the street-sharpened instincts of a reporter is invaluable on projects like ours. But Moriarity – let's describe him as a tenth-rate everything, with White Horse connections. "Reason I called," he went on, waving away with his big voice my comparatively feeble salutation, "is I want to be very careful on the Prospero business. You know what I mean."

"Sure, I know."

"What I mean is we ought to just keep this thing screwed down tight until the Cuban thing works itself out. So I don't want you going out with anything on Prospero being killed or the reasons behind it. Got me?"

"Yeah, I got you."

"I mean, we'll respond forthrightly to queries from the media. But only if they come to Sorel or you and I."

"That's fine."

"Has there been any contact at your end, Jake?" he boomed interrogatively.

"Let's see." I thought of Borg and his retrospective that had the Stormbat matter concealed somewhere within, the story that could really slap the Administration for its stupidity and cowardice in stopping Prospero, and took my first step down the duplicity trail. "Nope, not a thing. What about you?"

"Nothing so far. But, you know ..."

"Yeah, I know."

I waited for him to ask me about the growing storm, the prospects of our flying it, the availability of press seats on our planes. But Moriarity was too important to know a hurricane ripened south of Cuba. He just said, "Okay, Jake, many thanks," and slammed down the receiver, the time-honored reporter's goodbye, acquired by hanging around more experienced men.

Hearing me hang up, Bella yelled in, "Jake, Doc Hurricane's on line two."

I pushed the flashing button and said, "Hey, Chat."

"Nothing urgent, Jake," Chatham said, coming on the line with a voice that always sounded calm, but in which elements of excitement tumbled around below the surface. "The satellite shows that depression doing a little more than just breaking even. It looks to be intensifying some, and there's pretty good organization beginning around the center of low pressure. We're within an ace of naming it Dolly."

"Any recon yet?"

"Air Force has a C-130 on the way out from Keesler. It'll be a while before we have anything from it. You want a call?"

"I'd appreciate it. My home phone's on your list. We never close."

"We neither. Talk to you later."

The prospect of a hurricane flight sometime that week had come a little closer. I smiled to myself, letting my own excitement rise, and went out to the vending machine room for a cup of instant coffee. Jim Westheimer worked on some tea nearby, leaned over it, forcing it to steep – he did nothing with grace or ease. "Anything from the model?" I asked, using the premature question as greeting.

So he surprised me with news from his imaginary world: "There may be. We've had some preliminary runs on this storm, you know, matching the statistics of it with those of others, comparing the large-scale situation. Although it's much too soon for this to mean anything, the model tracks right down the history of Camille at this stage in her development."

"You think it'll hold up? Camille was a five-hundred-year storm ... "

" ... in Gulfport, Jake. In Gulfport. The 1935 Keys storm was a five-hundred-year storm too. Maybe we get one every generation."

"Okay," I conceded. Sorel had come into the room behind Westheimer and I wanted to shut down the discussion before he got into it. Something in Sorel's face told me he was still mad at Westheimer about their short exchange at the meeting that morning.

But Westheimer with something to say was the quintessential body in motion. "Atmospheric statistics don't really say much about the real atmosphere. You may not've known I understood that. But I do. A hurricane doesn't know what it is any more than one of my models knows how many times it's been spun up on the computer. Every storm, every evolving mathematical term, is a new experience. We can anticipate things happening in a general way, and learning to do that could be very important to understanding hurricanes. But the real storm always behaves like a large, very confident animal. It always will. That's what we can't model."

I started to say something like, Well said, to end it there. But
Sorel said from behind Westheimer, half frightening, half
surprising him, "You're right on one point, anyway, Jim."

"What's that?" Westheimer would not turn to look at Sorel.

"I didn't know you understood that." A bad thing to say
after a closed man opens to you a little. I think now it shows
the kind of web of tension Sorel could spin. After Sorel had got
his candy bar from the machine and left us I wanted to
apologize. But Westheimer had already snapped shut again.
He held his place in the room almost defiantly. "I'll see you
later, Jim," I said, and left him with his hurt.

Back in the office I finished the morning getting stuff ready.
I wrote down a call list to run through that afternoon, and
some items like crew sequencing and my choices for the
scientific assignments, and a handful of other remainders more
or less arranged around a small, scrawled "Borg" near the
center of the page. Then I realized, with something like a pang,
that I hadn't thought of Rory since we got back from the
meeting. I rang her intercom line and when she answered said,
"I'll be down to getcha in a taxi, honey."

"That's fine, whoever you are." We laughed. I told Bella,
"I'm taking Rory to lunch," and started to cross to her office.

"How's she taking the bad news about Prospero?" Bella
wanted to know.

"Fine."

"What'll it do to 'her science'?" Bella asked the question
drily. I knew she didn't admire Rory, whose life as a scientist
seemed to Bella to have no reality in it; and, in the way of
women who sacrificed a lot to children and to the trifling shit
that flows from poverty, she found Rory's life shallow and
self-centered. Maybe I did a little too, but I said, "Don't be
bitchy." Then Rory emerged from her room and we went out,
our backs swept by Bella's glare.

I said earlier that I loved Rory anyway, and I guess that, if you
had pressed me, I would have acknowledged it was more than
half true. It was definitely true I hadn't had much in the way of
results, although sometimes I had the feeling we had our
gravitational fields out, drawing one another in. Pressed
harder, I would have admitted that, on my side, love was right

around the corner, with a caveat or two about my reluctance to repeat a learning experience of the dimensions Lennie had given me. But – and I would tell this to nobody – I loved Rory the way a 14-year-old boy loves a certain 12-year-old girl: utterly, foolishly, crazily. She lived in my head like sound lives in a bell, nothing I did was done without some reference toward her. I saw her everywhere; and her indigo VW bug joined me on the highways of the world. So that, when it came time for me to choose between what was right and what was wrong (although no one knew *how* wrong back then, except perhaps the people at headquarters, the military men and the spooks), my decision and behaviour took form partly from my malarial affection for beautiful Aurora Merchant.

On her side, all ran along inscrutably. She had herself very much together, or seemed to; and her status as a free woman was uncertain, moot – as a protégée of Sorel's she had privileges around the lab. He acted as though she were his, and maybe she was, from time to time. You bump around in the back of a plane through enough experiments and eventually something – not love, necessarily, but something – blooms. The closest Rory and I had come had been on a mission that put down for a day in Barbados. But I lack the heavy-handed touch. (Lennie would have it another way: I'm insufficiently aggressive, or why am I still sitting on Sorel's left?)

We got shrimp baskets at a fish bar down by Dinner Key and sat out where we could watch the bay and the yachts and birds using the wind that pumped toward us from the east. Or where Rory could, for I found myself more and more watching only her. And listening. She had one of the fine, full voices in the world, and she ate her shrimps with hands that were long and rectangular, like Negro hands of a certain kind, which gestured delicately but with force to make a point. When I'd grabbed her in Barbados I'd learned her body was not merely small but wiry as well, and the little black cap of hair she wore was soft as something spiders weave. Her legs were above average, and her bosom had a classical curve. Her laugh, on those rare occasions when you heard it, pushed things toward rightness. She laughed now, saying, "if I'd known you'd be watching me this closely I'd have gotten something else."

"Watching you eat shrimp's no worse than a lot of things."

"Name one."

"Oh, lobsters eating eggs?"

"Mm."

"You eating crab?"

"People leave the room."

"Leaving you to me, m'dear. It could be worse." I looked as hard as I dared into the great blue clarity of her eyes. Windows of the clear blue mind. "It's always nice to have you around. Right now it happens about one percent as often as I'd like." There, something fairly serious; it made my hands tremble enough that I shoved them out of sight.

"One percent?"

"Or less."

"Can I say something about you?"

"Sure."

"I know what you're saying, and how hard it is for you to say it." She held up a hand to silence my protest. "But this is why I can't just banter back on it. You carry a lot of marks, Jake, and whenever you go up to D.C. you come back bleeding a little."

"Lacerations and contusions about the head and shoulders."

She frowned, teacher fashion. "More like the mind and spirit, old sport. So when you tell me more directly than usual that you like having me around, I have to crank in these other things that still drive you. You're still a sad old man over what's happened to your family. I've got a few bruises myself. One thing neither of us wants or needs is to have important emotions used up as a way-station. But –" Her smile returned for me. "I think we could increase the dosage to ten percent of optimum without getting any bad side-effects."

"Does that mean I get to take off your clothes?"

She shook her head. "It means hugs for extraordinary achievements. Increments of affection. A reach across the table by a trusting hand." Her hand touched mine gently, and stayed. "Small benefits like that."

"Despite my great disappointment – it sounds like a beginning."

"It is if we really want one, I guess."

"I may get a little silly about this from time to time. But trust me, Rory. Down deep, that happy inner man, thought dead, riseth."

She seemed to give herself a shake, which restored some of our emotional distance. "For now, I guess we have to work for a living."

"Saturday's children." I got up and paid, waving away her money.

"The next one's mine," she said, fussing gently over this hint of inequality.

"Well, lady, that would be dinner, wouldn't it?"

She laughed her wonderful laugh, and nodded. And, for a moment, I sensed how it might be to have her in my life, to be a happy, witty man who laughed a lot, who ached no longer, whose commitment had been valued and reciprocated by that person. It lasted me the afternoon.

For a time, that evening, I thought we'd had our last laugh of the day. She lived in a stuccoed and tile cottage on the southern fringe of Coconut Grove, just before it shades into large money. I went by for her in my ageing Saab, recently cleansed of Big Mac boxes and beer cans. Of course I had that twinge near the heart when she opened the door, done as she was in a white cotton handprint from the Keys, with a repeated freeform-floral design the color of her eyes. I've rarely had my breath taken clean away like that, and it was an hour or so before I realized that besides being beautiful tonight she was very, very quiet. The storm – the possibility of the storm – lay between us; we behaved like athletes with important games to play on an uncertain schedule, the hype already shoving us around. So when we sat at our table out on a gravel spit in Biscayne Bay with Miami glimmering back at us on tiny waves and the world looking fine and together, and a splendid filet behind us, we could barely speak through our preoccupations.

At last she said, 'We're not doing very well tonight, Jake."

"Nope. Too much too soon."

"Maybe so."

"Did I tell you Borg'd be out tomorrow?"

"Yep."

"What about your appearance tonight? Did I comment on that?"

"Nope."

"I said nothing about the extreme beautifulness of it?"

"Uh-uh."

"Rory, my friend, we're going to have to do better."

"I know."

"Look, if we fly, it won't be for another couple of days. It's way too soon to be brooding."

"You're right. But brood we do."

"Well, hell, I guess I'd rather be with you brooding than not be with you at all."

And on. We got out of the place after a cognac and headed back to the Grove. Our silence persisted, although now and then I caught the blue gleam of her gaze peripherally, and it cheered me to have her watchful, focused on me a little. "I guess," I said at last, "I guess I'm taking you home."

"I guess so."

We pulled into the sudden jungle of her street and into the clearing among the bamboos and hibiscus bushes and banyans where a few square meters of gravel gave her a place to park her bug and receive one other car. I switched off my machine and went around to let her out, but she'd got out ahead of me. "Can you come in?" she asked.

"Pop doesn't need the car back till ten."

She led me through an arbor dark with bougainvillaea and across a broad porch beneath the generous tile roof of the small, ochre-stuccoed structure, and then into the soft light of her living-room, where a bunch of big pillows did the work of furniture and a lot of art hung on the big wall that ascended to the apex of the high-pitched ceiling. The south side of the room disappeared in plants, and a door in that wall seemed to open on a small patio, dim in the darkness. I sat down on a pile of hand-done pillows the size of suitcases, soft handwovens in beiges and whites, and watched Rory. The light was only a candlepower or two above ambient, so that she seemed almost to glow in her white cotton, fluoresce, like a creature in the night-time sea. She left the room for a moment, and returned with a stuffed macaw from Bird World. Then, sitting near me in our nest of cushions, she unzipped the bird and took out a baggie of grass and some cigarette paper.

"Let us brood no more," she said

"Amen," I replied.

Rory rolled a cigarette-sized joint and lit up, then passed it to me. And so we spent the rest of the evening, sharing the grass and lowering our sights, and maybe letting the storm that had held us apart begin to push us together. She put on some music and as we went along the notes got farther and farther apart, and became important. The mission dissolved, along with any little pockets and residues of malice, and we sort of leaned into one another. Finally we made love in the timeless, slow, peaceful way one does when stoned, and lay around, and made love again.

I don't remember falling asleep. But the morning light seemed to catch me before I'd quite settled, and I sat up quickly, saying, "Jesus! Borg!" Rory didn't stir. She lay with her back against me, where we had curled up like two integral signs. Her dark short hair had been mussed a bit. In repose, her face seemed only frail, like the rest of her, all naked and creamy, with the faintest touch of sinew. Last night's blue and white sheath lay crumpled a surprising distance away, as though she had shed it in flight. I didn't wake her going out.

None of us lived very far from the lab. My apartment was over in Coral Gables, next door to Rory's neighborhood. It was a small but open set of rooms on one corner of a two-storey white-stuccoed structure that, among the ritzy estates of the Gables, looked

as comfortable in its setting as a beached river boat. I'd furnished it in what I thought of as Survivor Eclectic – the stuff a man rescues from a shattered home, plus the slurry of recently acquired necessities, empty of meaning, permanently unfamiliar.

I got home by seven and cleaned up and bolted a cinnamon roll and some juice and had Mr Coffee rumbling away while I cleaned up. Getting stoned almost always left me with the equivalent of a hangover, a restlessness, as though a not very important wire ·hung loose somewhere within. It had just about stopped sparking when someone rang the doorbell.

I opened the door on Sam Newman, who lived in the building next door, was one of the agency's more experienced pilots and had become a friend before anyone else had when I came down to Miami. "Hey, Sam, come in." He did. "You on your way in or on your way out?"

"Going out." Grinning at the suggestion that he would tom-cat his night away, he sat down and helped himself to the coffee. His accent was what you'd call Texas Aviator, eternally unruffled. "Reason I stopped by, I heard your phone ring off and on all night. Thought we might be flying today, but nobody said anything."

"Far's I know the storm hasn't changed."

"Best you check in, then. They'd named it Dolly by the late news last night," he said. I nodded. Sam seemed to have no life outside an airplane, and rarely displayed any humor or much of anything else away from a flight deck. Something had happened in the life of this small and compact and private man. He never spoke of it, but you could see behind the narrow squinting green eyes an acrimonious divorce, a parent's suicide, the death of a child – something as bad as that. One reason we were friends was our love of flying, and his generosity in sharing his Big Aviation with a light-plane driver like me. In the air, he was meticulous, without a tremor. Ask

him for a run twenty-five feet off the water and twenty-five feet
– not twenty-two, not thirty – was what you got. Now he
banked the conversation to a new heading. "You see Charlie
Whiskey in D.C.?"

"Nope. He was spending the night with friends. I think he
gets it from his mother." Sam frowned and I put up a hand. "I
hate myself for saying things like that."

"Me too."

"She's bringing him down this week. Jesus, I'd forgotten. If
we fly Dolly and Lennie's in Key West, how the hell can I take
Charlie?"

"If I'm not flying I'll take up the slack."

"That's very neighborly."

"Charlie's good company."

"You're right."

We left together and I offered him a ride up to the airport;
but he declined, saying it would screw up his carpool, which
had an elaborate point system for who drove and who rode,
and when. Really Sam just preserved a certain amount of
grumpy distance between us. We both understood that news of
my smashed little family was about the only family news he
ever had. He, or someone, a mother, a sweetheart, a daughter,
had burned some of his bridges long ago, so that he would
never marry now, never love; his fathering would be always
second-hand. It had flattered me, though, that such fathering
as he was willing to do went out to Charlie.

But I was just as happy not to have company on the way to
the airport, preferring to drive out alone with the news station
muttering from a rear speaker in the Saab. The back way takes
you out through Coral Gables and all the Spanishy houses with
red tile, bananas, bougainvillaea, and palms and huge banyans
grappling across the road; then through a patch of standard
concrete block Miami houses, shaped like children's sketches,
boxes colored blue and pink and green and white. This far into
the summer, even before nine in the morning, the awful heat of
southern Florida owned the town, gave it all a hot, brownish
tinge; the sky wriggled with sunlight, and heat bounced off
the flat, paved plate of the city. Miami is the only place I've
been where, from time to time in summer, you feel you could
fall off a barely curving earth.

The compensations of the route are mainly for airplane buffs. You come upon the airport from the south, deadending almost into the southern east-west runway; then, as you turn west to circle the field on a perimeter road, you get to take in all the aviation. As far as you can see, most times of the day, dark smudges over the horizon mark the line of incoming jets, settling fast and heavy onto the east-west strips; and, somehow, little planes like mine fluttering in for landings between the violent arrivals of the big guys.

The field also rates high as a museum, the grass areas and spare apron crowded with derelicts and tramps, old Douglases and Convairs and Lockheeds and Curtises and Boeings tucked wing to wing, some stripped of everything but airframe and skin, standing around in wing-deep grass and the oil-can debris mechanics leave around. You see old DC-8s and 707s out there now, to remind you how deep we are into the jet age. By the time Charlie's in college there should be a smattering of jumbos standing around, and maybe a Concorde, tape blinding their greenhouses and side windows, their engines plugged or pulled, their tires turned to dust. One of our old planes had been cast off for a while; then somebody figured out we wouldn't have flown hurricanes in a clunker and bought her for nothing, spruced her up with Indian colors and new paint, and flew her away to a new career as a lovely, ageing tramp in the enormous airplane graveyard of South America.

Past the derelicts I could see our new planes, their tails rising three storeys to show the flag and the agency roundel. They would go on and on, through the eighties and nineties. And then we – or someone – would get something a little better. Maybe.

Borg was there ahead of me, inside the fenced area with a stocky Cuban photographer, regarding one of our planes like a painter, his long, thin body arced back, one arm stretched out in a broad assessing gesture. His long rectangle of a face had seen some sun and he'd let his hair grow. For a moment I held back, regarding the airplane with them, once again acknowledging my more-than-routine affection for the blue, black and silver machines. Borg sensed something happening, I suppose, for he turned around and greeted me. I greeted him back and went over.

"This's Joe Arbenz," he said, waving at the photographer. "Joe, this's Dr Warner."

"Also known as Jake," I said, shaking hands. "Okay, Steve, what can I help you get?"

"I'd like to just do a walkthrough with Joe, and then let him go on and do his thing while we talk."

"Fine." I led them over to the ladder and up into the fuselage of Prospero Two, as the plane was known to people in the lab and to air traffic controllers. The two new airplanes still excited me. I couldn't enter one without a father's mix of awe and pride, although at best I was only an uncle to these wonders. "You remember how it was in the old planes, I guess." Borg nodded. "You can see there are some differences." We had large bubble windows and salmon-colored leatherette seats at each station. The interior was sheathed in beige metal panelling and pale, shaped polymer consoles; no open equipment racks disturbed the eye, no big auxiliary power unit thundered on the aisle.

"Christ," Borg said, "It looks like a starship."

"Works like one too, a little." I walked them up forward. "The mission scientist, usually Sorel on this plane, sits there, behind the pilot's seat on the flight deck. Then, moving aft, you have the gust probe and cloud physics station there on the right, the communications center on the left, and, behind it, the flight director's chair. That's where I generally sit." The station looked dead with nothing on the displays. "The view I have is a composite, fed from the Doppler navigation system and the belly and tail radars, which give me vertical and horizontal dimensions. Then the computer works the information into a false color display that shows our three-dimensional situation."

"Neat," said Borg.

"There's nothing like it anywhere else in civilian research, Steve. The military may have better on their all-weather interceptors," I went on, the Navy *Intruder* target I'd seen on Charlie's cork wall moving in on me momentarily, "but I'm not even sure of that. This is really a damned good system. On a mission I can monitor our flight level within a three-dimensional hurricane, and watch the other planes too, and even go in for close-ups of areas where minor differences in radar reflectivity mean important differences in what seeding will do." I took them farther aft, indicating where our computer specialist sat, and the guests. "These six seats belong to extra scientists and valued guests. If you fly with us you'll be in one of these."

The Cuban broke his silence. "What about the seeding?"

"All the way back." We went past the galley and foldup bunks to the dropsonde chute and seeding gun, a rectangular frame of stainless steel with a big plunger on top linked through an eccentric arm to a small electric motor. "It works like a Gatling gun. These are the rounds," I added, indicating a box of pencil-sized cylinders stacked in oblong magazines. "You just put the magazine into the larger rectangle, set the plunger, and presto, you've got a high-rate-of-fire silver-iodide machine."

"What, it spits them out?" Arbenz wanted to know.

"More or less. The plunger pushes them out the bottom of the magazine, where they hit a firing pin. This ignites the pyrotechnic which begins to burn as it falls, leaving a trail of smoke that's rich in silver iodide."

The photographer squatted by the gun, studying its form and function. As his interest brought him out of the background, I looked at him more closely. He wore his black hair long with sideburns that petered out just below the level of his eye; no beard grew until the chin, where whiskers sprouted randomly, like black barbs on a brown, pitted cactus. His eyes hid behind mirror-finished dark glasses, the heavy eyebrows arching away from the blue plastic rims that contained only reflections, like two holes in his face. When he raised his shades he revealed red-rimmed, moist brown eyes, longlashed, intelligent windows in a punk face. He wasn't very big, and a ring of fat trembled under his Star Wars T-shirt. "This the thing you guys used on Cuba?" he asked at last.

Borg laughed.

I said, "Come on."

"No, look," Arbenz said, "I don't care. You guys are heroes over on the Tamiami Trail, man, we hope you dry up the whole fucking island."

"You got it wrong, Joe."

"Okay, I got it wrong." Arbenz laughed. "But it would be

so, you know, *cold*, to have this plane in the parade Saturday.
Jesus, *que* float!"

"You really got it wrong."

"Sure, man. Like the CIA raising that, you know, Russian
sub, right? Like that trying to make Fidel's hair fall out, man. I
know I got it wrong, but don't, you know, try to straighten me
out. Tell your story to Fidel. *After* he catches you seeding his
clouds, you know?" He turned to Borg. "Okay, Steve-o, I'm
going to photograph the insides of this, you know, spy ship."

Borg nodded. "Fine. See you at the paper." We watched the
Cuban stalk forward and begin unpacking his denim camera
bag. Borg said, "No offense, Jake."

"That CIA link the thrust of your story?" The degree of
Arbenz's misconception angered me.

"No, hell no. You know how Cubans think about Cuba."

"Castro came to power five years before your boy was
born."

"Hey, come on. Every day of his life, old Joe has a thousand
reminders that he lives in the United States of America, an
Anglo nation, and has no native land, and less than oriental
splendor. But there his country is, a hundred miles south of us.
It twists you up to be so close, and still so far, from home. You
never get quite free. Here's an index of how poor the Miami
Cubans are. Castro gets to celebrate one of his many jubilees,
okay, with Mig flyovers and Soviet visitors and a couple of
divisions under arms. So the Miami Cubans are going to have a
'grand march' on Saturday, foot shuffling and speeches,
probably a lot of rum and two or three fatal shootings. What
Castro gets has a kind of reality. What these people get has to
be made up." He shook his head. "Of course, to see these
people here still trying to be a Cuba in exile after an entire
goddamned generation doesn't speak well for Castro's jubilee,
either."

I nodded, cooling off. "Okay, what else?"

"Okay," Borg replied. "Silver iodide." He uttered the
words like an incantation, steering us away from the
photographer. "Everybody uses silver iodide for seeding now,
right?"

"You can seed two ways. Either you lower the temperature
of water way below freezing to make it freeze without nuclei to

form on, which is the dry-ice way. Or you "persuade' supercooled water to freeze by providing a nucleus, or rather, millions of nuclei. That's the clean, neat silver-iodide way." I laughed. "Since you've done about fifty thousand words on weather mod, maybe I should move along."

"No, really, everything helps," Borg said, but his face told me I'd gone on too long. "Well," he said a moment later, "Joe needs to roam the plane. Can we get any crew aboard?"

"They'll be working on board shortly."

"Okay." Borg strode forward and talked to Arbenz in the cockpit about getting exteriors when he was through inside, and to make sure he got people at their stations. Then, returning to me, he said, "I guess I should talk to Sorel now."

"Fine."

We talked about Prospero on the way across town. I felt defensive, I think because the project had been killed and so carried the taint of the unfunded; or maybe because Borg pressed. "One thing I don't understand, Jake, is why a successful method for making hurricanes less bad doesn't get more support."

"That isn't exactly how things lie. Prospero's an experiment to see whether the technique works. There are uncertainties. Of course there'd be plenty of support for a sure thing."

"What kind of uncertainties?"

"Let me back off a moment. I should say that we don't understand hurricanes completely. But we're reasonably certain that the technique works, without a bunch of serious side-effects."

"Like changing the storm's track, or increasing storm surge, or drying up hurricane rainfall?"

"Your homework shows. But that's right. That kind of side-effect apparently doesn't happen." I hesitated, feeling my way again, waiting to see how Borg would move. He surprised me.

"Without trying to fart you off, Jake, what I hear you saying is that the fears are groundless as far as *you're* concerned – that you and Sorel and the other scientists here are satisfied. That sounds pretty relative to me."

"What you *should* hear me saying is we've done a hell of a lot of research on this particular set of questions and we're satisfied the technique will do no harm and probably will do a whole lot of good."

"Okay, tell me the benefits."

The benefits. In the lab we had chanted Prospero's benefits for years; it rose to the lips like catechisms. "It looks like we can reasonably expect seeding to reduce maximum winds twenty or thirty percent. Since wind force varies as the square of speed, reducing hurricane winds should lower damage significantly. And we're beginning to think reduced winds might also diminish storm surge."

"Does that translate into dollars, or lives?"

"Hurricanes don't kill a hell of a lot of people in this country anymore, although they still get a couple of hundred a year, even with a very good warning system." I cranked up the litany. "What we usually say is that if you seeded a major hurricane – one that would cause a billion dollars' worth of property damage – and reduced damage ten percent, you'd quickly pay off the money invested in Prospero."

"Invested. That isn't a word one associates with government spending."

"It's appropriate here," I finished, beginning to be mad at him.

Then he asked, "Okay, what about the experiment itself? Given what I saw at the airport and a reasonable expectation of progress, isn't Prospero really the same experiment they were running back in the sixties?"

"It's fundamentally changed."

"The technique?"

"That, and the hypothesis. They used to say they were going to weaken the storm by causing the eyewall to expand outward, and that this would smooth the pressure drop that drives the winds."

"How would seeding enlarge the eye?"

"It taps the heat stored in water. When you seed and make water freeze you release a lot of heat energy into the system, change the energy distribution in a hurricane, cause the eye to expand, and, through conservation of angular momentum, cause the winds to drop around the eyewall."

"So what has changed?"

"We now say we're going to seed immature centers of vertical circulation outside the eyewall, and that by seeding these we'll encourage their further development. The seeded cells ultimately grow into the high-altitude outflow layers, and become the main vertical conduit in the storm. The old eyewall dissipates. The result is an eye of greater diameter, and, again, conservation of momentum reduces wind speeds in the new eyeball."

"I hate to say it, but I don't hear any change."

"God-damn it, there are important differences. They're embedded in the microstructure of the storm. The key difference – this is not for your story – is that the old hypothesis was an informed hunch, and to the extent it seemed to work it was a good one. Now we've explained the physics and chemistry behind the hunch. We just about know where to seed, and why, and what will happen when we do. We badly need to test all this in the laboratory of a real hurricane. *That's* the difference you should be able to hear in the Prospero hypothesis now."

"Art into science."

"Sure."

"Ignore my bedside manner, okay?" He grinned at me, shaking his head at my small show of temper.

I had to laugh. "You're right. Absolutely right. Sorry."

"Can I continue my quest?"

"Sure."

"Okay. Given the benefits you've described, what about the question of liability? I mean, suppose you seed the storm and it comes ashore and greases a coastal town. Why wouldn't the locals be justified in saying, Hey, if that storm hadn't been seeded we'd still have roofs – and then sue the government? How do you handle that in Prospero?"

Liability was a minefield, and I waited a moment or two, giving myself back to the traffic long enough to think through my answer. Then I said, "I'm not a lawyer, so I can't really respond to all of your questions, Steve. Far's I know, anybody can sue anybody for anything in this country. But it would be *very* hard to establish that seeding had any effect – we have a hell of a time identifying the transient signal we think we produce by seeding. Here's an example. Debbie in 1969, after one seeding, showed a decrease in maximum winds of about 30 percent. But Allen, in 1980, did the same thing *without* being seeded. What part of the change do we cause? What is a hurricane's natural variability? We're on the way to finding out, but, right now, *nobody* knows.

"Okay. We're reasonably certain that no long-term changes are caused by seeding a hurricane. But we still try to keep clear of the liability issue. We wouldn't begin a seeding mission on any storm that had more than a ten percent chance of making landfall anywhere within the next 24 hours. This cuts our sample size way down. But it means we can say with pretty good assurance that nothing we do over the ocean has any effect on anyone ashore."

"But if you were seeding operationally ... "

"An operational hurricane modification is a whole 'nother kind of animal, Steve. And there, of course, the liability question becomes very big, very fast."

Let me ask what may be a stupid question."

"Why should we stop now?"

"Thanks a bunch. The last real seeding of a real storm was Debbie in 1969. Now, as I remember the situation, it was mid-August, and two hurricanes were out there: Debbie in the Atlantic, Camille in the Gulf. The government mounted a big seeding experiment out of Puerto Rico, but on Debbie, which was a 100-knot storm, not Camille, which was closer to a 200-knot storm. So, while they got interesting results from Debbie, Camille was killing hundreds of people in Mississippi. My question is, why didn't they try to get that 30 percent wind reduction in Camille?"

"Liability, I imagine. Suppose they'd seeded Camille and nothing had happened one way or another. The same 200-knot storm would drive into Gulfport, with the same ten-meter storm surge, and the same two-hundred-some casualties. A day later you wouldn't have been able to drive through Washington for the lawyers. That's something that just hasn't been resolved. That's why we stay out over the ocean."

"Is anyone studying the problem?"

"There's work in the universities and think tanks about risk decision-making, and hurricanes are in there somewhere. But there isn't a whole lot. That hasn't been where the money was."

Borg let up. I could feel his pressure on me relax. We pushed through traffic for a time in silence. Then he gave me his rabbit punch.

"Jake, you know how this sounds? It sounds like Prospero got killed just before it began to deliver on the large investment your agency's made over the last ten years. It doesn't track. I mean, it would be *crazy* to kill Prospero for budgetary reasons, even in these hard times. And, even allowing for the strong cowardly reflex in government agencies, I don't see them caving in because you get wildly inaccurate reports in the Mexican, Cuban and Russian press. So I've got to say, okay, they're pulling out because of Stormbat."

I shook my head. "No comment, Steve. Talk to Sorel about Stormbat." And then, possibly because we'd been talking about Camille just before, I added, "Talk to him about Camille, too." I was glad to get to the lab, and glad to leave Borg with Sorel who looked both meaner and more boyish than usual that morning. Then I went around to the hurricane room upstairs. Chatham was there, brooding over a dotted line on a wall map that crossed the Antilles at St Lucia, then, in a long, shallow wavelike motion, drifted through the Caribbean south of Jamaica, to a symbol near Grand Cayman. An infra-red satellite photograph tacked to the map showed a broad, ragged patch of white blotting out the sea between Cuba and Honduras. It looked violent as hell to me, with the cloud tops brilliant white, indicating some of the convection had pushed the weather into the lower stratosphere. A baby hurricane, with long lines of clouds forming up over hundreds of square miles of ocean as Dolly began to take over its corner of the atmosphere. You could see the storm spinning up on the television monitors in the forecasting areas, where the last twenty-four hours of high-resolution satellite imagery ran as a film loop; the clouds converged out by the Antilles, drawn to developing low pressure like pale leaves toward a whirlpool; then, crossing into the Caribbean, their rotation became more organized, and finally coalesced into the present big white whirlwind.

"Hi, Chat," I said to get his attention.

"Oh, hello, Jake. Tried to get you last night."

"Sam Newman told me. He's a neighbor."

"We're calling this thing Dolly. It went to a tropical storm late last night. Satellite shows a path of eighty-degree water to the north-west of her now, so we figure she'll spin up to hurricane strength tonight, maybe early tomorrow. She's also beginning to move right along."

"Air Force fly her yet?"

"They had a flight yesterday afternoon, before she got up tropical storm strength. Only thing they reported worth noting was extreme electrical activity. The winds sounded pretty routine."

He didn't look as though anything were routine, though. "If everything's so cool ... ?"

He almost grinned. "I don't know. I just worry. Well look. This thing's turning north-west now. Suppose it intensifies. Suppose it goes into something like Camille. And then suppose it recurves and heads up the Florida Keys. There's not much experience in bad storms down there anymore, and there's been a lot of construction. A real big one would put just about the whole chain underwater. So, naturally, I just – worry."

"Would you fire up Prospero Drill?"

"Oh, sure. You'll get a hurricane flight out of this one. I just can't say now whether it'll be on Thursday or Friday."

"Thanks."

"Sure. I'll keep you posted."

On the way back to my office I checked in at Westheimer's, partly to see what he had and partly to decant some guilt over the way he got shut down by Sorel the day before. He moved long computer printouts around on a conference table. "How's the modeling, Jim?" I asked.

"Interesting."

"More?"

"We've been adding data as it's come in and if we take the storm now and run the model backward, the model does what the storm's done thus far. So the fit seems to be a good one."

"What happens if you run it forward?"

"It turns into a hurricane tomorrow and begins to recurve up west of Cuba. And – it intensifies."

"It's got Chatham a little uptight."

"He's getting from his experience what we're getting from our model runs. That's a good sign."

"Sure it is." I left Westheimer to his printouts and headed for my office. Rory's office door was closed. "She in today?" I asked Bella.

She shook her head. "She called. She'll be in later on." You could see the temptation to zap move behind the wise brown eyes.

"Just the news, please," I told her.

Once at my desk I put the day off a minute or two, and thought about Rory and me and our evening. Moving her into the foreground of my mind brought a rush of excitement, and thoughts of her sweetness, and of how last night could have been a beginning for us; and then, on the backswing of these feelings, a lump near my heart: perhaps the night had been both the beginning and the end. Trouble with grass and love-making is you don't get quite the real article – great things happen, but the emotions are deformed. One's memory of something important glitters beyond a gauze of intense but often trivial perceptions. Mainly, I wished we'd had more of the night together, and the morning; and I wished she'd been at work so I could have caught her eye, read her drift …

Someone – it was Borg, but my eyes were focused on infinity and at first I just saw the movement towards me – came in and I jumped. "Oh. Steve." Embarrassed, I gave an awkward chuckle. "My mind was flat AWOL just now, so you startled me."

Borg sat down in the spare chair. "Day-dreaming civil servant deploys spirit into real world."

"Now that I'm back, how'd it go with Henry?"

"Fine." You could see Borg pulling his cards in a little closer. "He's a good interview. But, you know," and here Borg loosened up some, "I caught a twinkle, a gleam, something – I caught some hint that he isn't through. I mean, he could just go ahead and have the experiment, couldn't he?"

"Come on."

"But couldn't he? Of course, there'd be hell to pay when he got back, if anyone knew he'd done it. But meanwhile there'd be that seeded hurricane, and some life blown into Prospero maybe by favorable winds off Capitol Hill. You'll excuse all the metaphor."

"A government scientist doing that … "

"Would be as bad as a university biologist painting cancers on mice."

"It'd have the same effect on a career," I said. Then I shook my head emphatically, feeling too co-operative with Borg's troubling speculations. "Sorel wouldn't try to revive Prospero that way. He likes to work things up through a continuum, like someone building a city, over generations. He doesn't go for a priori field experiments. And you can't take one of our research flights, give it a bath and a haircut, and come out with a viable Prospero seeding experiment."

"Okay, but it's still possible to fly kind of a half-assed seeding mission that could have measurable effects on a storm, no?"

He began to worry me. "Jesus, I hope this isn't the direction your Prospero piece takes. Because if it is you'll be goddamned far off the mark, even for you. Farther than your Cuban photographer."

"Thanks." He got up. "On that sentimental note, I'll split. But I do want to fly next time you guys go out."

"Your name's on that list too."

"In addition to your shit list."

"Yep. Way it looks now, we'll be coming up on a thirty-six-hour alert sometime tonight. I'll let you know."

I was glad to see him go, partly because his hunch about Sorel illuminated thoughts I'd kept in a dark corner. Hell, yes, Henry would go for a seeding mission if he thought it would resurrect Prospero. Or even if he thought he could weaken a dangerous storm. Maybe. It would take the right hurricane, the right kind of opportunity; but if these came along, Sorel'd do exactly what Borg had sensed he'd do. Then, even if somebody knew his intentions, nobody would be able to stop the mission. Nobody could stop us once we were underway. And afterward, no one would know. There would only have been a shortlived perturbation in the huge energy of the storm.

Okay, then what good would a clandestine seeding do Prospero? If no one knew, there could be no papers written, no farming the data year after year at all the meetings – no

reward. And if, *when*, word leaked out that there had been a
seeding, Sorel and his accomplices would lose their
professional asses. Except – what the hell, Sorel could even
survive that with the kind of data, the right kind of support on
the Hill, maybe the right intentions, like trying to pull the fuze
on a killer storm on its way to landfall in Miami or New
Orleans or Mobile. And if he didn't survive professionally –
well, what a hell of a ride it would have been, right down the
centerline of the thin band of vitality that runs through the
bureaucracy. A hell of a ride.

About an hour after Borg left, Bella buzzed me on the
intercom to pick up one of the blinking lights on my phone,
and there was Lennie, all breathless and without significance,
which I took to be one beneficial side-effect of my night with
Rory."Jake!" she said with mock urgency. "Hi, it's Lennie. I
wanted to get back to you on that Key West trip. I tried to call
you last night, but you must have been out, so I had to call you
at work. We're still on,. but I wanted to make sure you could
take Charlie ... "

She meant she'd heard about the storm and wanted to seize
the initiative in our negotiations. "We've got a hurricane to fly
in another couple of days, Lennie," I said, feeling the tension
go into everything as she cocked the trap.

"Don't you *want* to see him?"

And old Jake trying to chew the thing off his leg. "It's just a
bad week for me."

"If it isn't going to work out Tom and I can make other
arrangements. I just thought you'd like to have Charlie for a
while."

Tom and I. "Of course I want him to come down. I'll work it
out. When do you get in?"

"Tom's flying down to Key West tomorrow from Patuxent.
Charlie and I'll be down on Eastern's noon flight."

"Tomorrow?"

"Yes."

"I'll pick you up."

"I'll be flying out ninety minutes later."

Then, thinking we could parlay the encounter into some
pleasure (and aviation) for Charlie and me, I said, "Look,
suppose I fly you down to Key West in the Skylane."

"Isn't that doing it the hard way?"

"Nope. I want to get Charlie up while he's here anyway."

"Okay." She could not help adding. "It might be fun."

"It might."

"Tomorrow, Jake?"

"Right."

"Bye bye."

She got off the line. I hung on a moment or two, relishing the hollow silence of the open long-distance line coming at the end of her voice and all the implied pressures she could put into it, talking to me. Did she do this to Tom? I doubted it. "Jesus Christ," I said, and put the receiver down.

"Look like you're having a day," Rory said from the door, the brighter outside light putting her in grey silhouette, destroying her outline.

"Ah, you caught me at vespers." It's a curse, always to talk, to kid, when what you want and need is to reach out, take hold … "Come in." I watched her cross the room's short diagonal, lithe and cautious as a cat. She sat down in the chair I kept pulled up at the corner of my desk, what I guess in loan companies would be the supplicant's chair. "You okay?"

"Sure." She gave me a smile. "You?"

"I'm fine about you. The day isn't the best."

"Let's talk about the day," she said.

"Okay. Borg was by this morning. Annoying presence."

"Are we flying?"

"Probably Thursday."

"Well," she said, "let's talk about that."

"Let's talk about us."

"No."

"Lennie called just now."

"Let's talk about that."

"I have less urge to brain her since your therapy."

"You're welcome."

"We going out tonight?"

"No."

"Well – can we curl up somewhere in the meantime?"

"No."

"Lennie's dropping Charlie off with me tomorrow. I'm taking her down to Key West and the boy'll stay with me through the weekend. I thought ..."

"I don't much want to start anything with Charlie."

"Okay." She'd begun to wear me out. "Other than the above, do we have a future?"

"I don't know."

And it came to me on her voice, in the sound of it, that she wanted me to shape this thing of ours too, and move her along in it. Something had made her tired in ways I recognized and shared; she needed me to do some of the driving. "I want us to, Rory," I said.

"I want us to too." The China blue teared up.

"Let's work something out, then."

"We've got to try."

Her translucent, long-fingered hand lay close to mine on the desk and I put my paw over it. Like weary dancers we stood and stepped into an embrace. I liked holding her tough little body and smelling her soapy smell, and I thought, We can stand like this eternally. "We're trying," I whispered. I felt her chin nod against my chest, but she said nothing. I said, "Come on," and moved us out of the office, telling Bella of a long lunch. We drove back to Rory's jungly pad in the Grove and made grassless love, and had tuna sandwiches, and murmured, and regarded one another from various distances. So that, for the interval of a noon hour, we were in love, fated, bound.

She decided to go out to the airport the rest of the afternoon, and I returned to the lab. I guess I should admit that the prospect of having Charlie enter my life just as this point did not elate me; and that the lack of enthusiasm pushed up guilt around the sides of the high I carried away from this time with Rory. So, barely able to think beyond these mixed feelings, I pushed papers around for an hour before finally getting serious and picking up the crew manifests for Prospero Drill.

Prospero Two would be flown by Sam Newman. Jim Peterson was down for copilot. Charlie Bruska at flight engineer. The usual bunch behind the flight deck.

Ordinarily I made the scientific assignments on both planes, so it surprised me to see Sorel had already made his list and attached it to Murchison's roster. Henry Sorel had the mission scientist's chair on Two, up behind the pilot, I had the flight director station aft of the flight deck, Archie McBride had the gust probe and cloud physics station; he flamed with red hair and freckles, but was a quiet man just 30, just married, just turned loose by Cal Tech with his new Ph.D. – as though his life had begun only about six months ago.

The surprise on the list was that Sorel had put Rory in at the dropsonde-seeker station back in the tail cone of Prospero Two. She should have been mission scientist on Prospero One.

I looked at the Prospero One roster. I knew these people, but not as well as the aircrew on my plane; they were about as familiar to me as soldiers in another platoon. Gil Bradenton commanded the airplane. Paul Wright, a recent Air Force transfer, flew copilot. They were our largest flight-deck combination, and our youngest. If we'd advertised they would have been on the poster; they *looked* like pilots, and were as alive and eager to fly as the men in a boy's book about aviation.

The rest of Murchison's recommended aircrew for Prospero One got only a quick look from me. But here again I found Sorel's personal assignments for the scientific positions. Dr Aurora Merchant had been crossed off in the mission scientist slot, and Dick Pettry had been written in. Carla Hendix was in the flight direcor position. Gary Himmell had the dropsonde-seeder station.

It occurred to me that this trio of young airborne scientists had one thing in common: they would go along. Pettry was on the way up, ambitious, about to stabilize as a coming atmospheric scientist. Hendrix had been sensitized to the possibility of discrimination, and was anxious not to fail. (Yes, and hurt; and hurt.) Himmell was black and about to enter Science. Well, hell yes they'd go along, and who could blame them? You work your butt off to get your doctorate in meterology, run errands for senior people and reduce data and read instruments out in the clouds of bugs that follow graduate students through their summers, and then – then, the professor, the Man, tells you he needs your help in some clandestine seeding, a little murder, something; and you don't know until the moment comes that you even have the option of not doing whatever has been asked, so easily will all your work be wiped away (you fear) if you don't. And your agony won't

even make your mentor blink. They'd do what Sorel wanted
them to.

And the aircrews? Our aviation facility was a little air force,
a vintage one, where officers did the large, technical things,
and sergeants did the mechanical, menial things. On the whole
it was very professional and really peerless for the quality and
quantity of flying we did. The sergeant figures would go a little
berserk in any new port; the pilots and other flight deck types
could merely have a good evening. In my memory the only
time any of the pilots arrived even red-eyed for a mission was
when the new boy, Paul Wright, had almost had to be carried
aboard Prospero Nine Five. Gil Bradenton, his pilot, had
explained extensively how they were no longer in the
goddamned Air Force and nothing like that happened again.
They were pros, not latter-day mail carriers, and they'd behave
like pros if Sorel wanted to seed. They would tell him,
courteously, to kiss their ass, they weren't going against the
administrator and God to help him out.

But if we flew a seeding drill, who'd know whether we were
really seeding? Sorel and Rory and I on our plane, Pettry and
Hendrix and Himmell on Prosper One. Jesus. I shook my
head fiercely to clear it of Borg's destructive ideas, wishing he'd
laid them in someone else's mind. ·

I called Murchison and told him my choices. He remarked
that we still had five scientist stations unfilled. I told him no
one had asked to go and we hadn't invited anyone, so Borg
would be our only outsider, riding the first scientist station on
Prospero Two.

"How far toward a real mission we need to be, Jake?" he
asked.

"I don't know. Henry wants a full simulation, so I'd think
both planes should be taken up to the full Prospero
configuration."

"Pyrotechnics and all?" I didn't blame him for trying to
leave the seeding pyrotechnics home. Although they only
produce silver-iodide smoke, they can be a lot of trouble in an
airplane. They were flares, after all, and burned hot enough to
eat a big hole in the aluminum hind end of a plane. But what
the hell, sailors can strap 500-pounders under a wing on a
pitching deck; we ought to be able to load ten thousand

pencil-sized flares without setting ourselves on fire. "Can't be anything but valuable experience."

"Roger." He hung up, mad.

On the way out I gave Bella my rough draft crew sheets and asked her to smooth them and make the thirty-six-hour notifications, with an effective time of 06.00 local time – 10.00 Greenwich – on Thursday, with a nominal first-seed time – T_0 – was set at 10.00 hours, eastern daylight time, Thursday. Then I went upstairs to see how our hurricane was doing.

Dolly was fine, but Chatham had begun to wilt some; he'd been on duty too long, and put too much of himself between Dolly and the mainland, as though sheer will and body English would keep the storm at sea. Dolly had moved on the map. As of an hour earlier, the satellite showed the unruly bunch of clouds just south-west of Jamaica, and a shade north of her position that morning. "I don't know what to tell you," Chatham said. "This morning I *knew* we'd have a hurricane by now, but surface winds near the center are only about fifty knots and pressure's nothing remarkable. The Air Force flew her again late this morning and they still report high electrical activity, and very bad turbulence. Will you settle for a tropical storm with character?"

"Maybe we'll have to. You going to be around tonight?"

"I'll be around off and on until this thing goes away, I reckon."

"If I'm nearby around midnight I'll run you up a liter of adrenaline."

"Make that on rye, Jake."

Westheimer came in then and looked at the satellite photos and the storm's position. "What do you think?" he asked Chatham in a tone that suggested he didn't give a shit what Chatham thought. It was a tone Westheimer used a lot.

"She'll develop."

"The model's less certain of that. We plugged in the last batch of data from the Hurricane Hunter and everything seemed to calm down." Westheimer frowned. "I think it calmed down too much. Could they be getting bad data?"

I laughed. "Could you be getting a bad motel run?"

"Very funny. But seriously, they may have some calibration problem."

"You're right, Jim." To Chatham I said, "Let's ask the Air Force to check the instrumentation on the 130 that flew into Dolly this morning, before it makes another flight. This thing looks ugly as hell in the satellite images. Maybe Jim's model is trying to tell us something. You know, 'Take me to your leader,' or something."

Chatham came dangerously close to laughing. Westheimer looked away, too annoyed to look at me. Never treat lightly a man's religion, political party, child or numerical model. "Later," I said.

I caught Sorel as he was throwing some stuff into a worn-shiny leather satchel, about to bail out for the day. He looked up when I came in and I saw, or thought I saw, something unfamiliar in his look – a kind of greed shone in his boy face; it was a look you see in the worst of the upperclassmen in a military school. "How'd it go with Borg?" I asked, for openers.

"Fine. He takes an adversary position, of course. I don't enjoy his interviews."

"He's flying with us, if we fly."

"Are we scheduled?"

"Bella's sending out the thirty-six hour alert for 06.00 Thursday."

Sorel nodded. "I talked to Chatham about an hour ago. Dolly doesn't seem to want to turn into anything. Perhaps we'll stay down."

"Maybe. Westheimer thinks the Air Force data may be off."

"His model relaxed too soon, or something."

"He's probably right."

"We'll see." Then I added, "I'll be gone tomorrow afternoon. Lennie's bringing the boy down and I thought I'd fly them down to Key West."

"Whatever. What about the Drill?"

"We're all set. Planes are configured for a seeding mission."

"Good. I wish we were flying one."

I dug my heels in some and said, "I figure we are."

"Oh?" His face hid nothing; its round, healthy cheeks flared crimson.

"Your crew selection looked like loaded dice to me, Henry."

"I sense a certain pissed-offedness at not getting to make the assignments yourself."

"I sense a certain putting people in key stations to ensure that a seeding goes down during the Drill." It made me nervous to argue with Sorel, and to know we'd barely begun. "The tip-off's putting Rory in at tail-gunner. She ought to be running Prospero One."

"What is it, don't you trust yourself with Dr Merchant on your plane, Jake? What's happening with you two, anyway?"

Ah, there we go. I flushed. "Why?"

"She's mine, you know," He had gone back to packing his satchel, his eyebrows arched, his rosy cheeks rosier, his eyes on what he packed.

"She's hers." Brave talk, merely. What he'd said, his proprietory tone, his look, all told me he had reason to be confident. If we'd been fencing he would have scored with that.

"I mean she's mine as much as she's likely to be anyone's. And that isn't very likely." He went on, explaining patiently to his brief-case, "I give her a kind of sheltered harbor she likes to return to from time to time. So I want you to keep clear, Jake."

"You speaking master to minion, Henry?"

"Man to man."

"Well, I can't do it."

"Then there will be some personal trouble between us."

"You're right."

"Look, Jake, I'm really not asking you," he said then, flashing an angry look at me before returning to the satchel. "I don't think you wish to share her with me. So – keep clear." He turned intently toward me then, the greedy look illuminated by a gleam of exasperated understanding, his tall spare frame curved against the windowlight, his long hands cupping the brief leather bag. The distinguished scientist.

And I, playing a goddamned adolescent, said, "Fuck you," and left him there.

I went back to my office. Bella had gone home so I kicked some furniture around in the privacy of my room. After a while I called Rory at home. "Can I come by tonight?" I asked when she'd answered.

She hesitated before telling me no.

I hung up and sulked for a time in my chair. Then, feeling

dumb and outmaneuvered, I hauled myself out of the office. I couldn't drink my sorrows away because I'd be flying the Skylane on Wednesday, so I did some shopping and chores and got the place supplied and clean enough for Charlie. And all the while, I ran my resentments back and forth, like a film loop, always ending with a questioning of Rory; and yet, as the end of the loop approached, always hoping she would say whatever could be said to chase away the woman Sorel had evoked that afternoon.

On the purely emotional front, everything was simple: I ached and missed my Person. So that, around midnight, I did the kind of thing kids do when they are horribly, obsessively, in love. I drove out to her house with the idea of getting close to the source of my anguish, and, luck and nerve permitting, to encounter it, hold it, spend the night in its soft arms. When I reached her driveway I saw dim lights inside, and would have turned in except Sorel's BMW glittered in the shadows near the porch.

So I did a cheap thing. I went to Carla Hendrix, looked into her pretty wolf eyes and gently touched her honey-colored hair, and asked if I could lie in her lap, and ended asleep in her arms. When I awoke my head rested against her abdomen, the big artery there throbbing the rhythms of her large, golden heart; my arms cleaved to her as though I were a castaway and she were a rock in the sea. I hung on until the sky began to flicker with dawn, and then got up and kissed her. She had not slept, or spoken. When I left she only watched me go with her lovely yellow-brown eyes, that said: Yes, I will even drink your poison.

"Prospero Two, this is Prospero One," Bradenton calls.

"Hello, Gil," I reply.

"We're in the eye about ten nautical behind you at four o'clock. Where's your damage?"

"Mostly the right side and along the belly."

"Okay, we're going to come up below you and take a look, then move on up so we can see your right side."

"Roger."

"After that we'll go to work."

"Okay."

"While we're moving up, I need some information," Bradenton says.

"Okay."

"I know you fly but I don't know what your level of experience is. Can you fill me in?"

"I've got about five hundred hours, all single-engine, all under four thousand gross."

"Instrument rated?"

"Nope."

"Other ratings?"

"Seaplane."

Bradenton is quiet. I brood. I hear him shake his head. I hear his sadness over the silent earphones. My confidence sinks in the pitiful little pool of experience I outlined to him. He has given up. He has gone off the air to whisper Hail Marys for me, for the people I doom with my small knowledge. The airplane looms around me; it has never seemed so large, so heavy, so incapable of flight. The engines beat the air perhaps twenty feet behind my chair, the tail is more than a hundred feet behind me. The center of gravity is way the hell back in the fuselage somewhere, and Borg and I and Bruska's covered body occupy a small, ruined, cylindrical room at the end of a fifty-foot cantilever. At take-off we weighed more than a hundred forty thousand pounds, and carried sixty thousand pounds of fuel. Zero Charlie Whiskey grosses a fiftieth of that, and carries only five hundred pounds of avgas. I look at the engine and fuel gauges. We have nearly half our fuel left. We are a great Molotov cocktail hurtling through an afternoon, waiting for the match, and the throw, and the bursting.

"Jake?" Bradenton returns from his prayers.

"Yep?"

"These next couple hours are really going to dress up your log-book." A moment later he comes on again. "We're coming up behind and under your airplane now. We're under you. Looks like you took a bunch of rounds along the belly, radome's all tattered. We're going to rise off your starboard wing in a second, stand by."

"Roger."

The other plane floats into view off the right wing, his wingtip barely the length of a wing away. I swallow hard. Bradenton is visible in the left-hand cockpit window. He waves. I wave back. Borg waves too. The plane rises farther and Bradenton looks down at us. "Yeah, you got stitched pretty good along the right front, and your number three and four nacelle's have some damage," he says. "Say – Jake – what happened to Peterson?"

"He got blown out the window when we depressurized." I shut my eyes, envisioning the smear down our fuselage where the copilot was swept away ...

"Yeah, I see. Who's in your gust probe station?"

"McBride." My scalp moves. Sickness touches my stomach with a cold finger. Borg is already ripping away his seat straps.

"He okay?" Bradenton asks.

"I – don't know." I get my strap off and run back, leaping the covered mound. Borg precedes me, and I see Rory turn toward us from Newman's bunk.

McBride sits at his station. The tubes and flasks connecting his cloud physics gear to the environment hang in ruins, like pale snakes, violently killed. The gust probe panel has been torn apart, as by a powerful hand within. The great wind in the cockpit echoes here, where three fist-sized holes gape at the atmosphere. McBride is imperturbable, he seems to watch his ruined instruments. But he is pale beneath the freckles and red hair. Sorel lies across the entrance to this station, which wraps around its occupant. Borg steps across the long, still body, then draws back, cries, "Oh, Christ!" into the noise, turns away; his foot is richly red, for Sorel's body dams a reservoir of blood. I lean into the area. From this perspective I see the hole in the fuselage hidden by McBride's pale profile; an intercostal from the airframe, sprung inward by the explosion, has piked him in the brain on this far side, and holds him where he sits watching dead instruments with sightless eyes.

Rory arrives on the scene, but does not look for long; I see the added death turn her grey and signal Borg to help her. Saperelli hurries forward from where Newman lies doped and bound, and I tell him, "Get some blankets, soak this up." Then I reach past Sorel and take McBride's head gently in my hands, and pull it towards me. The intercostal, so jagged it is slightly barbed, resists; then the metal releases and I begin to lift him out. Borg and Saperelli reach in to help me, I deliver McBride's body over to them, and they walk it to another bunk near Newman's, leaving a trail of brain and blood.

I wipe trembling hands on my trousers and lean against the flight director console; Rory sits there now with her head in her hands. "Sorry," I say.

She looks up. "You didn't do it."

"I'm beginning to wonder."

"We thought he was just sitting there."

"He was always – quiet."

"God."

"Best I get back." But I run in sand, McBride riding me, his death, the sense that death is all around us now, weighing me down. I try to remember who has spoken, who has been seen, since the attack. Weld, Mattson, Saperelli, Chesney, Borg. Rory. And our dead.

When I have my headset on I call Bradenton. "McBride was dead. We …" I want to say, A fuselage member hooked him in the brain, but it chills, put so directly. I want to say, His head was cold to my touch. I want to say, He was always so quiet. And, He'd only been alive about six months. But nothing comes, except a shiver of sickness and fatigue …

"Bad news," Bradenton says. "How do you feel, Jake? As well as can be expected?"

"Yeah."

"Back when I was in a ward after the war, that was how we described our condition to the doc. As well as can be expected. Sir." He seemed old and wise, and I remember with surprise that his war is Vietnam. He goes on, trying to unwrinkle me with conversation. "Some were, some weren't."

"Always the way." But my response is mere courtesy. The discovery of McBride, another death, has rattled me. Death, I think, will begin springing at us from suddenly opened doors.

"Ye-ep." I sense him trying to gauge my real state of mind. At last he says, "Well, best we go to work."

"Fine." My voice still shakes, though.

"First thing I want you to do is get comfortable in that left seat, Jake. Move it around until the wheel, the pedals, the power levers, everything feels like you could fly the plane from there." He pauses before adding, in a tone too even to rattle me, but cold enough to make me listen, "You want to be *real* comfortable in that seat, because that's where you stay till you're on the ground and stopped. You leave that wheel unattended and you're gonna kill all those good people over there. Okay?"

"Okay." It shames me, to have forgotten to fly.

"I understand why you left, Jake," Bradenton adds in a gentler voice, becoming the instructor again.

I fiddle around with the seat, making small adjustments, then tighten my straps; they must support me if my spine should fail. "All right," I say.

"Good. Now tell me your altitude, airspeed and heading." I tell him; nothing has changed, our heading shifts instant by instant as we circle in the eye. "Now, on the panel right ahead of you are your flight instruments. You seem to know where they are, but run through them again for me." I comply, moving from black disc to black disc, and I feel myself laying claim to the cockpit once more. Bradenton goes on. "Everything's like your plane, Jake, just a little bigger, little heavier and faster. We won't be doing anything today you haven't done in your Cessna, except maybe land at a hundred knots – and, uh, maybe lose an engine and stay airborne. Those holes in your number four nacelle could drop out that engine any time. If it does, you'll get a fire light up by those emergency handles – those red and white striped handles along the top center panel. They go from left to right, one, two, three, four. You see a warning light, or hear me say *pull number four*! kind of loud, pull that E-handle on the far right. That shuts everything down – fuel, air, oil, everything, and feathers the prop. And that should, uh, put out the fire."

"If it doesn't … ?" I begin.

"If it doesn't," Bradenton puts in quickly, "in the remote chance it doesn't, you get another shot. When you pull the E-handle you expose a fire extinguisher switch – the high-rate discharge button. If the E-handle doesn't put it out, you hit the HRD button."

"And then?"

"HRD bottle's your last shot." Silence. "Uh, let's move along."

"Roger."

"Okay, you're in a plane that's just a bit bigger and hotter than your Cessna. You've got about the same fuel we do, which is fuel OTA for what we have to do. We could stay up there until you're ready to solo that machine if we had to. But you've got some wounded aboard, so best we go on and take you in after a (pardon the expression) crash course. Ready for some flying?"

"Ready," I reply, my mind snugly blanketed by his words, hypnotically reassuring. And yet, beneath the blanket, I am numb to the prospect of flight. I see our plane in flames, spinning down and down, like the broken bombers in World War II combat films. Except we carry no parachutes. Nothing blossoms from us but little balloons of surprised conversation.

"Okay, Jake, just reach down there on your right and turn the autopilot switch to *off*."

I wrap the control wheel with my left hand, willing myself to hold it gently, then lean over and turn off the autopilot. Instantly, the mechanical aviator opens his dead hand; the wheel revives, and the rudder pedals. Although servos and circuits separate me from the air flowing over the distant control surfaces and stabilizers of this vessel, I feel these artificial added boundaries in the controls. The instruments say nothing has changed. But, unmistakably, the big ship now hangs from my left hand, where my fingers touch the wheel. I seem to control nothing but the nose of the airplane, and feel the need to somehow compensate for my extreme forward position and think backward, fly closer to the center of the aircraft.

Bradenton, reading minds, comes in. "Jake, you flying now?"

"Yep."

"Don't worry about flying the whole ship from way up front. In a little plane, they're *your* wings. Here you just fly your chair and sort of bring the rest of the plane along."

"Roger," I say.

"Okay, let's try a standard two-minute three-sixty to the left."

Timidly, I roll the plane into a left turn, watching the little airplane on the artificial horizon and the altimeter and rate of climb and turn coordinator to balance out my deficiencies and excesses – too much or too little back pressure on the wheel once into the turn, too much opposite aileron. The circle, once completed, is deformed in space, one side higher than the other; but it is not terrible. I think of my Charlie's perfect three-sixties in the Skylane, flying the airplane that *he* can't really fly. Yesterday. Only yesterday.

Outside, the wallcloud rushes at us, and I turn away, begin the long circle that will keep us in the eye until Bradenton thinks (or is willing to say he thinks) I can take us through. Now he says, "Not too bad," echoing my feelings: nothing irreparably bad has happened. The airplane has not flipped over in an accelerated stall. We do not spin toward the sea. I look back at Borg, shake my head. He grins, gives a thumbs-up.

"Okay," says Bradenton, "do a ninety-degree turn to the left to get out in the middle of the eye again, and then try a three-sixty to the right."

Going left I descend; rolling to the right I climb. But it is better. I begin to get the sense of the airplane through the wheel. It is gargantuan, heavy, and you must *move* the controls; but my hands tingle with new intuitions of the broad spectrum of its performance, like the muscles felt beneath the loose skin of a cat.

"How the turns feel?" Bradenton asks.

"Better."

"They look pretty good from over here." The other plane floats off our right wing about two hundred feet. "I think your directional control's pretty good. Now let's get into how it behaves when you add or subtract power."

"Okay."

"Take a good look at that pedestal on your right – then, as I

call them out, touch them – power levers – elevator trim ..."
He orders my hands around the pedestal; it moves like an
enthusiastic blind man's, touching the levers and wheels that
sprout from the grey metal console. "Got them?"

"Yep."

"Then let's get basic. You've got a standard pitch and power
situation, even in that big machine. Add power and the plane'll
climb if you don't pitch the nose down to maintain level flight.
Reduce power and the plane'll dive if you don't pitch up to
maintain level flight. If you hold level with added power, your
airspeed comes up. Stay level with less power, it drops. Just like
a Skylane."

"Right." He takes me back to fundamentals. In a way I
resent the simplicity: it says I have no instincts.

Bradenton hears something in my voice, intuits. "Here's a
cautionary note, Jake. Turns are just a hand on the wheel, like
a kid steering a car. You aren't flying the plane until you're
running those engines."

Embarrassed by my transparency, I reply a muttered,
"Roger."

"Let's do some pitch and power problems."

Bradenton asks a lot. He wants me to move the four levers
that control the amount of power from the engines. Not just
move them, but disturb the careful equilibrium which is the
last bequest of Sam Newman. It is sacrilege; it invites
punishment. "Christ," I say, clutching the clustered levers.

"Hold those things like a little child's fingers," he says,
making me wonder how many children's fingers he's held
lately. But I relax my death grip. "Now pull back slowly until
you hit the stops. That's your flight idle position." I comply.
The airspeed declines swiftly. "Maintain two twenty,"
Bradenton says, "and notice how she doesn't glide." I put
forward pressure on the wheel, chase the airspeed needle until
it's captured and begins to rise. I release some of the wheel
pressure. The airspeed stabilizes. "Now the trim, trim her up."
I rotate the trim wheel until the pressure goes out of the
controls. "You need a little left rudder going down, just a tad."
We are diving gently; the slipstream is a muted scream, a hint
of the shriek you would hear in a steep, terminal dive. The
altimeter unwinds. We are down to eight thousand five,

eight ... "Okay, leave the power alone and level out – and you best turn away from that wallcloud." The white wall hurtles toward us. I pull the wheel back, drive the airplane into a shallow left turn and try to get the artificial horizon and its toy plane level, the altimeter steady. The airspeed decays to two hundred knots, a hundred eighty, hundred seventy; the controls begin to thicken their response. "Okay, hold that altitude and add power so you come back to two hundred."

As the power comes up I push the nose forward slightly. The airspeed rises. "Go on and open her up now. Watch your attitude." I advance the power levers. We accelerate perceptibly, and begin to climb. "Get that nose down, hold seventy-five hundred." The airspeed passes two hundred fifty, two hundred seventy-five knots, the wallcloud flies toward us. "Okay, pull her up in about a twenty-degree climb." The climb is exhilarating, a wonder. I want to go up and up; I want never to land. "That's good. Go on and get level at ten thousand, Jake and set the autopilot, turn on the altitude hold, and crank in a shallow turn to stay clear of the wallcloud. We've got to figure the best way to get you out of this hurricane.

Dolly was officially promoted to a hurricane early that morning, while I slept a shallow, anxious sleep full of Sorel and Rory and Charlie and Carla – Carla doing some forgotten violence, acting out the pain I'd handed her ...

MIAMI
Wednesday
T + 28 h 30 m
Lat 25.5 N
Long 80.2 W

Chatham called me at home about six-thirty Wednesday morning. "We had an early Hurricane Hunter flight into Dolly," he said after I'd made a sleepy response to his greeting. "She's still small. Not much more than ten miles across the eye, and not a lot of strong peripheral circulation. We got surface winds of about ninety knots, flight level winds about a hundred. Surface pressure in the eye's 980 millibars."

The news shook me awake. "That's a hell of a lot more storm than we had yesterday."

"Jim Westheimer was right," Chatham went on. "The Air Force ran a check and found a calibration problem that undermeasured everything. Dolly probably went over hurricane force about sundown yesterday."

"Where is she now?"

"Air Force fixed her west of Cuba, just entering the Yucatan Straits."

"So we'll fly her in the Gulf," I said. "How convenient."

"But you may have to land somewhere besides Miami."

"You serious?"

"About halfway. I see Dolly coming up past Yucatan, then veering to the north-east, where high pressure should constrain her to more of an eastward course. So then you've got a storm on a north-east-to-east heading that has to come out of the Gulf somewhere between Havana and Jacksonville. I imagine we'll get her through here."

"We'll be mustering at ten at the airport. Will you have more by then?"

"We're getting high-rate pictures off the satellite now, so I'll have some fresh stuff for the meeting. But the Air Force won't be flying the storm again until this afternoon."

"Thanks, Chat." I returned to my last stale cinnamon roll and coffee.

What really lay most upon my mind was the prospect of flying the Skylane down to Key West. Even with Rory haunting my thoughts like a lost loved one, even with the taint of last night's selfish trip to Carla, even with my unfortunate son only a few hours away from my care, even with Dolly drifting out by Yucatan, getting more violent by the minute – my primary view of the future filled with a couple of hours' flying over the blue and green sea.

As I went out Sam Newman fell in alongside. Apparently he'd waited until he heard my door, reluctant to come in for coffee two days running, in the way of lonely, diffident men. I told him about Charlie's coming down and the flight to Key West, and the hurricane. I wanted to ask him to join us for dinner that night, and he seemed to want an invitation; but I couldn't bring another person into a life that had become so crowded.

"We're both flying tomorrow," he said finally, "what you plan to do about Charlie?"

"I guess I'll try Bella."

"Lots of luck." He took up his carpool vigil. "See you at the briefing."

"Right. So long." There was disappointment on both sides.

Driving over to the office I fretted about asking Bella to take Charlie for the day. It sounds easy, and for some boss-secretary relationships it would have been. But Bella and I had quietly stressed the human qualities of her job; she didn't dial my calls or wax my desk or fetch my coffee. So asking for a personal favor exceeded our guidelines, and it bothered me to have no option but to ask her.

She was there when I arrived – she seemed always to be there – this big chocolate-colored woman who would rise exuberantly from what I perceived as sad reveries of life in and around the Grove. She was anachronistic, a fifties-style black woman, and not a friend of mine in the usual sense. We didn't talk about her husband, who had a reputation in the lab of being an idler, or about my divorce. But we now and then responded to each other in a way that suggested more than superficial friendship.

"Hi, Bella," I began.

"Hi, Jake."

"You muster everybody for ten o'clock at the airport?"

"Yep."

"Good. Look – I've got an unusual request, old thing."

"What you got?" A jovial tone, but you could see her defenses go up; a slight focal change of the eyes.

"Charlie's coming in today. I've got him through the weekend. But I need somebody to take him while I'm flying tomorrow."

"So naturally you thought of me."

"Well – I don't like to ask you. If I weren't in a jam I wouldn't."

She laughed. "Jake, I know you're not trying to domesticate me or anything. I'm glad to take your Charlie if he doesn't mind spending time in my part of the Grove. I don't want to do it at work, you see."

"Fair enough." I added, "Chatham thinks the hurricane could turn this way. We might not be able to get back into Miami."

"Sure enough?"

"So you and Charlie may go through hell together."

"Oh, we been *there* before, no doubt. But we're on high ground, and the house is up off the ground eight feet. So with some water and food we ought to ride out most anything." I thought of Charlie and Bella with a category-five hurricane whipping away cars and roofs all around them and gradually mashing this house into the "high ground" of the Grove. Probably I frowned because she added, "You'll get your Charlie back afterward, Jake, I promise."

I gave a guilty grin. "Okay." Then, glancing at Rory's office, "She in?"

"Was, but she went on out to the airport. With Dr Sorel." Bella watched me closely as she spoke and I, still inclined – still fated – to do the adolescent thing, flushed and turned away, hoping my disappointment wasn't all that visible.

"I guess I'll do the same," I said. "I'm taking Lennie and Charlie down to Key West this afternoon so you probably won't see me again till I bring him by. It'll be early, like six thirty."

"That's fine." She'd been writing something and handed me the note with an address and telephone number. "Can you find this all right?"

"Sure."

I puttered at the stack of weather maps and satellite photos on my desk, then, near nine, headed for the aviation facility. Only this time I turned off at the general aviation ramp and drove over beside Three Charlie Whiskey. The tanks had been topped off, and I checked the oil and poked around in the cabin to pick up charts and gum wrappers, and stowed a surprise for Charlie; then went through a careful preflight, taking longer than one needs to going over the plane, making sure the windows were clean and the cabin fresh (people sweat a lot in airplanes). Mainly I was putting my aviation between the world and its people and me; the touch and smell and prospect of the Skylane was my antidote for anything.

The whistle of a taxiing jet made me turn to look, as all aircraft sounds make all pilots turn. A gull-grey Navy A-3D bomber waddled across the ramp on its narrow undercarriage, its stubby wings folded, incongruous and violent among the gentle singles and bizjets, a great, droop-winged carnivore of a bird, browsing among finches. The pilot's hatch had been popped and a two-star admiral's ensign fluttered on a short mast. I watched the bomber stalk the line boy flagging it in, and pivot into one of the ramp parking spaces nearby. As the engines spun down a ground crew hooked an auxiliary powe unit to the plane; then it just sat there buttoned up in the awful turbine scream, I shook my head with mild wonder and went back to my own little machine, restoring the protective barriers of my aviation. It took me far enough away that the sudden, peripheral appearance of a dark flight-suited figure made me jump; it might have been Death. "Dr Warner?" it asked. I nodded. "Admiral requests the pleasure of your company, sir …" I looked around the ramp, and wondered what he meant. Then he added, "Will you come aboard, sir?"

It made me gin, as such puzzling incongruities invariably must, and I followed this deferential young spectre over to the Navy plane. The bomb-bay doors dropped open and an aluminium ladder uncoiled from the forward bulkhead. I had to stoop under the fuselage to reach the steps, then climbed up into a small room built into the bay. The stairs hissed back up into the fuselage, and I heard electric motors seal the doors; the roaring power unit outside was suddenly lost in silence.

The room was a very comfortable office. A U-shaped sofa

ran around three sides of it, with seat-belts poking out of the maroon leather cushions at intervals. Several polished wooden table-tops extended on aluminum arms to give the passengers a place to read and write in little pools of high-intensity light from overhead lamps. The floor – the deck, they would say – was concealed by a thick black carpet, which someone kept free of lint and footprints. And all of this was set in a great quilt of silvery soundproofing material covering the walls, except where two large oval windows had been cut into the fuselage. Admiral Carney occupied the far corner of the U, somnolent, eternally calm, watchful. "Hello, Warner," he said, without extending a hand to shake or making any other welcoming movement; he seemed instead to wait, like a spider testing the vibrations of his web.

"Morning, Admiral," I said. "Nice transportation."

"Fine ship." I saw the Navy wings on the tieless khaki uniform and thought he probably did more than just ride along in his upholstered den. "Fast. Comfortable. Uh, highly maneuverable. That yours?" He pointed his sharp little chin at the side window, in the general direction of Three Charlie Whiskey. I nodded. "Fine ship," he murmured.

I took a seat at the other corner of the U. "May I?"

"Of course. Rude of me. Yes, please be seated. Drink?"

"No, thanks. Then I added, perhaps to retrieve my own aviation in the face of this flying whore-house of his, "I'm flying this afternoon."

"Yes, of course. In the old days, used to drink the brandy halfway down to get an artificial horizon. But not now, not in America. French pilots drink all the time. But not us. Coffee, tea?"

"Coffee."

He turned to a grill behind him in the quilted wall. "We'll have coffee," he told it. A moment later the young crew chief who'd summoned me appeared, wearing a starched white jacket over his flight suit and carrying a silver coffee service and plate of cookies. "We'll serve ourselves," the admiral said, and the boy set down his things on a table-top between us.

"Yessir," he replied, backing toward the flight deck.

Carney leaned forward and began pouring out our coffee, asking about cream or sugar and handing mine over to me.

While he occupied himself with his, I took a closer look at the paper littering the table-tops: they were satellite photos of Dolly, yellow rectangles ripped from weather teletypes, facsimile weather maps showing the great fingerprint-like patterns of pressure, the barbed arrows of wind, the meteorological world in which the smaller coil of the hurricane drifted like a cloudy man-of-war. I asked, "What brings you to Miami, Admiral?"

"*En route* Key West. Had to put down here briefly."

He made me uncomfortable. It was as though he'd come by just to see me, at a place and time only I knew, and he was going where I was this afternoon. It made the world too small, and him too powerful. Itching to get away, I said, "I can't stay long, there's a meeting ..." My voice carried a vague, annoying apology.

"Meeting?" His eyebrows moved a centimeter upwards. "Meeting?"

"On Prospero Drill."

"Ah," he said. "Ah." He watched me sleepily. "The rehearsal."

"The drill, yes."

"I should attend your meeting," he said, adding, after noting my disappointment, "But no time, no time." Then, after a short, watchful silence, he asked, "When do you fly?"

"This afternoon. Also to Key West."

His laugh was softly metallic. "I know about Key West – I meant your hurricane flight."

So he'd known I would be on the ramp sometime today. It frightened me, to be made so predictable. "Looks like tomorrow morning," I said.

"Tomorrow morning. Very good. I should go with you. Never flown a hurricane." He shook his head. "But I can't go. No time."

"It's a long flight," I replied, thinking of the prospect of ten bone-rattling hours inside Dolly.

"Interesting possibilities with Dolly," he muttered, staring dreamily out the window at nothing at all. "*Very* interesting." He turned his deceptively sleepy little eyes on me then. "Stormbat. Will the Cubans launch a research flight? Ideal chance to show us planes are kosher, not combat. But, you know, they've had some days of Dolly passing to the south, recurving west of them, but no flights. No movement. Stormbat sits under tarps on the ramp at San Antonio de los Banos. We are very close to telling Russia this huricane-research ploy is a crock of shit. But not until Dolly is gone. What do you think, Warner? Will they put Stormbat into Dolly?"

I shrugged. "That's not my department, Admiral." Or my way, I thought.

"If they do, get a picture. Like to know more. Just a bit more."

He drowsed, musing. "As you see from all this litter," he said at last, "I have great interest in Dolly. Rare storm. Track like Camille. Intensity like Camille." Then, abruptly, "How's Sorel?"

I flinched, understanding his question. "What do you mean?"

"Come on, Warner. That, uh, medical gap in mid-career after Camille. Look." He slid a photograph out of papers on his table and handed it to me. It showed a thin-faced man of about 40, blond, his eyes flat, his face empty, as though untouched by life, like an unfinished etching; no one I had ever seen. "Well?"

"Sorel," Carney said, smiling his spidery smile. "Sorel in that unfortunate gap, after Camille, before he got into hurricanes. Took numerous volts to the head of this unrecognizable young man to exorcize Camille. Many volts. Many woven baskets. Many conversations. You know why?"

I nodded, and thought, Ah, you nasty little angel of death, what is it you want?

"One wonders. Very stressful, flying these storms at all. But for your lab director, much worse. All that voltage getting over Camille, you see. All those baskets. All that talk. What happens when he meets Camille again? Interesting, isn't it?"

"It's carrion," I said.

"No program here, Warner. Just interesting possibilities. One studies men, one finds such coincidences wonderful, in the old sense of that word. No program to discredit, however." He added sleepily, "After all, he bounced back very well finally. Very well."

"Yes, he did."

"Still must be quite wrenching emotionally, to come upon such a storm. You agree?"

"I think he's fine. No problems." I wanted badly to add, No residual cracks, nothing like what you're describing. But Carney had laid his eggs now, and irresistibly I would have to see this aspect of Sorel in everything he did – in terms of the crack Camille had left him. The admiral had given me a glimpse of his prediction, as though alerting me – I still wonder why. Perhaps he wanted someone half ready, half expecting what would come. I don't know.

"Glad to hear it. Fine man. Fine scientist. Sorry about Prospero. Great disappointment."

"Yes, it was."

Having done what he intended, he hurried us apart. "Well, Warner, thanks for coming by. Must go now. You have your meeting. I have my business in Key West." He made the expression that passed for a smile and added, "Good luck tomorrow." But something in his voice said we had none. I shivered at this step upon my grave.

"Thanks for the coffee, Admiral." I watched him for a moment, then stood up. The bomb-bay opened beneath us, the ladder unfolded for me and the office filled with the sound of the auxiliary power unit. I left him in his plush, evil nest and headed for the meeting. Even before I left the ramp, the A-3D was taxiing, its folded wings extending like a waking bird's as it rolled across the concrete, the little Navy flag flickering dark as death in the bright light. I watched them trundle away, watched their take-off, watched until the admiral's plane was just a black speck in a grey cloud of jet exhaust. "Jesus," I whispered. "Jesus." The contact had left me nearly sick.

Everybody except Chatham waited for the meeting when I arrived. We'd gathered in the flight facility's conference room, a plush alcove on a mezzanine in the big hangar; incongruously, hangar racket flowed in whenever the door opened, then stopped as abruptly as cartoon sound-track when it closed.

These meetings were the coming together – sometimes the confrontation – of two worlds. There was always some degree of polarization between the lab people and the airplane people, since the former didn't want their science run by airplane drivers and technicians, and the latter didn't want their airplanes commanded by scientists. When we met at the lab, Sorel chaired. Out here, Murchison did the honors, his face almost lost in the frown that had grown with the possibility of Prospero Drill. I sat down across the table from Murchison, on Sorel's side but not at his end, with Chatham's chair and Carla, Pettry, Himmell and a couple of young forecasters between me and Sorel and Rory and a pair of other lab people, including Jim Westheimer. Carla watched everything but me. Rory looked at me for a time, showing how her face could be as neutral as a stranger's. Finding nothing anywhere but pain, I turned to Murchison, who'd decided to start without Chatham.

He opened with logistics, radio frequencies and procedures, and schedules, then gradually shifted to where we'd pick up the storm. "Looks like the mission will intercept Dolly when she's north of western Cuba on a north-easterly heading. That close to home, you can have a full eight hours in the storm, if you want it, and still divert to MacDill or Keesler if Miami goes down in weather. At Dr Sorel's request, we've staggered the flights so that Prospero One will get off here about an hour ahead of Two, and return about the same time, so you won't meet until you're both in the hurricane. But that'll give One a chance to scout the storm and set up the Prospero sequence."

Sorel had the next spot. He told us about this being a kind of work we'd done in earlier flights, and earlier simulations, but that Thursday's drill would stress timing and coordination. "What our house admiral calls the choreography," he said. "We may get funded one of these years, so we may as well know how to do what we have proposed doing." He nodded at a grad student across the room, who dimmed the lights and flicked on an overhead projector. Sorel slid a film positive into place that showed a greatly enlarged satellite view of Dolly. "Prospero One will fly at endurance cruise to Dolly, arriving there about half an hour ahead of Prospero Two. You'll enter along the rainbands," he went on, looking from Bradenton and his copilot to Pettry and Carla, and added a transparent overlay to this hurricane picture that showed a flight path shaped like a squared-off figure eight – what we called a butterfly. "At fifteen hundred feet you'll fly this butterfly pattern, then climb to twenty-three thousand in the eye." He added another overlay replaced the low-level butterfly with a high altitude pattern. "Then you re-enter the storm at about the two o'clock radius to begin, uh, simulated seeding. For two hours you'll fly a network of seeding legs back and forth between two and twelve o'clock. Okay?" he asked the room. When there were no questions, he cleared the Prospero One overlays and turned off the projector. The student brought up the house lights.

"Prospero Two will fly a butterfly at fifteen hundred, then climb to nineteen thousand for another cloud physics butterfly at that level, then go on up to twenty-three thousand. You'll climb in the eye. While Two is in the seeding area, One will fly a cloud physics butterfly at thirty thousand.

"We'll wait an hour after the second simulated seeding, and both planes will monitor at the seeding level and thirty thousand. Then Two will simulate another two-hour seeding, followed consecutively by One for a third hour. In a genuine Prospero mission we'd break off after eight hours in the storm, refuel and recrew, and be off again in an hour. But for Prospero Drill, we'll do just the one eight-hour sequence. Questions?"

Nobody else asked him so I did. "If we aren't seeding, Henry, why fly the full eight-hour cycle? We could rehearse four hours and have it down."

Sorel's mouth went mean. Rory put on a slapped look. But his voice kept cordial. "Good question, Jake. We need the full mission. We don't know how we'll do once we're in the hurricane together. I think you and Carla Hendrix, for example, are going to need the full drill to sort out the best way to monitor your plane, the other plane, and the storm, and keep everybody efficient at the same time. It's new ground. I think everybody will benefit."

"Okay," I replied. But that cruel upperclassman cast to his ageless face kept me suspicious, if you can call a vague ache near the heart suspicious. Hell, it was more likely jealousy, and grief, seeing Rory leashed to Sorel, seeing our beginning cave inward.

"Thanks, Henry," Murchison put in, pulling us all back to the room. "You all have copies of the crew assignments and ops plans. We've got only one visitor, a Mr Borg from the *Herald*, who has the number one visiting scientist station on Two. I believe he's the only one on this mission." There was murmured agreement.

Chatham came in then, flustered at coming upon the meeting already in motion, and a bit annoyed we'd gone on without him. But Murchison picked up on it, and quickly passed the floor to "Dr Chatham". His mood improved once he got back into hurricane meteorology, the violent vineyard where he'd labored these twenty-five years; the life of this slight sunburned Floridian was reckoned in hurricane seasons, and the spaghetti of their overlapping tracks had four dimensions in his memory – he could remember that jog Camille made south of Cuba that straightened out the track toward Mississippi, or the hesitations of Eloise. Long after the ruined cities had been reassembled and the dead put out of mind, the storms thrashed in Chatham's reverie.

He told us about what he'd told me at six-thirty, except that Dolly had drifted a degree to the north and east, indicating she'd begun to recurve nearly at the lower boundary of the Gulf. He still thought that, given the weather systems flanking her, the storm would head on up to the north-east, crossing the west coast of Florida probably no earlier than noon Friday. "We've put out a hurricane watch from the Keys to St Pete. After this afternoon's Air Force fix we'll adjust that. But I'm really counting on an early flight tomorrow, and your flight, to give us what we need to narrow the predicted track for our warning."

"What's your gut feeling?" Sorel asked. When he used American slang it always resounded, like a challenge.

"My gut feeling is that this thing's going to rip up the Keys pretty bad. She was down to 980 millibars this morning, and the satellite shows her really beginning to deepen – a very tight, swift little vortex."

Peterson, the Prospero Two copilot, laughed. "I used to date a very tight little vortex up in Appalachicola." Everyone but Sorel and Chatham thought it was funny.

Sam Newman put in, "She's going to be a hard flight." He'd

flown better than two hundred hurricane penetrations, including the last flight into Camille before she came ashore. Coming from him, a storm would take it as a compliment.

"I think you're right, Sam," Chatham said. "I think it'll be a very hard flight. It won't surprise me if you find yourself in something like Camille."

"Shit," said Bruska, the flight engineer on Two, starting a ripple of laughter and conversation along the aviation side of the table.

But I wasn't looking at Bruska, who tried to preserve his funniness by dropping expletives into the air that drifted down the table. Sorel had that odd, greedy look I'd seen before. Everyone in the laboratory knew why Camille would have more than average interest for Sorel; but I don't think he himself had talked it over with anyone there except me, and perhaps Rory.

Camille had killed his family.

Sorel told me about Camille one night in Bermuda, where we stood down after a bad flight into Emma, which had been not much more than a collection of violent thunderstorms by the time we got there, and which had given us and our old airplanes a frightening time. We always pretended the machines couldn't be made to crash in a hurricane, that we could not be driven out of our aluminum shells into rubber boats to endure the wind and lightning and rain and mountainous waves that surged like blood in a great, grey heart ... But the Emma flight shook our faith some, and that night in the officers' club at Kindley and around the pretty town of St George a goodly amount of alcohol went down our relieved throats.

Sorel and I did our drinking above the swimming deck of our hotel, the sea off to the south-west, the town lights and gibbous moon illuminating Emma's cape of cirrus clouds, retreating toward the northern sea.

"Look there," Sorel said in a thick voice. "Look there. The bitch is going to die."

I nodded. "A hard case."

"They're all hard cases, one way or another." Sorel leaned toward me over the table. "I hate the fuckers. I really hate the fuckers."

His vehemence surprised and embarrassed me; it opened the

way to responses he wanted that I didn't know how (and didn't want) to make. I guess I sensed he would end by telling me about his family, and I didn't need it, especially then, with my own little home in ruins. And something else: I half loved the big storms. I even liked their having a gender: it seemed to compliment everyone concerned. On the other hand, I knew they were just wind and water, energy in the atmosphere, and worse – unintelligent takers of life and the things of life. So my view had no extreme position. I said, "Nobody loves a hurricane."

"No, I mean I hate them, Jake. It's too much feeling to take into the bloody atmosphere, you know. But there it is."

Well, when someone talks like that to me my first impulse is to say it's eight parts bullshit and let it go; but beneath that obvious layer I understood Sorel had something going on, that he wouldn't let me not listen to his story. So I asked him why.

And he told me.

We still consider Camille the worst hurricane on record to have touched the Unites States, a five-hundred-year storm, an atmospheric event of inconceivable violence. In August 1969 she curved up around the western tip of Cuba, jogged slightly to the east, straightened out and headed across the Gulf into the shallow beaches between Biloxi and Bay Saint Louis. She hit the coastline with winds too high to measure; one anemometer recorded 230-mile-an-hour winds before Camille blew it away – the winds of a huge tornado. Camille *was* more a whirlwind than most huricanes; her eye wasn't but five or six miles in diameter. But violent as hell.

She brought a lot of ocean up the barely sloping beach, across the sea-wall, and better than a quarter-mile into the little Gulf-front communities west of Biloxi. Big, steel ships were turned into gargantuan beach litter. Land less than ten feet above mean sea level was swept by a surge nearly twenty-five feet deep. The arithmetic of such destruction is elementary.

You can still see the scratches on the land down there. All of a sudden the parade of old homes along the beach stops, just east of Gulfport, and you get a run of vacant lots everywhere the land is low, all the way down to Pass Christian. Then you

see the ruins. Driveways turn off into empty lots, concrete steps
rise to nowhere from stands of brush, foundation slabs wiped
clean by some great force lie among the weeds. Only the old
oaks and pines survived the surge west of Long Beach.
Probably there will always be some sight that once, long ago,
the people there had to absorb America's worst hurricane.

Sorel had been down at Bay Saint Louis for a NASA
conference on remote sensing. They'd brought him down, he
said, because they wanted somebody from the private sector to
say what kind of sensors would do the weather-modification
community the most good. His family went with him to get
some Gulf of Mexico water and sun. Then Camille had begun
to turn into a hurricane down south of Cuba.

"Meteorologists find approaching storms irresistible," Sorel
told me that night in Bermuda. "I watched the bitch come in,
listened to the reports and called the Weather Bureau people
over in New Orleans about it. God, I knew everything there
was to know about that storm. We knew we had a bad one, a
hundred-year storm or something. The meteorologists were
talking about a fifteen-foot surge and winds a hundred fifty
miles an hour. Then they got better information from one of
the Hurricane Hunter flights and called to say it looked more
like twenty feet of surge and two-hundred-mile-an-hour
winds. An incredible hurricane, you see?"

I nodded.

"Well, I didn't want to just get in the car and flee the
goddamned thing. I'm a research meteorologist. I ought to be
able to evaluate the hazard, right? So I found a church that'd
been in the same place for more than a century and I got my
family – I got Maria and Teddy and James and little India into
that old stone church."

The names conjured faces for me. The winter before Camille
there'd been a cloud physics conference in Fort Collins and I'd
attended with Lennie. Sorel had been the putative host of the
conference, and the cocktail party on the second night had
been held at his house, a large, modern stone and cedar
structure on a low hill west of town. His family had all
participated. Teddy and James, the two big boys who had the
fair look of England, and their dad, ran the bar, and played to
India, a lovely, dark and, I thought, unexpected girl ten years

their junior. She had Maria's looks, the skin faintly olive, the eyes and hair dark and Latiny; the mother came from somewhere between the tropics, but I never knew where and never got to ask. The memory of that evening stayed clear for me because of the gentle household behind it. I think that glimpse into his private life weighed against his reputation as a big ego and let me persuade myself to go to work for him. So when he paraded the names I saw the gentle faces, the sweetness of a vanished family, all gone in the whirlwind.

"Seeing them safe, Jake, I went on back to help the locals put their emergency together. We evacuated people by the scores along that beach. We did a damned fine day's work before Camille came in that night, and we rode it out, somehow. Near midnight the main surge came in. People would call and say they were neck deep in water and the house going down and you could hear the kids crying in the background ... Then we lost power and everything just lay beneath Camille and blew around, and drowned."

He looked fiercely away from me, watching with a sad boy's expression the remnant of Emma on the northeastern horizon. "We were still there in the morning, but everything else in the world had turned to shit. And that old stone church was gone."

For a moment he drifted in reverie, then returned to me. "But think of this, Jake, As Camille was coming in on us down in Mississippi, the government was mobilizing to seed Debbie in the Atlantic. Debbie, for God's sake, when they had Camille! I remember all that day wondering why they didn't shift their operations to the Gulf and just seed the *shit* out of Camille. But the bloody cowards didn't, and everybody died."

With that evening behind us, I knew something about what Sorel felt when Chatham tied our mission to "something like Camille". It was like telling your captain about a whale something like that big white fellow, or being brushed by a great shadow while examining the sandaled footprint of Goliath – you would hear the Fates.

I didn't put much on Sorel's obsession then, despite the dirty interview with Carney. It seemed to me that a scientist of any seriousness at all could never take the subject of his specialty so personally. Cancer researchers may feel anger and futility, but they must rage at God, not the virus. And yet – you would have to have said, knowing nothing else, that Sorel lived in the upper range of the obsessiveness available to him. I had made it my policy to undervalue his stated hatred of the big storms, not trusting a senior scientist to be pushed around by natural phenomena. And yet, Carney had made it impossible not to remember that. It *had* been since Camille, and after a hole in his career afterward, that his work in tropical meteorology narrowed its focus to hurricanes, and his research turned fully to the prospect of modifying them. Of course he didn't brood endlessly, surreally, about hurricanes. But the science of them flowed into the empty center where there had been that small circle of friends, the wife, the children, the gentle interactions. From there, the storms might drive him. He might come to wear that greedy, focused look I saw then at the Wednesday briefing. And I realized what he wanted that expression to say to me: You know how I came to the hurricane business, you know something about what drives me, for I've told you more than I have the others; now please keep your insights to yourself a little longer.

I watched him for a moment, then, almost imperceptibly, shook my head. He drew back as though he'd been touched.

I realized suddenly what he'd been telling me in Bermuda: next time he would make his try upon such a storm, seed the shit out of it, gambling his science and instincts against a killer hurricane. It was a flaw that went right to Sorel's core, a crack that time, treatment, *nothing* could heal. How many baskets had this man had to weave before they let him back to the world of hurricanes? How much dissembling had he done to get loose, during that "gap in his career" after Camille? Jesus, I thought, in a sense Prospero is just his arming himself for such an opportunity, the scientific manifestation of all this internal breakage. Of *course* he wouldn't care about my adolescent trading for Rory, or about Westheimer's speculations, or anything else. *That storm* had arrived. No – *Camille* had *returned*, and now nothing would keep him from trying to kill it.

And it came to me then, as it had to Admiral Carney much earlier, that a crack like that moves the man – wiggle the crack, manipulate the man. I knew all this speculatively, not the way Carney must have. I see him listening to tapes and reading manuscripts, talking Sorel over with former doctors, all in the national interest; and then I see him gambling that, given the right storm, in the right place, Sorel could not help but commit his crime; and that this crime would generate consequences from which Carney and his spooks could extract a groat's worth of intelligence ... But I must be careful not to sound too prescient. At the time, all I had were my speculations about the size and depth of Sorel's crack.

I thought of Borg, then. He had smelled the Ahab on Sorel. Now I smelled it too.

Westheimer was talking. " ... doubt that this particular hurricane would be a candidate for Prospero treatment. One reason the hyptheis has changed is that our models suggest – and I emphasize the word "suggest" – that seeding across the eyewall could actually cause the storm to intensify. In the Prospero hypothesis, we seed outboard of the eyewall in an effort to intensify vertical development there, at the eventual expense of the original eyewall.

"But in a Camille-type storm, where you have a small, tight system that's essentially all eyewall, our models show a high probability of intensifying the storm no matter where you seed." He hesitated, sensing a growing restlessness around the table, and laughed uncomfortably. "That's academic, since we're not seeding tomorrow. But I thought I'd throw it in."

Murchison stepped into the silence quickly, ran through the aircrew assignments for the record and described the provisioning of the airplanes. Then he looked at me and asked, "Anything to add, Jake?"

I shook my head. "They've said it all."

"Okay," he resumed. "Takeoff times are zero seven eastern daylight time for Prospero One, zero eight for Two. Each aircraft commander will file a flight plan to a set of coordinates the Hurricane Center will supply in the morning, the predicted position of the storm at thirteen Zulu time, which is T, tango, for the beginning of the simulated seeding. We'll be shutting the doors on both birds about fifteen minutes before taxi. All altitudes will be pressure altitudes above a thousand feet in the operating area. Below that we'll use radar altitudes. Communications frequencies are in the ops plan." He ended at a cliff of silence, almost embarrassed for a moment; then, his frown relaxing briefly, he added, "Good luck and good hunting." He always sounded as if he expected fifty percent casualties on every mission. It ended the meeting.

Sorel went by me without speaking, with Rory in a sort of trailing heel position. She looked unhappy and nervous, and glanced at me as though I were a potent enemy. I wished I could tap the sources of such power; and approached the lovely stranger. "Care to reconsider for tonight?"

"I guess not." The blue eyes darted off.

"Okay." To my surprise I felt more relief than disappointment. I guess I didn't want to have Charlie and a spiritually deformed Rory at the same table. "What's wrong?"

"Nothing." She gave a calm imitation of a wild look around. "Hasn't Henry talked to you?"

"Oh, right. He talked to me only yesterday."

"What are you going to do?"

"Nothing."

She frowned. "He was sure you'd go along."

"You're not his."

"Is *that* what you talked about?" She yielded up some gloom.

"Yep. Apples and oranges, no?"

"Yep." She laughed. "He talked to me about the mission."

"You're more businesslike than I am."

"Jake, do you know about the mission?"

"Lady …" I shook my head and smiled for her. "Lady, I know all there is to know about Henry Sorel and the Drill. I see it in his greed-filled eyes, and the worse Dolly gets, the more of it I see. If he wants me in, however," and here I was conscious of improvising on the grand scale, "he will have to give me your title and plates, if he has them. Or something of equal value, if possible."

"It could be most anything, Jake. I'm not a very special person."

So there wouldn't be any serious misunderstanding between us, I said, "Well, sometimes you are and sometimes you aren't. But I still intend to wrassle your tall, boy-faced, Limey friend for you."

"Are you cooperating on the mission?"

"I don't know. Even if I were an enthusiastic co-operator, which I definitely am not, we have Borg on the plane. How's Sorel going to run more than a drill with the *Herald*'s finest right there watching?"

"Maybe Henry has a plan."

"Sure he has. But if it disregards or underestimates Borg, it's a dumb plan." All of this sounds assured; but my assurance against Sorel was pretty weak. Natural selection pushes mutations in deputy directors as well as other creatures. Being around Sorel, if it fostered confidence in the working world of atmospheric research, eroded confidence within. Still, my blustery talk had its value, for my lady's eyes began to brighten once more, and she leaned (spiritually anyway) again in my direction. "I think, m'dear, you must stop letting that fellow hypnotize you," I said.

She shook her head, half-grim again. "It isn't that he has power over me, Jake. Or maybe it is. But it isn't what it seems. My science is very important to me; I look and there it is, coloring everything. It fills my future. But it's all been intertwined with Henry Sorel. I see it, I see him. *You're* the anomaly in my life. Even if I could say, I'm in love with Jake Warner, the science and the Henry Sorel in my life would shrug and reply, So what? that is how he wears me down."

These were unattractive sounds to me. "That's why he thinks you're his," I said.

"I'm more likely yours."

"That's good to know, but you have a funny way of showing it."

"But all I am right now is somebody else for you to feel bad about."

"You're right."

We stood a few feet apart in the plush room with the hangar noise beating upon the soundproofed door; stood like unhappy statues for a moment. We might have touched, or made another mitigating gesture, except that someone fumbled at the doorknob, greater noise leaked in and Murchison stuck his head into the room. "Henry's waiting for you outside, Rory."

"Okay." She went brittle, moved to follow him away, drawn by her work. Her science. Pausing, she said to me, "Don't worry about us too much."

"Sure." It saddened me to see her walk – to see her *able* to walk – away. I watched her out of sight down the catwalk that crawled along this wall of the hangar, down the ladder-like stairs and out into the unnerving brightness of the ramp, where Sorel waited in silhouette. His shadow gave him eight limbs.

I called Bella to check on who'd called me. Pete Thompson had left the message that we were funded for twenty-five airplane hours, period. Shit, Pete, we can blow up the world in about twelve hours. He didn't need a call back. Borg had checked in and I returned his call at the *Herald*. When he came on I said, "Jack Warner, Steve."

"Hi, Jake." His voice held tiny remnants of our mild clash the day before. I ignored them.

"We're flying tomorrow morning. Take-off time for us is eight."

"The wire's talking about Dolly," he said. "There's a watch out."

"Yeah, she's spinning up. We expect an uncomfortable flight."

He sent out a slight frost. "That a hint for me to stand down?"

"You're too sensitive," I told him. "The storm may be a mean one, that's all."

"It coming through here?"

"Nobody knows. It has to pop out of the Gulf somewhere. It could drift north east and come across between the Keys and St Pete, or chug through the Straits and out to sea. One reason we're flying is to help the forecasters focus their warning."

"Can we get back to Miami?"

"I don't know."

"Doesn't matter. Look, Jake, something's been bugging me since yesterday, about the theory behind Prospero. You got a minute to talk about it?"

"I really don't right now. I've got people coming in on Eastern in about an hour and I'm kind of scrambling around. But what the hell, we'll be bumping around in the plane for about twelve hours tomrrow. Let's do it then." I knew what he wanted to do – he wanted to review our uncertainties. "Okay?"

"Okay." He had been deferred, and didn't like it.

I rang up Miami flight service and filed VFR to Key West International and back, got the forecast – essentially zero weather beyond a few afternoon cumuli building into thunderclouds – and felt myself relax into the idea of going somewhere in my plane. Then I ran out and got a Big Mac and an orange drink and ate on the way to the terminal.

To a lot of people, the airport terminal at Miami International *is* Miami. I'd spent a lot of time waiting for odd connections on the way through before they'd sent me down to live there, and the interior of the building had changed very little over the years; it just got longer. The major difference was the jerry-rigged stations where the broad concourses nozzled down to magnetometer walkthroughs and cordoned security areas. I'd changed planes in Miami as a kid and my memory of it had been of bright stuccoed structures and light and palm trees and air. Now you can't see people to their planes in Miami, or meet them. They emerge from a concourse, or vanish into one; it could be prison, or a kink in time. I find it unfriendly.

I waited behind velveteen ropes near the magnetometer, watching through the crowd around me the waves of people moving up the concourse. The security people ran passengers through, sending a backscatter of human waves down the long hall. Very tidal and impersonal. Perhaps the impersonality knocked me out for a moment, or perhaps my estrangement from them had become so complete that they no longer leapt at me from crowds. But my people – the big strawberry blonde with the hard face and great figure and the little 9-year-old man beside her – saw me before I did them. Yes, and how long had my son been waving before my eyes unglazed? "Hey, Charlie," I called out, and waved back with more eagerness than was necessary. The first sight of him could make my throat constrict painfully and bring a gloss of tears. He strode along beside his big mama, a boy just a shade on the small side (forty-eighth percentile as his pediatrician would say) with shoulder-length strawberry-blond hair from the Lenore gene. She had dressed him like a boy that day, and as her escort: he wore a bush suit kind of deal with Nike running shoes that looked enormous beneath the trim, cuffless trousers; she had on the movie-star equivalent, a pants outfit of khaki-colored satiny material that exposed her long, pale throat and emphasized her big breasts and body – you wanted to help her out of those clothes. She saw me looking at her then and her mean look – a red-faced aspect she got from wearing too much make-up of the wrong colour – went into a smile. "Jake, Jake," she yelled. "Hi."

"Hi, Lenny," I said. Then, "Hey, Charlie," planting myself in his path to gather him in for a hug.

"Hi, Dad," he said in his clear boy's voice, indicating he was too big to call me Daddy anymore and maybe should be less hugged. But I held him where I could see his face up close a while longer. It was a fine face, well-featured and, in the summers at least, colored in pale reds and golds, like paintings of healthy Anglo kids. He was so much less dark than I, and generally frailer, that our friends had used to kid me about repressed genes, until the marriage turned to shit. When I looked into his big intelligent chocolate-brown eyes I peered into a mind much like my own, and that was what lay between us, a shared way of viewing things, and thinking. "I'm glad to see you, old boy," I said.

"Me too," he replied solemnly, but with a small smile of pleasure.

I turned to Lennie. "You're looking pretty edible yourself, Mama." It was unexpectedly pleasant to have her nearby.

"Thanks. Nice to see you too, Jake."

As we talked we wheeled away from the security fence and off toward the baggage claim, while another wave of incomers beat toward us down the concourse. I said, "I don't know how much time you'll have in Key West."

"The hurricane?"

"Yep, she's ..."

"I'd rather you didn't call an it a she."

I nearly rose to the fight; then, reflecting quickly, I decided to abort the complaint, ignore it and just be a little sad the enjoyment I'd got from being with her had been a spurious surprise. "Okay."

"What about it?" She'd expected more response, and so she flared at me, out of phase.

"There's a watch out from Key West to St Pete. She could come right up the Keys." I caught Charlie watching me and

gave him a clandestine wink, to the effect that we would take
no shit off this woman today. He smiled back his troubled
smile.

I left them in the baggage area and hiked out to where I'd
parked the Saab. By the time I'd made the terminal loop and
got in front of the eastern door, Charlie was outside to signal
me. I double-parked and ran in and got their four pieces –
Lennie had two beige leather two-suiters and an oversized
flight bag, and Charlie had the old grey cardboard job we'd
bought for our honeymoon. "You're looking prosperous," I
ventured to Lennie, once we were loaded and moving out
through traffic.

"I guess we're doing okay."

"That's good."

I felt her looking me over and studiously watched the road
ahead. After a minute she said, "You seem to have it together,
Jake."

"I'm just a cool customer."

"That's how you seem."

"Must be the storm."

"Or someone?" She was trying to be friends again. I
laughed, not wanting to pursue it.

We went down 36th through the little metropolis that's
grown up along the northern borders of Miami International,
made the jog onto the perimeter road and drove over to Three
Charlie Whiskey on the general-aviation ramp. This late in a
Miami summer day the concrete danced with heat; the sun
made everything on the plane too hot to touch. We gathered in
the shadow of the wing while I opened the cabin and windows
and stashed the luggage. Then I parked the Saab over by the
line shack. When I ushered them aboard, Lennie took the front
right hand seat, which disappointed Charlie and me. He
climbed up behind the pilot's seat. I walked around the plane
to see if anyone had run into it with a truck since the morning
preflight, checked the oil one last time and got in. Going
through the checklist I was aware of Lennie, tense and trying
not to be. I looked at her a moment, took in the well-formed
chin, the throat and torso good enough to grace the bowsprit
of a clipper ship. "It's been a while," I said to her.

"Since what?"

"Since we've gone anywhere together in a plane."

"Oh."

The last time had been when we were trying to restore some slack to our relationship and rented a plane and flew to Rehoboth for a night and part of a day. It had been fine, the sea and the seafood and the night in an old knotty pine motel, like an affair. That had also been the last time we had a good time together in bed. I caught her watching me again. "Well – I'm an even better pilot now."

Three Charlie Whiskey came alive nicely, the big six-cylinder powerplant burbling its fine deep sound. I called clearance delivery and got our transponder code and departure clearance, then turned to Miami ground and told them we were ready to taxi for take-off. They eased us into the line of jets moving clumsily as beetles crawling on the taxiways. I did the run-up and check-list while we taxied out behind a chartreuse and white DC-3 about my age. I told the tower we were ready in our turn and they cleared us to go ahead of the old Douglas. There was a light crosswind, the surface winds from the north east, feeding down into the Gulf, into Dolly. We took off short to stay out of any random vortices floating on the field, got cleaned up and level at about a thousand feet to cross the coast just north of downtown Miami.

I'd planned the flight to take us east across the beach, then fly down more or less parallel to the shoreline, to give my passengers the best view of the city. It added a few miles to the route a crow would take, but it opened Miami as it cannot be from the ground or the sea.

The rowed condominiums and glass-walled hotels marched southward on our right. I smiled, thinking of Chatham. He went around trying to get people to take hurricanes seriously, hammered at the condos and made a bunch of enemies among real estate people and shoreline developers. Sometimes he'd pose as a prospect and ask the salesperson whether there was a hurricane hazard on some flat slab of fill two feet above mean sea level. Usually they said, Heck no. "You ask about pilings," he'd tell an audience, "and they'll tell you those buildings are standing on 'compressed sand pilings'. Well, I've talked to some structural engineers about compressed sand pilings and they can't think what those are, unless they're just the sand

compressed by the weight of the structure sitting on top of it."
His spiel took those who would listen on a tour of
condominiums from New Jersey to Padre Island, always
stressing that the tall, thin towers were rising where a decade, a
generation, a century ago a hurricane had eaten all the sand
away. "On most of these units," he'd tell retired people from
up north, "the first thing that'll happen is you'll be sitting in
your living-room with the wind and rain of the storm outside,
then *bam*!, that sliding glass door is going to buckle inwards
and shower the room with big sharp blades of glass. And then
you're going to see such rainfall you'll think you're
underwater. And you'll feel that wind."

Chatham lived with spectres. Patio doors were one. He
didn't care whether the door opened onto an ocean view at
fifteen stories or on a ground-level garden; big panes of glass
were just lethal debris waiting for the motive power of a
hurricane. Low-lying developments were another Chatham
ghost. Off to our right I saw the skeletal roads and nearly
contiguous stuccoed boxes of a tract built on filled land
crowding the shoreline south of Miami Beach. Some of the
homes had been there awhile, but most were newish. No one
could predict how they'd do in a storm; they might ride out the
wind and rain. But even an average storm surge would eat a
bunch of them, next time around. Some of the condos would
survive on deep-driven pilings; and some would have their
ground floors and foundations washed out by the surge, then
cave in like something made of sugar – or built on sand.

We passed Key Biscayne, then sailed suddenly out over the
blue water of Biscayne Bay, all laced with the wakes of pleasure
craft. I let the Skylane drift down to five hundred feet. Soldier
Key and its residues of wrecked boats went by, and we began
picking up the rocks that point the way into Elliot Key, and
then the intermittent elongated slabs of mangrove and coral,
not quite land and not quite water, curving south and west
toward the end at Key West. The Everglades filled the earth to
its horizon on our right, all ponds and hammocks cut by a few
roads strung between the bug-infested towns like Flamingo.
The water gleamed on this day, given to patches of pale bluish
white, and deeper pools the color of sapphires in the coral
floor, and long tongues and freeforms of tropical green.

"Beautiful, isn't it?" I said to Lennie over the sound of the engine. She nodded. I looked back at Charlie. "How're you doing, boy?"

He grinned and made a circle of his thumb and forefinger. That was the way he and I rocked along, always reacting a little more than necessary. When things were okay we tended to upgrade them to A-okay, just to keep from disappointing the other. God.

There was nothing in the sky with us but scattered cumuli, one or two off to seaward mature enough to drop a shaft of rain. Such wind as there was flowed from the northeast, helping us on its way into the coils of the hurricane that spun behind the southwest horizon.

I watched the Keys move by. Sparsely settled developments, mere sketches of communities that never took hold in the hot, waterless land of the Keys, went off the main road, lined the shore. Chatham had lots to say about hurricanes and these isolated, low-flying chunks of coral. "You get a category five storm through there, the only land above water's going to be a couple of points on Key West and the centerline of Largo, and maybe a point or two on Vaca, although don't bet on it.

"And, see, people will try to get out and they'll start pulling out of places like Key West and Big Pine Key and heading north. Well, you've got maybe sixty thousand people down there, and two-lane highway, mostly on a *causeway*. You've got to keep one lane open for emergency vehicles. So you've got one lane to carry sixty thousand people. Let's be optimistic and say each car has four people in it. That's still fifteen thousand cars.

"Okay, pretty soon that little road is completely choked with cars coming north, moving slow enough that here and there you get one overheating. So the road begins to get blocked. Out in the mobile home developments in the Keys those people'll begin thinking they should get out too. So they'll hitch up their trailers and pull those things out on the highway. But, you know, a lot of those homes haven't been pulled anywhere in years, and those tires are just rotted through by now. So pretty soon you get some of these trailers blocking the highway, or maybe blocking seven-mile bridge, where you can't go anywhere but into the water. And coming up behind all these people is a category five hurricane with a twenty-foot surge. Why, it's going to be just awful next time around."

Next time around could be in another day or two.

"We're about there," I told Lennie, and she nodded to acknowledge, then looked out to the west with fresh interest. Coming toward Key West the islands change their orientation, so that the lower Keys lie at right angles to your approach, like the fossil rib-cage of a giant fish. Over Sugarloaf Key I called Key West tower and told them where we were and what we wanted to do. They brought us in just south of the cluster of dark blue buildings and long runways of Key West Naval Air Station. I asked Lennie and Charlie about their seat-belts and ran through my memorized landing checklist. The tower cleared us to land as we came up along the runway heading west, then turned a short base and final and fluttered down to what I thought was a pretty fair landing. We taxied over to the terminal, a white block structure that trembled in the sunlight. I got the window open for the air, but the heat was already clawing at me. "Welcome to Key West," I said.

"Thanks," she replied. She'd begun to droop. Her hair had gone a trifle stringy on her, and dark patches stained her shiny blouse at the armpits. "That was a nice flight, Jake," she added, using the tone the lady of the house uses for small talk with the gardener.

"Yes, ma'am it sho' nuff was."

"What?"

"Nothing. Is that your Tom?" A big figure stepped out of the palm shadows around the terminal as I shut down the Skylane. It was Gordineer, large and special in his O.D. green and black flight suit, all zippers and pockets. He came over grinning and we shook hands and greeted one another; then he gave Lennie a big welcoming hug. Charlie, careful not to wound his dad, ignored Gordineer almost rudely: at the time I welcomed it. I began hauling her baggage out and piling it on the crushed coral around the ramp.

Gordineer broke his clinch and came over. "What's happening with Dolly?" he asked, without quite looking me in the eye. He knew how it would go, up to a point, even then.

"She's a hurricane, she may be a very bad one. They've got her coming ashore somewhere between here and St Pete, maybe day after tomorrow, maybe tomorrow night."

"You guys going to fly her?" Again, I remember his eyes skewing away from mine here. Never ask a good man to do your dirty work, Admiral Carney.

"Tomorrow." Then to keep the conversation going, I asked, "What're you flying?"

"A-6. Running some tests."

"There an all-weather squadron at Key West?"

"Nope, just us. The fairweather jocks have us figured for something between a Ford Trimotor and Apollo Seven."

I laughed for him, and we carried Lennie's bags over closer to the terminal, and put them in a humid pool of shade. "Look," I said then, "seriously, if that storm comes through here, the whole reef'll be underwater."

"Not to worry. I'll take care of her." He gave a proud grin over his shoulder at Lennie.

"I mean, if you have to get out, I hope you start early."

"Okay." The repetition annoyed him.

Okay, I thought, so drown. But, looking at Lennie, I reconsidered. "Really, Lennie, be careful. This storm's no joke."

She didn't want to hear it either. People who worried about weather had always bored her. "Sure, Jake. Thanks for the lift."

"Sure. So long." I took a long look at her while she kissed Charlie goodbye. Maybe it was the patches of sweat and the droopiness, or maybe just that dumb choice of make-up, but she touched me at that moment. This big, sweet-bodied woman would be forty in another year, and time worked her like fish worrying something weak and drifting in the sea. She had her Tom, her big boy a year or two younger than she, who'd waste what time she had. There had been other Toms, and there would be others after he tired of her and went his way: and they would be younger, and still greater wasters of her time. "So long," I said again, and, "Take care." They were talking, though, and didn't hear.

We got in the Skylane, Charlie in the right-hand seat and forward far enough that he could reach the pedals and the wheel. We fired up and while the oil pressure rose I tested the controls and got the plane generally ready to fly. Then I told the tower we were ready to taxi for take-off, and, after a quick mag check on the way out and one cycling of the prop, got their clearance. "Okay, Charlie," I said, "You do this one and I'll follow through."

He gave a big grin and I put on power until we were accelerating down the hot white runway. He had the plane, just about – I helped keep us straight since I could see over the glare shield, and put a little forward pressure on the wheel as we began to fly. But you have to call it Charlie's take-off.

We turned back to the north-east at about five hundred feet and ran along the Keys, the air speed moving up to about a hundred twenty-five knots indicated. I gave him his heading and he stuck with it, flying instruments, really, with his nose almost on the panel, his thin little shoulder-blades distended like wings by the tension of this important work we were teaching him to do.

"How's you swimming?" I asked.

He nodded vigorously, but wouldn't look away from his instruments.

"That mean good?"

He nodded again.

"Okay, let's stop at Marathon. Steer about two zero. Getting tired?"

"Nope."

"Let me know."

"Okay."

"You eat on the plane coming down?"

"Yep."

We fell in beside the long bridge to Vaca Key. After a minute or two of this I said, "Here, try some turns, and then I'll take it."

Charlie nodded and, with great earnestness and some grace, rolled the Skylane over in a sixty-degree bank to the right, flew a circle, then reversed it, flying through his turbulent wake both times. Then he held up his hands. "Your airplane," he said, with a look that admitted he knew he'd done fine turns.

"You do good work, boy."

We came in on a long final to the east at Marathon and taxied over the concrete and crushed coral to a tiedown on the ramp. After shutting down we got out and unloaded what we'd need, including what I'd stowed earlier, a bundle of black rubber. "What's that?" he wanted to know.

"I thought we'd do some diving." It always embarrassed me, to catch myself trying to manage a child's surprise. "Open it up."

And he, wanting to match what he perceived to be my expectations, put on a surprised child's face and took the bundle apart. When he had the wet-suit trunks and flippers and a snorkelling mask and cork-handled knife spread out, he said, "Oh, this is – wonderful. Really, thanks – Daddy." Beneath his trying you could see the genuine pleasure; you had to go by the eyes.

We caught a cab from the airport over to a motel I'd fished from a couple of times on the Gulf side of the key, where you could rent cabanas and use the small artificial beach and snorkel around what remained of their reef. I showed Charlie how to use the snorkel and we did some inshore paddling around until he got the hang of spitting the water out after diving; then we moved farther out, where the motel management had dug a forty-foot pit and rolled the metal skeleton of an Edsel into it, a rusty castle for legions of fish. Around the edge of the pit there wasn't more than four feet of water for a long way from shore, and we flew over this underwater grassland where gars watched us as patiently as barracuda, and crabs fled our great shadows. Pale sediments from all the dredging and filling along this part of the Keys choked the grasses, but they still did the graceful dance plants do in the dense winds of the sea.

It was a lovely time for us. I watched this slender, important little man plunge not quite awkwardly down from the surface, his skinny legs thrashing him downward in a brilliant column of bubbles; then he would surface, blow out his snorkel and look to me for confirmation of his skill. This diffident boy had my whole heart, forever; he occupied the central chambers of my life. And I thought then with regret that such certainties only came in these netural settings, where nothing stressed his loyalty to me or Lennie, or mine to him, where we moved closely but out along the rim of one another's consciousness, making (and seeming to make) no demands.

As we drifted farther from shore, the ocean moved us too. At first I took it to be just a little chop driven past us by the wind. But the rhythm had the feel of depth and distance, the beat of the gravity waves on which the shorter waves are travellers. We could feel the swell, the oceanic resonance.

It was Dolly's heartbeat.

Charlie and I had a hell of a good time snorkelling. Then, flying back to Miami, weather had forced us around some thunderstorms before we entered the hive of International. So we'd shared some excitements. After Charlie had settled in at my place a little we got Sam Newman to eat with us down by Dinner Key, and my quiet son and my quiet friend chattered and got tickled and laughed like young room-mates. I don't know just what happened between them, but I liked to hear it going on. It turned out that Sam had once been a kid after all. At the end of the evening Charlie and I almost had to start over. And Sam, alone, must have had his problems too ...

Finally, Charlie slept, his copper-colored hair spread against the pillow, his eyes closed; he started now and then, like a dreaming dog, but his mouth held a smile. I decided he must be back in the ocean off Vaca Key, and adjusted his covers gently, not to wake him.

I expected a call from Sorel, so when the phone rang I took my time answering it, and was surprised to hear Jim Westheimer's complaining voice, uncharacteristically slurred, as though he'd been drinking (although he didn't drink), the precision broken. Mixed excitement and fatigue. "Henry's going to seed that thing," he said.

"It remains to be seen, Jim."

"You're probably in it with him."

"I'm flying the Drill tomorrow. Period."

"If he seeds that thing he's a goddamned criminal. We've modeled Dolly – I'm back at the lab now – and every run tells us the same thing: if you seed it you'll get what environmentalists have always said you'd get, a change in track and an increase in intensity."

"Come on, Jim. They've seeded storms before, and the only result they ever got was a reduction in winds." But he had already gone a ways toward spooking me about this storm.

"Dolly's different. She's like Camille, possibly worse. There just isn't that much outboard of the eyewall to seed. Our models show that seeding will produce higher winds in the eyewall and in the area of seeding, where intensification occurs."

"What about storm track?"

"We get some anomalous movement off to the south and east. You know what that means?" His voice rose in the question.

"It means your model storm turns into Cuba."

"It means World War III, Jake!"

"Oh, *bullshit!*" The term hit him like a slap; I felt him flinch at the other end of the line, and sensed he was getting calmer. "You're talking models, and what happens when you add or subtract heat. Dolly's a big, fat, living, breathing hurricane. She'd spit out a massive seeding in a few hours."

"Look," he said then with an earnestness I'd never heard from him before, "Jake, look, the model's followed Dolly very closely thus far. I know it's only a model. I know Dolly's a real hurricane and the model oversimplifies the real world. Give me credit, I know that. But the model is what we've based our hypothesis on, and now the model's showing changes in the storm that should make us wait, and go back to real hurricane data, and see what's happening."

"What do you suggest?"

"Stand down tomorrow."

"Come on."

"Then tell the aircrew about it. Tell Murchison. Tell the administrator."

"Jim," I said, trying to be cool and objective, "I'll do what I can. I don't think Henry's going to seed anything tomorrow. Don't worry about it."

"I'm still worried about it." Westheimer had begun to whine. "He's asked me for a continuous series of model runs tomorrow while you're in the storm. I think that says he's going to seed."

"It only says he's kicking it around. Look he's a scientist too, and quite a good one. He isn't going to seed if your model says Dolly'll turn into a monster." He seemed to quiet down, but only a little. "Really, it isn't going to happen." I said it, but I didn't mean it. I hadn't said anything to turn him off, either;

he'd spend the night brooding among his worlds made of numbers. But I felt childish anger that he would intrude at all. If Sorel wanted to seed, he needed my cooperation; I would give it for a price. I didn't want my trading interrupted by Westheimer's scruples.

After Westheimer hung up I had time to open a beer and get comfortable by the phone before the call I'd been expecting came from Sorel. He'd been drinking, but less, I think, than he wanted to seem to have been, possibly wanting to have all kinds of latitude without much responsibility a day later; he had reached the point where he had nothing preliminary to say. So, about a sentence into our conversation, he said, "Look, Jake, I know you know what's coming on the mission tomorrow. I've meant to talk it over with you ..."

"No need to do that, Henry."

"But Rory says you said it won't happen. Because a reporter's on board."

"I think it won't happen for a number of reasons, and that's one of them."

"It might be good to have him along."

"It might."

"Jake, my needs are pretty simple on this thing, but I will need some people to be with me."

"Rory and three people on Prospero One. And me."

"Are you with me?"

"Nope."

"Will you try to stop me?"

"I'm willing to trade." And here we reached the parts of the dialogue I'd prepared for, the mean-spirited beginnings of my cooperation.

"Trade?" A deflected sound, as though this simple but hard-hearted solution moved him off his track.

"I want you to give up Rory. Forever. Completely."

He laughed contemptuously, relieved. "Jesus Christ, a white slaver."

"Or I call the administrator tonight and tell him you're planning to seed."

"He wouldn't believe you."

"But he'd begin to doubt you, Henry. And he'd look into it. The planes wouldn't launch tomorrow."

"So you'll try to stop it?"

"I said I'd trade."

"What if Rory doesn't go along?"

"It isn't up to her. It's up to you."

"Well – if I agree, how far do you go?"

"I fly the mission as Prospero Drill. If you want to seed while we're drilling I won't blow the whistle on you and I won't intercede."

"You know, just because I give up Rory doesn't mean you get her."

"I know that."

"Well, it seems to me you're putting a lot into being a dog in the manger, Jake."

"How's it going to be?"

"Oh, I'll give her up. This thing's too important not to. I don't see her leaving her science, though, or the lab, and I don't see a very brilliant future here for you. Perhaps you'll have a rich correspondence."

"Maybe so."

He laughed a couple of harsh notes. "Do I have to bring over a signed document, or what?"

"Just tell me what you're going to do, Henry."

"I'm – going to give up my attachment to Dr Aurora Merchant, for all time."

"And you'll discourage her from seeking a renewal of it."

"Yes, I'll discourage her in that."

"And keep your after-hours contact with her down to zero."

"And not see her outside the lab."

"It's a deal, Henry."

He hung up, and I leaned against the telephone table for a time, feeling dirty and stupid, half bewildered by what I'd done, only half satisfied at the outcome. I suppose everyone, handling love that has such fever in it, is at some point willing to perform that act which causes irreversible damage, which taints, contaminates, destroys. I fiddled some more with Charlie's covers, and worked on my beer, and thought about the mild, growing insanity of Sorel, and our dealing, and how no matter how one perceived my part in all of this, it was always wrong, wrong, wrong. God knows, though, against the desperate acts I was willing to commit for Rory, this seems just moderately bad behavior.

And I thought of Dolly, drifting on the sea, vast and unintelligent. She brought me just the slightest chill of fear, which kept me awake a while longer. When I slept finally I dreamed of tomorrow's hurricane flight, a routine mission that flew and flew into a turbulent world which got as black as space, a Flying Dutchman of a routine mission, endless as a journey to the stars.

Bella lived in the black half of the Grove, down one of the narrow mango-lined streets where tiny painted frame cottages rest on concrete blocks that seem to have grown on narrow lots; remembering hurricane damage surveys along the Gulf coast, I always see

these slabs swept clean. Some people, perhaps unnerved by the endless day of sodium vapor crime lights, steel themselves to cross from Coral Gables to Dinner Key and the boutiques and whatnot shops and galleries in the rich quadrants of the Grove. But they overlook something sleepy and southern that lives beneath the glaring light, that peeks out in the early morning, when the place looks like all the little towns down through the Keys, with a touch of coastal Georgia and Alabama thrown in.

Charlie gave a puzzled look when we turned off Grand into the Grove and I laughed for him. "Don't worry. I didn't sell you to a Cuban plantation."

He laughed back. Then, glancing around, he asked, rhetorically, "Does Bella *live* down here?"

"Yep. I think it can be kind of a hard life."

He watched the thin patches of morning people and a few leftover night people while a red light suspended us for half a minute. "I bet it's rough at night."

"Maybe. There're worse places, though."

"Yeah, I guess so."

We'd started early, with a fine breakfast in a motel restaurant where we could sit and watch the charter boats get ready to go out the Coral Gables canal. We tended to be rather man-to-man that morning. I had on my flight suit with the big hurricane emblem on the breast pocket, and Charlie wore a hurricane-emblemed baseball cap with his blue workshirt and Levis, so we made a kind of hip father-son ensemble, and were conscious of it. And we were up because our visit was successful.

We swung into a thin street overhung with big mangos and banyans, and found Bella's number. It was a smallish green wooden structure back behind a fenced, dog-ruined yard rimmed with hibiscus and nasturtiums, the house set up on concrete posts that made a narrow carport underneath the place. I parked and got Charlie and the pair of books he'd decided to bring and we entered through a white metal gate and took the buried concrete block walkway to a single set of stairs going up the entry. As we got closer I noticed a black man of about 50, thin and with the spiritually mashed look of the failed person, red-eyed and angry. I nodded at him and he turned away. I felt we'd invaded Bella's privacy by having even this slight contact with what must be her husband. She came out, then, looking very West Indian (home was New Orleans) in a bold-printed white shift, and stepped toward us with her Bella smile. "Hi, Jake. Hi, Charlie. I'm Bella." I kept looking at the black man, who hovered, waiting to be introduced. "This is my husband, Thomas Moore; Thomas, this is Dr Warner from work." We nodded back and forth, too far apart to shake hands.

"Is this still okay, Bella?" I asked.

"Oh, don't worry about Thomas. He never stays around much once Grand Avenue opens up."

"Sure. I owe you for this one."

"Don't worry about that, either. I'm glad to have Charlie here. We'll have a good time."

I leaned down to hug Charlie goodbye, and, once I'd gathered him in, something internal whispered to me: You may not see your son again. I had trouble letting go, and I was shaken when I did.

Bella saw the problem. "This is some bad storm, isn't it?"

"Pretty bad."

"Well, you don't worry about anything but getting home. Your Charlie's going to be just fine."

"Thanks, Bella. So long. So long, son."

"Bye, Daddy."

I drove away quickly, angry with myself for caving in. Dolly was just another storm, maybe a little more violent than the ones we'd flown before, but not sinister or intelligently bad, or – personal. Besides, there were limits to the winds and water in any storm. And yet, she'd begun to spook me, as though there were more than just processes in the atmosphere. Okay, I thought, I'm slightly haunted. That comes close to what I felt, that and shoddy and soul-selling from my deal with Sorel; I was on my way to conspire in an ugly crime.

The tropical sun was already powerful when I dropped

Charlie, and the heat and humidity of the Miami summer touched everything with headachy brightness and moisture by the time I reached the Hurricane Center. Chatham, finally forced home to rest, had left packets of barely dry satellite photos of Dolly and a summary of the storm's position at 6 a.m. Miami time, central pressure, and maximum winds – she had deepened to 950 millibars and winds up over 110 knots. Dolly began to look like a real honest-to-Christ category five storm. Chatham had Dolly curving slightly more to the north and east than he had the day before, probably tracking along the Keys and then moving offshore at a tangent to the arc of devastation she'd leave from Key West northward. But for the moment – and in fact since Wednesday morning – Dolly had kept to a trackline that, if you extended it past Miami into the Atlantic, drew a centerline through the Florida Straits. Another twenty-four hours of that and all we'd get in Miami and the Keys and Cuba would be a rough fanning with high winds and water.

Prospero One was buttoning up when I got to the airplane facility. I drove over close to the plane and got out and had them hold the ladder long enough for me to run up into the fuselage and get one of the data packages to Carla Hendrix, who occupied the flight director's station behind the navigator. She took the packet and we nodded to one another like colleagues. But we didn't seal our eyes, and in hers I saw my own vague fears about the flight, the storm, the essential wrongness of what we were about to do, for different reasons, for Sorel. "Don't worry," I said.

She said nothing. But the fear went out of her eyes. Probably out of mine too.

"Come on, Jake," Gil Bradenton yelled on his way forward, "you shoulda thoughta that before you left home. Haha."

"You're an inspiration, Gil," I said, adding, "Good luck with whatever it is you plan to do today."

"Same to you, fella."

I hurried off the plane. They'd started their engines before I got the car off the ramp and were taxiing by the time I returned to watch them. The plane waddled toward the active runway, insect-fashion, the candy-striped probes extended like stingers, the black thorax of the belly radome retracted, the tail radome elongated and slightly curved, like the drooping tail of a wasp. I saw Carla's face as the plane turned past me, the pale, window-framed mask of a stranger wheeling by. She waved. I waved back, then stood like a Greek waiting for omens, feeling no courage about the flight.

Sorel was in Murchison's office, a wedge-shaped room in the thick wall of our hangar, when I got there. I told them hello and Murch said Hi. Sorel nodded, being cold. I gave them their packets of current Dolly information, and then, as Murchison began to get busy and drift away, I told Sorel about Westheimer's call. "I think you've got a problem, Henry."

"Then I'll just have to have a problem." He wouldn't look at me; his smooth cheeks burned with anger.

"Suit yourself."

"Of course I will. It sounds as if you've forgotten whose lab this is, old sport."

If he meant I'd forgotten my place, he was right. It no longer occurred to me to defer, to be second (or twentieth, or two hundredth, however inferiorities are reckoned). He might still be the Jupiter in our small planetary family, but his gravitational field could sweep me now without raising an additional millimeter of tide – I had seen his insanity too clearly.

But if he meant we were talking about a fiefdom of his – and he did – he was so wrong I had to comment on it. "It's everybody's lab. You just run it." He went pale, and I gave him another stanza. "It's academic anyway. After today we'll probably get somebody else."

"I doubt that."

Still, I'd hit a chord; it reverberated in his voice. I decided to pursue it. "You're pulling everything down around you if you seed that storm. Blind, pissed off and driven mad. That's how they'll remember you."

"*No!*" Within the confines of coolness the word was shouted. "No, they'll remember a category five hurricane that got knocked down to a category three before it could destroy Key West and a fourth of Miami. And they'll remember it was done because someone had the bloody vision and the bloody balls to go round the bureaucracy to do it. I don't think that's half bad."

"The new Billy Mitchell."

"Sure."

"What if Westheimer's model is right? What if seeding makes Dolly rev up to something much worse? What about the goddamned Cubans when they see us out there seeding the storm?"

He flashed a grimace intended to be a tough smile. "Then we shall all be on the outside looking in, old man."

"So will our victims."

"What victims? Look, I don't believe Westheimer's model can simulate a Camille-type storm. I think the high values in Dolly are confusing the model. We've got a running model back here and we'll check what it says against what we get in the storm, continuously. If it looks to me like seeding will blow up the world then I'll probably not do it."

"I don't believe that, Henry."

"Then call the administrator. Kill the game."

"I don't have to. Westheimer will."

"Fine. We'll be in the storm and busy as hell. I don't see the administrator reaching us until the mission's over; by then we'll have our data and we can show people that Prospero deserves a better run than it's had." He glared at me, conscious that he'd begun to turn his argument around. "Look, if your conscience is so bloody uneasy, why don't you stand down?"

"We have a deal."

"Christ, and what a deal it is. I'll tell you, Jake, I don't see tuppence between my attempting something I believe in deeply and your trading what you seem to believe in for a rather average bit of pussy. I rather see myself as better than you. I can work this without you in the plane. Why don't you stand down and keep your hands clean? The cunt is yours, whether you fly the mission or not."

"No. I'm going." I nodded to Murchison, who'd come back close enough to be embarrassed by such rough fragments of our conversation as he could hear. Then I went out to the ramp and climbed the ladder to Prospero Two.

The beige metal and leatherette interior hummed, everything driven by the big auxiliary power unit down in the hull. Sam Newman and Peterson occupied their cockpit positions, flicking switches as they went through the

pre-mission checks. Charlie Bruska did the same from his
flight engineer's jump seat behind the power pedestal between
the two pilots. Back where I sat Ed Mattson had got the
computers up to speed and nursed his system from the big,
intricate panel across the aisle from me. One position ahead of
me Don Chesney laid out his navigational tools. Ira Weld had
the radios going, but nothing much to do. I got up and went
toward the back of the cabin. Rory punched instructions into
the panel that controlled the plane's automatic time-lapse
cameras. The oblong, stainless-steel frame of the seeding gun
gleamed nearby, and magazines filled with pyrotechnics
covered the left-hand bulkhead. I waited, watching her march
through her tasks, sensing her love of this work she did in the
laboratory of the sky. She bloomed that morning; her body,
lithe and free-breasted, moved visibly behind the pale blue
flight suit, and I thought of grabbing her. But she turned to me
and smiled a welcome. "What's a nice girl like you doing in a
plane like this?" I asked.

"Hi, Jake." She had the vague nervousness of a not quite
seasoned shoplifter.

"All set?"

"Sure."

"Funny having you in steerage."

"Funny being in steerage."

"Sorel moves in mysterious ways."

"Enough said." She returned to her panel and continued
punching in her programs.

"You going to use that thing today?" I nodded toward the
seeding gun.

"Henry's asked me to."

I laughed. "Jesus, is there a chance you won't?"

"Nobody's perfect."

"Hey, look – I'm glad we're on the same plane."

"Me too," she said. "I'll come up for a tour later on."

"Good."

I'd forgotten about Borg. I met him on the way forward,
and it surprised me to encounter him suddenly on this
particular turf. He also had some problems about being there
– he had come aboard tentatively, almost shyly, very much at
loose ends in the aisle, hoping he would disturb nothing. He

wore a Nikon bag, chinos, a white shirt, and Wallabees, and looked 13. We saw one another at about the same moment, and both of us grinned as if to say, Hey, I've got a friend on this thing. The sentiment surprised us both.

"Right on time, Steve," I ventured, shaking his hand.

"Wouldn't have missed it for anything." He carried a lot of excitement about the flight, and no detectable fear, which was the optimum combination. We got a lot of people so cool or so frightened they missed the hurricane experience. He said, "I guess the first plane's already off."

"Yep. We'll be taxiing in a few minutes. Everything okay?"

He laughed. "I was going to ask you the same thing."

"Just high-strung."

"Sure."

"Come meet the cast." I took up to the flight deck and introduced him to Newman and Peterson, who broke the soft incantations of their pre-start sequence to greet him. Pete was a long Nordic who'd taught the aircraft type in the Navy, and had drifted into the hurricane-flying business as naturally as a sensitive boy grows toward priesthood. Both he and Sam qualified as airplane commanders and in a full Prospero season they would have rotated the left seat between them and a third pilot.

Borg winced when he shook hands with Charlie Bruska, Prospero Two's flight engineer, a huge man of about 45 with arms that looked like muscular, hairy legs; Bruska spoke an eloquently blue tongue, but was helplessly devoted to any woman, especially the bar girls, whores and various other tough-minded females with whom he spent short intervals of what must have been a lonely life.

Back of the flight deck, Borg met Don Chesney, who rode as navigator – retired Air Force, a young-seeming grandfather who dressed like a golf pro when we weren't flying, and sometimes when we were. Tall, tanned and blandly handsome, Chesney always carried a whining note in his high athlete's voice; I never could tell if the complaint were real or merely tonal.

Ira Weld had communications. He was completing his fifties, the oldest and in many respects the stablest man on either plane. A small person, stocky, very direct, the black eyes young and questing under a bunch of grey eyebrow and silver hair, the other grandfather on the plane. I think of Weld in terms of his generosity with his radios, his gruff giving of opportunities to all hands to talk to wives and children and girl-friends during the long grinds out and back across the tropical Atlantic.

Ed Mattson had the computer station, which meant he controlled the electronics on the plane. Our hillbilly, the man you always expected to stick a clodhopper through a delicate panel, and who never did. This moon-faced giant boy of about 30 hulked over both of our airborne computers and the radar electronics and everything else that used electricity in the plane with something like grace, and loved his diverse and complicated gear like a string of mules.

Gino Saperelli served as man of all work, a chubby loadmaster-cum-steward, who spent the flights roaming the plane, carrying soft drinks and coffee, providing ground crew for out-of-town starts, a perennial airman second class, and a bit of a bum, this soft-eyed flabby little man whose flabby olive face always asked for a shave.

McBride gave Borg a characteristically gentle greeting from the cloud physics booth and we went on back to Rory at the dropsonde-seeder station behind the galley. "Steve Borg, Rory Merchant."

"Hi," he nodded. You could tell he sensed something special here, without quite knowing what it was.

"Hi, Steve," she replied.

He noticed the pyrotechnic magazines racked up on one side of the cubicle. "Those seeding rounds?"

"Right," Rory said.

"You've really got a shitload – I'm sorry – a bunch of them." He went a little on the offensive and asked me, "Going to seed?"

"It'll be a realistic drill."

"Sounds like." He kept friendly, but moved just out of focus too, seeing his story ramify in strange ways, and not wanting to ruin anything, like a naturalist in a habitat at a rare and sensitive moment.

I steered him to his seat, which was the first visiting scientist station behind the power panel. It gave him a bubble window and I showed him how to call things up on his video display. "Just punch buttons the way the code tells you and you can get the speed and direction of ambient winds, or the airplane track, or radar displays of the storm with our position marked by an airplane-shaped blip." I got him a headset and plugged it into one of the overhead communications boxes. "This'll let you listen to what's going on. We also make a tape of the flight, so that's available if you need to check anything later. If you need coffee or a doughnut or anything it's back in the galley. Anything else, ask Gino. I'm going to go get my station together."

As I started forward to the flight director's station, Sorel vaulted aboard through the hatch. Saperelli seated the door in the fuselage and dogged it shut and the ground crew began moving the ladder away. Sorel nodded to Borg but went by me without speaking. I looked at Borg, who had noticed the coldness.

Back at my station, I'd begun to strap in when Ira Weld yelled over at me, "Jake, you got a call on the radiophone."

The call was from Chatham. "Jake, I'm sorry to call you this way, but I knew you'd be buttoning up and I needed to pass something along."

"Sure, Chat."

"I would have put this in your data packs, but I didn't hear about it until a little while ago. The Air Force man here says Dolly just about swallowed their C-130 this morning. It popped a bunch of wing rivets and sprung a nacelle. They also took some lightning strikes."

"You're just telling me this to make me feel good, right?"

"Sure. But seriously, I wanted you to know the storm doesn't *seem* all that bad. Plenty bad, you understand, but there's nothing in the conventional pressure gradient or winds or other data to suggest that level of turbulence. I suspect it's kind of a dry storm, so the convective clouds near the eye are more like your continental thunderheads than tropical systems. You know, higher and harder. Like Camille."

Camille. I shivered, for a moment sharing Sorel's insanity. "I'll monitor the radar contours with that in mind, Chat. But one question – how come you didn't tell Sorel?"

"I did. But, you know, I got the feeling he wasn't

interested." I didn't know how to respond, and he heard my hesitation. "Jake – is something happening you'd like me to stop?"

It made me smile to hear his offer. Chatham was one of the best-wired scientists in the agency. All of us knew the administrator and all of us could call him at home, although diffidently. But Chatham and Ted Grose went back twenty years or more, and his call would have social as well as scientific weight. Chatham made such calls, I knew, to register a complaint, or reinforce a plea for funding, or divert a brazenly wrong-headed move at the headquarters level. He hoarded his opportunities, and used them like face cards; so it was not an offer of anything small, lightly made. "Thanks," I told him. "I think we'll be okay." And again, my message to the world. "Don't worry."

"Take care," Chatham said.

"You too."

I finished strapping myself in and put on a headset, which moved me out of the surface world of the ramp at Miami International and into the quiet, technical one of the mission, the world of flight in which voices have the crisp sound of radios, and the background is the whine of auxiliary power units and engines and the electronic singing of the data system. My station began to come to life. I punched in zeroing information and in a moment the big screen showed the southern half of the Florida peninsula as a bright green outline against a one-degree grid of latitude and longitude. The northern coast of Cuba rose into the picture at the bottom of the frame. On the intercom I asked, "What's Prospero One squawking?"

"Four eights, Jake," whined Chesney. "Our computer's got their Doppler course now."

"Okay." I put the transponder code into my system and asked the computer to show me Prospero One. A small blue light shaped like an airplane appeared just beyond Key West, moving slowly toward the south-west. The hurricane didn't show on my display yet because the aircraft radars weren't turned on; but I thought the other plane must be coming under the outer edges of the cirrus cloud cap blowing off the top of the storm, and the low-level clouds would be just

beggining to show the arc that would curve more and more
until you could see the spin into the atmospheric whirlpool
that circled the eye. I wondered whether Chatham's
information had reached them and decided that probably it
had not.

The cockpit crew still murmured their check-list, like men in
a quiet card game. Trailing his headset cables, Saperelli went
through the plane checking his manifest against the occupied
seats; he disappeared into the cockpit for a moment to give
Newman the current body count and weight and balance. He
moved around the plane more than anyone else during a
mission, like a spirit doomed always to search for work. And
even here, on the ground, he kept one hand on the overhead
rail as though it supplied his motive current. He'd been
thrown against the overhead a couple of seasons back, and his
grip had tightened some since then.

Peterson got clearances over the radio and in a moment we
were moving with that clumsy gait a big plane has on the
ground. The pilots continued their calm exchange. The wind
flowed from the north-east and as we turned toward the end of
Nine Left the tower told us to get in position and hold. The
plane made the turn and stopped on the centerline. Then we
were cleared for take-off.

I always second-guessed these high-time pilots; my own
experience was just enough to make me want a placebo stick
and rudder at my station for take-offs and landings. We
accelerated down the runway, rotated and leapt off, climbing
on the screaming turboprops out over Miami and Miami
Beach. Our Doppler navigation system had got its zero at the
end of the runway, and added us to my display: a bright red
airplane blip appeared on the screen and drifted down the
Atlantic coast of Florida, turning slowly back to the southwest.
We crossed into the Gulf of Mexico just above Key Largo. The
blue blip of Prospero One held its course south-westward. I
needed to see the storm. "Sam, it's Jake."

"Yeah, Jake," the pilot replied.

"Can you extend the belly radome now?"

"It's going down."

"Thanks."

The ship vibrated as the black hemisphere of the radome

pushed into the slipstream. A green light flashed on my panel, and the horizontal sweep of the belly antenna repeated as a faint line of brightness on my screen, which clouded with the dim amber fireflies of other traffic. I adjusted the antenna sweep, dimmed the non-Prospero traffic and told the computer to give me one-minute updates of the radar information. Dolly appeared, an evil-looking curl of white blossoming and fading slowly on the scope. The eye looked farther south than Chatham's prediction, and I moved the pointer and asked the computer for the geographic coordinates of the storm center. It put

    LAT 23.5N
    LONG 84.8W

in the displayed eye. I asked the computer when and where we'd intercept a storm moving east-north-east at twenty knots. It wrote

    LAT 23.6N
    LONG 84.5W

The blue dot of the other plane was still clear of the storm. I called Newman. "Sam, Jake again."

"Go ahead."

"Did Chatham talk to you this morning?"

"Negative."

"He called me just before take-off and said the morning Air Force flight had a very bad time, with some structural damage and several lightning strikes. He said there wasn't anything in the winds or central pressure to signal those conditions and wanted to let us know."

"Any theories?"

"He thought Dolly could be a dry storm, so that the towers outside the eyewall are more like continental thunderheads."

"Ouch."

"If I get anymore good news I'll call."

"Thanks a bunch." Then, to Weld, "Ira, let's get the other plane on HF."

"Roger," Weld said. "Prospero One, this is Two on HF, over."

The thin Georgia voice of Donaldson, the other plane's communications man, came back. "Go ahead, Two."

"Stand by for Newman," Weld said.

Newman got on. "Gil Bradenton, Sam Newman here."

"Hey, Sam," Bradenton replied in the shrewd countrified voice of a Disney wildlife narrator. "What's up?"

"Warner heard from the Hurricane Center that Dolly isn't very nice." Newman went on to give Bradenton the bad word on the storm. "So, you know, handle with care."

"Sure," Bradenton said.

Sorel came on the line then, breaking his silence. "Bradenton, Sorel here. Is Pettry available?"

"I'm on, Dr Sorel," Pettry said.

"How close to the storm are you?"

"We're passing beneath some cirrus outflow and the middle clouds've begun to, you know, build. We can see cloud lines turning in toward the storm center. Hendrix puts us about a hundred nautical from the eye. It must be a compact storm, because we're still contact. We've passed our radar eye position back to the hurricane center."

"Good," Sorel said. "Do you see anything that might explain Chatham's report of severe turbulence?"

"Negative. It looks like a standard bad hurricane. We've got some light chop right now, moderate washboard. But Carla isn't painting anything remarkable on the radar. Some amber contours north-east of the eyewall. Nothing that makes this storm uglier than any other ugly hurricane." You could hear him liking his work.

"Thanks, Dick," Sorel said. "Two out."

We flew in silence then, except for occasional terse sentences over the intercom. The two-lane link between the Keys and the world went out across the ocean on our left and I watched the traffic on it. Chatham would have the area under a hurricane warning, and people would have begun thinking about staying or getting out. I could see tiny cars trying to move tiny mobile homes. Police and emergency vehicles flashed on the causeway a couple of miles below us. Traffic already looked dense, like a weekend. Key West lay out of sight in haze to the south-east of us. I hoped the Keys would be there day after tomorrow. I hoped Lennie would get out.

On my screen, our red dot slowly overtook the slower-flying blue one, which crossed the outer rainbands of the storm. "Easy does it," I whispered.

Borg came over then and plugged in his headset, holding one earphone up to catch the radio transmissions, leaving an ear free to talk to me off the intercom. "How's it going?"

"Fine."

He looked at my screen. "Some view you've got."

"You should see it in the hurricane."

"I'll bet."

"Big fat Technicolor and 3-D. Look." I told the computer to give me a closeup. The image wiped out for half a second, then the display came back. This time it showed the eye of Dolly in the lower left-hand corner, with the rainbands spreading out in the familiar counterclockwise pinwheel toward the upper right. Our red blip wasn't in the picture at this scale, but the blue blip was there, moving along the rainbands. Then I called for contoured radar images. The display wiped out again and returned a moment later with the same display except that the thunderstorm cells around the eyewall were color-contoured for intensity.

Borg asked, "The colors mean anything?" He had the Nikon out with a wide-angle lens on it and photographed me at work while he talked.

"They're false, but so are traffic lights."

"We see danger in red because we're taught to, and safety in green." Click. Click.

"Right. We use red to indicate bad cells, like you'd find in a severe Oklahoma thunderstorm, one of those High Plains rain and hail machines. You wouldn't fly an airplane into one lightly. Then we have violet, for less bad. Then amber." The display abruptly took me away from Borg. We didn't ordinarily see many red cells in hurricanes, and Carla Hendrix, who had my position on the other plane, had apparently seen none. But on my display red freeforms circled the eye to a depth of about thirty nautical miles, brutally turbulent islands in violet and amber lagoons. On the intercom I said, "Henry, it's Jake. I don't know what Carla's got on her screen but I got lots of red, pretty close together. She better check her radar."

Sorel answered, "Maybe you'd better check yours."

"I'll do that. But they're entering the storm now. If their radar's underestimating those cells I'll have to vector them through."

"Okay," he said after a slight pause. Then, "Sorel, to Prospero One. Is Carla Hendrix on?"

She came back, "Right here."

"Warner says he has a lot of red on his display. What does yours show?"

"Nothing worse than amber anywhere on ours."

"Could your computer be malfunctioning?"

"It doesn't look like it."

"Carla, Jake Warner here." I was watching their blip head for a severe storm cell while they talked things over. "I show you flying into a red cell right now. Steer two five five to pass north-west of it."

"I can see the system on the forward-looking video. It looks softer than that." But while Carla resisted the idea of a violent cell ahead of them, Bradenton acted; the blue blip on my display had already turned to the new heading.

"Okay, One," I said, "you're moving past it now."

Carla said, "I can't check out the radar unless we break away or get in the eye."

Sorel came in quickly. "Don't break off. We'll vector you in."

"Roger," Bradenton answered for his aicraft.

I said, "Okay, continue with that two five five heading."

"Jake, this is Gil Bradenton. We're in the soup now, barely contact just below the cloud bases at fifteen hundred. We're going in. We've got lots of lightning off to port, nearly continuous, moderate turbulence, we're coming back to our turbulence penetration speed just in the event. Appreciate your keeping us out of trouble."

"Anytime." I looked at Borg. "I'd say we demonstrated this machine for you at the propitious moment."

"I guess so. Was it as close as it sounded?"

"It was if my radar's working." I punched the test sequence and the radar display ran through a series of display that matched echo intensity and color. Everything looked fine. "Yeah," I told him, "it was close." Then, remembering where he worked, I added, "I don't mean the airplane would've been torn apart. But you risk some damage, like broken windscreens and dented wings."

"And maybe worse?"

"Maybe." The real-time display returned and I watched the blue blip. I went back on the radio. "Gil, Jake Warner here. Turn to two one zero." Prospero One was flying blind now, unable to pull the embedded bad cells out of the general bad weather with its radars.

"One to two one zero," Bradenton echoed. The blip moved more to the south, between two large red freeforms. "Anything specially bad between us and the eye now?" he asked.

"Negative, One."

Borg asked. "What's he mean, especially bad?"

"We'll find out in a minute."

Sorel was on the radio. "Prospero One, this is Sorel. Say your winds and pressure, please."

Pettry replied. "Hendrix has us about fifty nautical from the eye. Winds here are four zero meters per second, pressure nine five seven millibars. We're beginning to get updrafts and downdrafts of five meters per second or better even out this far. Lightning is almost continuous on both sides of our line of flight."

"Dick Pettry," I said, "Have Carla check her radar."

She replied, "I'll check it in the eye."

"Check it now. I can vector you into the eye."

"Roger," Carla said.

I told Borg, "For hurricane winds I guess anything much over seventy meters a second – that's about a hundred forty knots – you'd have to consider 'specially bad'. One hundred fifty-five knots is the threshold of a category five hurricane. For updrafts and downdrafts, I guess anything much over ten meters a second would be bad, although the airplanes can absorb much more punishment than that."

"So even without the red echoes on your radar, it's still a severe hurricane."

"Right. If Dolly keeps revving up and comes ashore she'll likely be our new worst-case storm. The new Camille. So what we're doing is flying the worst storm we're likely to get more than once in many, many years, and avoid the worst parts of her."

"Need I say, I wish you luck." He unplugged and returned to his station, where he strapped in and brooded out the bubble window at the turquoise sea.

I went back to work, adjusting the display so that the eye of the storm was approximately centered. The blue blip of Prospero One would pop into the clear in a few minutes. Our red blip crawled south-west, not yet to the outer rainbands.

Pettry counted down on the radio. "We're about five minutes from the eye. Winds one seven zero knots and rising. Pressure – Jesus, we've got nine zero five millibars. Ten nautical to the eye, eight nautical – six nautical – winds one eight zero knots, pressure nine zero three – two nautical – winds one nine zero knots – pressure nine zero one. We're in the eye. Our position, on the minute, is – 85.0 west – 23.3 north – mark."

I said, "It's a record."

"No," Sorel responded, "it's just a measured storm. Camille was worse. She just blew everything away that could have proved it."

Weld came on the intercom, uncomfortably following Sorel's harsh assessment. "Dr Sorel, you've got a call on the radiophone."

There were three radiophone outlets on the ship, one at the mission scientist position, one at mine, and the third on Weld's communications panel. I picked up my phone to listen in, hoping Sorel wouldn't hear me on the line. It was Westheimer.

"Henry?" The voice came faintly to us. He must be calling commercial, I thought, to sound so distant, like a pre-war call from London.

"Yes, Jim, go ahead. Over."

"Henry, we've completed the current run on the model. It shows the strongest negative result thus far."

"Can you be more specific, Jim?"

"I'm not sure I should."

"You should."

"Any treatment of the storm throws it to the south-east and causes winds to intensify." A pause. Then, self-consciously, "Over."

"What kind of moisture parameters are you using, Jim?"

"We're using the Camille interpolations."

"Do you have anything yet from Prospero One? Over."

"We have. But the run with that data won't be ready for another couple of hours."

"Then let me know what happens in a couple of hours. Over."

"In an hour you'll have started."

"No, we'll wait for your data."

"I don't believe you. Over."

"What are you going to do?"

"I'm going to stop you. Over."

Sorel gave a metallic laugh. "No way to do that now, Jim. Just get me the model run, won't you?"

"No, I meant it, Henry. Westheimer out."

I replaced my phone. Westheimer ran pretty much on schedule. He'd screw around for a few minutes, and call the administrator.

Sorel stormed aft then, and stopped at my station. "What does this thing look like on your set, anyway?"

"Lots of intense cells scattered to quite a distance around the eye," I told him. "My hunch is there's more ice than water in the towers, so if you seed to promote freezing it won't have much effect. I took the liberty of listening in on Westheimer's call, Henry."

"That doesn't surprise me. Do you have an opinion?"

"I think Dolly's the wrong storm to seed."

"No, she's the right storm. She's – the *one*."

"Okay."

"What're they going to do, come in here after us?"

"If Ted Grose tells Newman to turn the plane around, he'll turn the plane around."

"We'll be monitoring by then. We'll have our experiment."

"Wonderful." I unplugged and stood up. "I need to take a leak. How about watching the screen awhile? Prospero One's climbing in the eye and I guess Carla's trying to get her radar up."

"Sure." Sorel took my station and I went after to the head, then looked in on Rory. "Can I buy you a cup of coffee?"

"Sure can."

In the galley I poured a couple of cups from the aluminum air-liner fixture and we sat down at the four-person table that had been crowded into the small eating area. "Funny," I said, "Sorel and I are right on the edge of tearing out the other's throat, but we're still working together. Like dogs on a sled team." She laughed, and I was grinning at the image this evoked, of Sorel and me getting ready to have it out once we got to put down our goddamned sled, when Borg came in. "Have some coffee, Steve," I said.

"Thanks." He poured himself a cup and sat down next to Rory, fiddled with a plastic spoon. After a time he said, "Can we talk?"

"On or off the record?"

"Off. This is a kind of philosophical quest, okay?"

"I didn't know the *Herald* did philosophical quests," Rory said.

He laughed. "I'll let that pass. Now – I don't understand why you're interested in a five-hundred-year hurricane, which is an anomaly in nature. What'll you learn here that can be applied in the year-to-year stuff, the category fours and threes and twos?"

"Dolly may be a five-hundred-year storm," I said, "but you can get that storm in any year, or get them back-to-back in any pair of years. Camille was one, and that was 1969. The Keys storm in 1935 was another. Allen in 1980 just about qualified out over the Gulf. Dolly is another. That's four in a generation. Probably terms like five-hundred-year storm are meaningless, except that they emphasize the unusual power of the event they describe. As to what we'll get out of it, we'll learn something more about how a very severe hurricane functions. Maybe we'll bring back something that will improve our models in important ways. And maybe you're right. Maybe there's no application. We get no help from nature in these things. It's hard to predict the benefit."

"Okay. Now. The other day you said the new hypothesis seeded the storm outboard of the eyewall, to intensify systems there. But in the old days they seeded across the eyewall, didn't they?"

"That's right." I knew what he'd come to. He really wasn't bad at his work.

"So isn't it possible that seeding across the eyewall could have intensified instead of weakened the storm?"

"That's how they seeded Debbie, and her winds diminished. But I'd have to say yes. Nobody ever intensified one by seeding across the eyewall, but theoretically it could happen."

"But, see, you guys had this possibility and you went ahead and seeded anyway."

"The possibility hadn't been recognized then."

"Yeah, but *see?* You didn't *know*, and you still seeded."

"Okay."

He shifted gears. "Let's talk about seeding."

"Okay."

"Your radar helps me understand it. You find, like, an amber cell, which is a cloud tower outside the eyewall that hasn't developed into part of the upper-level outflow of the storm."

"Right."

"So you seed the amber cell and after a while it turns violet, which means it's intensified."

"Right."

"Then maybe it turns red?"

"We don't see much red in hurricanes."

"You wouldn't seed a red."

"No."

"Then what the fuck are we doing here?"

Rory laughed. "That's the most intelligent question anyone's asked all day."

"It's no joke. We're out here in a ten-, fifteen-million-dollar plane, tagging after another ten-, fifteen-million-dollar plane. We're flying into the worst hurricane in a long time to explore a world that doesn't usually exist and maybe doesn't require our exploration. Why, because there's money to do it?"

"That distorts it," I said, beginning to heat up.

"Would you like to hear Borg's Hypothesis of Evil in Publicly Supported Science?"

"Not especially," Rory said. She'd been quiet, but Borg and I were pervasively aware of her; she occupied the galley like a watchful spirit, whose silent presence couldn't be ignored.

"Come on. I'm not doing a story. I just want to see how my theory holds up in this big silver test tube today."

"So go ahead," I said.

"My theory is that scientists will always do what there is money to do. I don't mean they'll do anything for money. I mean they'll do anything they've been funded to do, and, further, they will push their science into shapes which they believe will entice this funding.

"Everything's put on an empirical basis, and you go along toward this goal you're funded to approach, really approaching it the hard way usually. The scientific method, in the Borg Hypothesis, is equivalent to the Hard Way. But what really concerns me (as a builder of hypotheses) is the evasion of consequences. Real consequences, I mean, not some intramural administrative bullshit.

"So if you're funded to smash a cat's balls to check out cat pain in terms of cat testicles, you'll smash their balls; and no amount of perfectly perceptible cat fear and cat cries will deter you from the path of empiricism. Many cats will have their balls smashed before you achieve statistical significance.

"Or you'd teach a gorilla to sign language and write passably good English prose, and smoke a pipe, and go to the opera, and frequent four-star whorehouses; but nothing in your work would apply your discoveries with that gorilla to save any other primate from disagreeable and debasing experiments.

"Things only connect up when you care about the consequences of what you do. You don't see that in science much. There are platoons of scientists working away on a reason to go ahead with genetic experimentation. Peenemunde is classical publicly supported science, man."

I waited for Rory to respond, expected her to; but she kept her silence. So I said, "Steve, you sound like you flunked calculus at Cal Tech."

He shook his head. "Hell no." Then, "What do you think of the Borg Hypothesis?"

"I think it needs work," I said.

"But it applies here. You and Sorel are on this plane today. I think you're going to seed this storm illegally. After all, you're *funded* to seed the storm today. And you don't care about the consequences."

"That's unfair," Rory said.

"No, really. I've been watching Jake and Sorel, and listening to them on the intercom. They're carrying this thing out as though it only concerns them. Maybe you are too. Jesus, what if you make this a worse hurricane, or tip it into Cuba and wipe out a couple of coastal villages that wouldn't have been wiped out? Shit, where are we, a hundred miles northwest of Cuba?

The clouds you seed, the seeded air, will flow out over the island in a matter of hours. That's what *they're* thinking about, watching us on their radars, monitoring us on their radios. They're thinking about those reports that the CIA tried to seed them out of sugar. Given all the tension over Stormbat we could be a very provocative little Pearl Harbor for World War III. But neither of you nor Sorel has really thought much, or cares, about such things."

"You're wrong, Steve," I said. Not nearly wrong enough, but wrong.

"Explain."

"Let me tell you how things lie, okay?"

"Fine."

"Still off the record."

"Right."

"Sorel plans to seed. I'm passive about it. I don't think seeding will have much effect on a storm this bad. And I don't see Russia launching a world war because of it. The risk of doing anything bad is very small. We believe. Now – back at the lab, one of our colleagues has a mathematical model that responds dramatically to seeding. It intensifies. It turns to the south-east. Maybe the model is right. Now, we don't want this storm to drop into Cuba, or turn north and wash away the Keys. If we thought it would because of us we wouldn't be here. But that isn't the whole story.

"Our scientist with the model has empiricism out the ying yang. But he has to pay for it by giving away the storm's complexities to get it down to something you can simulate with basic thermodynamic equations. And we have something he doesn't: we have instruments and experienced eyeballs right there in the hurricane. My instincts are pretty good where hurricanes are concerned. Rory's are better. And ours are nothing to Sorel's. He's kind of crazy, driven. Camille killed his family, and here she is again. Maybe that cracked him incurably. Maybe he made the dead a promise."

Rory came in then. "The point is that Henry Sorel's still a brilliant scientist, and his instincts about these things are as sharp as a predator's about food. He doesn't use data and go through his work by the numbers. He has hunches, gut feelings, maybe *visions*, and all of these steer and shape his work. I don't say scientists can't be everything you say. I'm only saying they – we – are relatively free of evil. As a class we tend not to sell our kids to queers and do murder and spawn great wars. To be scientific about it, I bet we don't contribute more than ten or twenty percent of the evil in the world. So – I think the Borg Hypothesis is shit."

Borg laughed. "You're in the wrong field."

"I've never thought so," she replied.

"I don't buy your defence of Sorel, or your hunches. I think if you cared about the consequences of your work you wouldn't go along. I mean, it doesn't figure that either of you'd go along with him. Why are you, Jake?"

"I – can't tell you."

"But there is something?" Borg wanted to know.

"Nothing that would change either argument."

"What about you, Rory?"

"No comment."

"I'm beginning to regret going off the record."

"Think of the benefits," Rory said, "we can't call your paper and tell them you were on a philosophical quest when you were supposed to be getting the Prospero story."

"Whatever that is," Borg said, trying to end the discussion without tension between us. It ebbed, but didn't go away.

Sorel got up when he saw me coming, and said, "Hell of a leak." I thanked him from a distance and he acknowledged it with a nod on his way back to the flight deck. I looked at the radar display. The blue blip of the other plane circled slowly as a fly within the circle of Dolly's eye. I told the computer to say altitude and numbers appeared next to the blip, counting off the feet; they were climbing to twenty-three thousand.

Then Peterson came on the radio to sever our connection with air traffic control. "Miami Center," he said, "this is Prospero Two."

"Go ahead, Prospero," a female voice replied.

"We're coming up on the Prospero airspace now and leaving center control."

"Roger, Prospero."

"We'll be leaving fifteen thousand for one thousand five hundred now."

"Roger, Prospero Two out of one five zero for one five."

The turboprops quieted as the big blades reduced their bite. We dropped toward the sea, which moved like grey-blue terrain, hatched with foam. My readout from the nose camera showed cloud bands converging ahead of us, and the course shifted from southwest to south, so that the center of convergence moved off to our left.

And there, a great darkness that seemed to eat the inward-flowing clouds, was Dolly, a young hurricane standing some ten miles high, an atmospheric pinwheel made of violent storms within storms, covering tens of thousands of square miles with high winds, heavy rains, and a storm surge that could swallow the seaward part of a coastal community. We sailed for a time along the edge of this whirlpool of air and water, then turned inward along the rainbands. Even this far from the center, the storm kicked at our shell. We pushed into rain, rain so dense, so plentiful, that we might have been at the bottom of the sea. We lost the sun to the sudden night beneath the dense rainbands, the light of a partial eclipse, green, filtered, broken only by the sudden glow of lightning. Thick sheets of rain and wind-ragged clouds blew in the half-light. Above us, out of sight in cloud, the rainbands stepped upward toward the storm center, rising higher and higher until they reached the eyewall, where low-level air ascended into the high atmosphere, feeding the violent thermal engine of the hurricane its diet of energy from the sea.

Ah, the sea. That is what you watch on the low-level legs of a hurricane flight, that is what tips you to the power of the storm. Beneath us great waves heaved beneath the wind, which cleaved and shredded them into long spumes of spray. The water boiled and broke and seemed to pluck at us. You could sense the storm reaching several hundred meters into the warm sea for its fuel, and taking out so much heat that the whole Gulf could cool a couple of degrees. The ocean seemed to resist this robbery of heat, contorting, heaving, railing at the winds. Lightning strobed the violence below, froze the waves and horizontal clouds of blowing white water in yellow-blue light. Then darkness. Then the illuminated, angry sea.

We began our low-level butterfly pass, flying the thin, dark zone between the cloud bases and the water. The heavy, demon hands of Dolly tore at the airplane; and our ship, stiff-winged and powerful, drove unyieldingly through the wind and water and artillery of lightning flashing everywhere around us. The intercom quieted as it always did with that first penetration into the fierce heart of a hurricane.

I asked the computer to give me a higher-resolution closeup of the storm around the eye, and to the southeast, where Prospero One would soon begin to seed. The screen blanked, and the closeup appeared. At this scale the computer added wind barbs and retained the airplane track, so that our two blips left red and blue tracks.

Outside the storm had settled into a turbulent steady state. The ocean disappeared in rain. The wind barbs indicated seventy-meter-per-second winds – one hundred forty knots pushing us to the southeast. But our machine bulled on. Ten minutes would bring us to the eye.

The blue blip of Prospero One had climbed to seeding altitude but still circled in the eye. I got on the radio. "Dick Pettry, this is Jake. What's happening?"

Pettry's voice came back broken and incoherent with static. Weld said on the intercom, "This static is killing us on HF, Jake. I'm going back to Prospero VHF." There were clicks on the intercom as everybody made the change to the new frequency.

Pettry tried again. "Hendrix still trying to get her radar up. It tests okay but it isn't, you know, giving us those red cells."

"Do you want me to give her cell positions?"

"Gil?" Pettry asked his pilot.

"If you think you can do it, Jake, that's fine," Bradenton said. "We've got our cockpit radar display, which isn't as fancy as yours. But between us we might get through okay. What's it look like in the seeding area?"

"You've got red cells spaced all the way around the eyewall, not quite overlapping. Violet to amber in between. In the seeding area you've got red cells along the eyewall side, then widely separated red cells about forty nautical farther out. Can Carla Hendrix get on?"

"I'm on," she said.

"Okay," I went on. "Let me give you the scope positions of those cells." I told her their azimuth and distance from the center of the eye, and their size at this scale on our display –

nickel size, dime size, BB size. She grease-pencilled them on her
scope and I did the same. "If they change significantly I'll give
you a holler."

"We're set," she said.

"Okay," Pettry came on then, "we'll pick up the mission
and go in for a seeding pattern at twenty-three thousand."

I looked at winds. We were getting a hundred seventy knots
now, with gusts twenty knots above that. Atmospheric
pressure, which had dropped steadily since we left Miami,
veered steeply downward. At the bottom of its plunge we
would come upon the eye.

"We're about five minutes from the eye," I said for the
record. "Winds one seven zero knots, gusts to one nine zero.
Pressure – nine zero three millibars – ten nautical to the eye,
winds one seven five, pressure nine zero two – eight nautical –
six nautical – two nautical miles, winds one eight five, pressure
– nine hundred millibars." Dolly had deepened since Prospero
One came this way, although her winds had dropped a few
knots.

Suddenly we floated in the eye.

The intercom revived with the fireworks-watching *Ah*s a
really well-made eye elicited from us. Dolly was one of the best.
The eye couldn't have been more than ten miles across;
around this narrow, almost cloudless, almost windless span of
whitecapped ocean rose the white cylinder of the hurricane,
gleaming blue and violent and golden in the restored blaze of
the sun, bright as an exploding star above the towers of water
and ice and air that churned around us.

"Jesus," Borg said on the intercom, surprising me with his
visitor's voice.

"Jake," Sorel said, "if Steve Borg wants to come forward
and take a look at this from the bridge, now's a good time to
do it."

"He can have my chair," Peterson added.

Borg unbuckled and went to the cockpit, uncovering his
Nikon as he passed Peterson in the narrow aisle. "Thanks,
Pete," I told the copilot as he went back toward the galley.

"*De nada*, Jake."

Everybody stretched and rubbed arse while we orbited in the
eye. Then Borg came back to his place and Pete returned to his

and we all strapped in for another go at Dolly. Newman banked the airplane toward the eyewall, and I had a familiar tickle of fear, wondering whether the big white stadium would part for the aircraft. This time Dolly didn't seem to want us back. The plane pressed the eyewall, and the turbulence pushed back, so that our tough machine skittered in an awkward slipping motion along the hard edge of the eye. Peterson said, "Son of a bitch!" on the intercom, and Newman turned us away, flew a gentle three-sixty, lined us up with the airplane crabbed something like forty degrees into the wind, and banged into the darkness and noise and awesome turbulence that marked the worst of Dolly.

We began a series of passes through the storm at fifteen-hundred feet, flying out nearly to the edges of hurricane-force winds, then back to the eye and out the other side, the ocean boiling beneath us. It took an hour to do it. Prospero One was in the seeding area, and the red cells held about where they had been relative to the eye. We kept quiet and took our data. Dolly hammered at us so persistently that I – probably all of us – became more sharply aware of the violence outside than we usually did. We began to feel a little like people in a car being rocked by a mob, like crewmen sinking in a sub: it was a contest we could lose. The storm banging at the aluminium tube of our airplane, twisting its thin wings, blasting at it with bright explosions of lightning, seemed to say Dolly would tolerate only so much of this buzzing around inside her. There was an old lady who swallowed a fly ... Charlie had this song in illustrated form, funny and grotesque. I focused on the memory of a child's book to wall my dread of Dolly.

Again we popped back into the eye. I looked for Prospero One, but the scope showed it still in the seeding area. The long radio silence, the silence of Sorel, told me they were seeding.

Ira Weld came on the intercom. "Dr Sorel, you've got a call on Prospero HF, static's pretty bad."

I turned my selector to the HF band while Sorel got on. Through the static I could just make out the sharp baritone of the administrator, speaking along the edges of his anger. "Henry, this is Ted Grose."

"Yes, Ted." Sorel's voice had an unfamiliar, nervous sound;

you could hear his fear that Grose could *make* him pack it in, and leave Dolly to spin herself to death without our intervention.

"Henry, I've had a call from your man Westheimer. Have you talked to him?"

"Yes."

"What do you think?"

"I think the storm is confusing his model. It's a very intense storm, Camille strength or better, and his model doesn't simulate such storms very well."

"Do you know that?"

"I believe it," Sorel said. His voice had stabilized.

"Westheimer thinks you're out there to seed."

"I know what he thinks."

"Are you, Henry?"

"I'm sorry, Ted, the static is very bad. I'm not reading you at all."

"Come on, Henry, for God's sake. Don't turn this into a game." There had been some residual good humor behind Grose's words; now that drained away and you heard the anger, the force behind the emotion. If he could have at that instant, Grose would have reached out like Zeus and pulled us from the sky.

"Say again, please?" Sorel said, acting deaf.

"Henry, we have some very serious problems developing back here. The Cubans copied your talk with Westheimer. They are copying our talk right now. They are understandably upset. So is the State Department. So is the Department of Defense. The call from Westheimer to me was almost an anticlimax. Do you read any of this, Henry?"

"The static is very bad, Ted."

"Okay. I'm ordering you to abort the mission and return to Miami. Immediately. When you get back we'll determine what action should be taken. I repeat, Henry, I am ordering you to return to Miami, *now*."

"Ted, when we get back within VHF range I'll call in. The static is really very bad."

"Henry, you have my order to return. We're watching you on Navy radar remoted from Key West. I want to see your airplanes on their way home right away. Otherwise ... " His voice sounded hollow and tired and sad. It evoked the uniforms who shared his office that afternoon, the guy from State Admiral Carney, the telephone calls from power to power, cascading down into our middling agency and bringing a riunous head of pressure with it. "otherwise," Grose went on, "I – the agency – will not be able to control this situation. Repeat, return to Miami immediately, or I cannot control this situation."

Grose got off the radio. I wondered who else on the plane had listened. Weld had apparently stayed off, giving Sorel his privacy. I waited for Newman to swing the airplane back toward the northeast and home. But nothing happened. Everybody had stayed on the VHF channel we used to talk to Prospero One. What about Borg? He was abstracted, staring out the window at the eye. I couldn't believe Sorel's luck.

I switched back to the VHF channel in time to hear Pettry say, "We're leaving the seeding area and returning to the eye."

"Good," Sorel said. Then, testing, "I just had a call from Grose." A pause. "He – just wanted to be in touch." Another pause, waiting for the contradiction, which never came. "So – we're climbing to nineteen thousand now. We'll fly the cloud physics butterfly pattern under the seeding area."

"Roger," Pettry replied. "We're coming up on the eye and will be climbing to twenty-seven thousand for a cloud physics butterfly above you." Then he added, "Jake, Carla's got her radar going again. We can see."

"Good." The blue blip of the other plane floated in the eye of the display, made its slow climbing turn to altitude, and plunged back into the wide world beyond the wall-cloud. We followed moments later at our lower altitude. Our probing would tell us the amount and form of water below the seeding level, give us an inventory of what could be seeded, persuaded into ice, coaxed into giving the storm its energy; higher, the other plane would see what seeding had done to this inventory. I called our pilot. "Sam, those cells on your cockpit radar are bright red."

"I thought they looked sort of unfriendly. We'll move amongst them."

"Okay." I punched in a read-out of environmental conditions. The water content was disappointing – most of it was already frozen. "Not much liquid down here."

"I see that," Sorel said.

"I imagine Grose will be looking for us to turn northeast."

"Listening again?"

"You bet," I replied. "They're right." .

"If they can work out a way for us to take that heading we'll be glad to take it."

Newman came on. "I get the impression you guys're talking around everybody on something. Is there something we should know about that call from the administrator?"

"Ask Sorel," I said.

"Henry?"

"No, nothing."

We finished the butterfly and the storm spat us back into the calm cylinder of the eye.

"Okay, Sam," Sorel said. "Let's go to twenty-three thousand for the seeding pattern." His voice had gone steady and quiet. The worst thing he'd anticipated had happened; he had slipped past it on luck, the mission went on.

I told the computer to give me a broader view of Dolly. It blinked back to the earlier picture, with southern Florida down to Key West descending from the upper righthand corner, the northern backbone of Cuba rearing into the lefthand portion of the display. I thought about the Cubans. They had little information. They'd monitored Westheimer's transmission, and the administrator's call. They were too far away to copy our VHF transmissions. So they only knew a little, had only enough pieces to suggest there was some kind of puzzle. Well, they knew Americans had been presumptuous enough to try to use the weather as a weapon in Vietnam; they'd begin to twitch, hearing us argue on the air over whether we were seeding. They'd come to a tentative alert, their radars and radios focused on us and their paranoia – except, you aren't paranoid unless you're wrong.

My radar showed the traffic sliding down the airways into Miami International and the other airports there, swarms of dim amber dots, slowed by distance and by scale. As I watched, an amber blip gathered like a drop of water coalescing over Key West. It didn't follow the airways, but turned to the southwest, toward Dolly, toward us. "Sam," I said on the intercom, "we've got traffic coming this way. Very fast." The amber blip cut across the normal grain of air traffic, anomalous, frightening.

"Keep me posted," the pilot said.

I told the computer to give me back the color-contoured close-up of the hurricane. "You listening, Henry?" I asked.

"Affirmative," muttered Sorel. He had gone still quieter.

"Level at twenty-three," Newman said.

"Prospero One, this is Sorel."

"This is Pettry."

"We're at twenty-three thousand, turning into the seeding area for a run now."

"Roger," Pettry said. "We're returning to the eye. We'll climb to thirty thousand for a cloud physics butterfly above the seeding area."

Dolly smacked us hard as we pushed into the eyewall, flying to the southeastern quadrant of the storm, where the seeding area was an imaginary band about ten nautical miles wide and maybe fifty long, like a segment from a gargantuan race-track. The turbulence was bad this high in the storm, and the plane washboarded through it, with some dramatic ups and downs that had us holding on. The old piston planes had been more malleable, had seemed to give a little, get a little from the storm. This machine had no respect for hurricanes. I pulled my seat straps in to keep the ride from being worse than a wild trot.

Sorel went back on the intercom. "Rory Merchant, stand by."

There was no response from the tail.

"Rory?" Sorel's voice rose slightly.

"Yes, Henry," she replied.

"We're beginning our run. Stand by."

"Roger." Sorel heard none of the reluctance in that courteous voice. Rory wasn't going to seed anything. She'd *heard* Borg, and thought his hypothesis so much cruel bullshit; now she had an opportunity to prove it. As between protecting Henry Sorel and redeeming science, she'd gone for science.

I gripped the corners of my small metal desk against the whipping motion of the ship. Our red blip moved slowly past great crimson freeforms on the scope, closer to the intense cells than we needed to be. The vertical speed indicator spun crazily, three thousand feet per minute up, three thousand feet per minute down. Dolly had begun a serious effort to shred us.

The computer added the bent rectangle of the seeding area to my display. Our red blip curved toward the southern end of it. Sorel said, "Seed in five, counting, five, four, three, two, one – fire." Hair rose on my neck

We waited for the rapid *chung-chung-chung* and the floor vibration that meant the dispenser was flinging ignited pyrotechnic pencils from a chute in the belly of the plane. Nothing came.

"Rory!" Sorel shouted on the intercom. "What the hell's going on?"

"Nothing, Henry," the calm mutineer's voice replied.

"Shit!" A moment later Sorel ran aft from the flight deck, keeping himself braced between the overhead rail and the floor against Dolly's efforts to pry him loose and crack him on the hull. He looked wild and suddenly I feared for Rory. I tore away my straps and unplugged, and followed him as fast as I could walk the tossing tightrope of the aisle back toward the tail, where you were far enough from the center of gravity that the airplane's motions became grossly amplified.

I got there half a second after he slapped her. They held their positions like statues: she leaned away from him, her eyes squeezed shut above a gathering patch of deep red, her body crushed into the web of straps that held her in the chair; he bent toward he with his limbs braced against the heaving deck, his left arm at the extended maximum point of his swing. "Son of a bitch," I yelled, wondering how to attack. Sorel turned to meet me – turned really to meet the Enemy, for at this point I don't think individual identities meant a hell of a lot to him – and I hung onto the overhead rail and kicked him hard in the chin. The kick and a sudden lurch of the floor threw him against the aft bulkhead, where he grabbed some braces to keep from being hurt, and looked around for a weapon. I pursued him, far enough into anger and some adrenaline-producing fear that I forgot to hang on. The airplane bucked me against the dropsonde cases, where I dug in with fingerholds, hoping my breathing would resume before Sorel reached me. But it didn't. I felt myself lifted by the combined forces of Sorel and the sinking plane; then I flew

into the after bulkhead pulling enough gravity to weigh three
hundred pounds landing. But the bump also threw him to the
far side of the small enclosure. We paused for that instant, like
tired cats fighting in a barrel some boys had set rolling down a
hill, our movements amplified or cancelled by sudden shifts of
our container. Sorel moved on me again and I neglected pain
and let go long enough to bring my clenched hands up from
my knees to his chin; then, as his head snapped back, I
smashed the double fist back across his nose, which somehow
didn't break. He dropped to all fours and the airplane flipped
him into a yellow rubber nest of survival gear. I didn't go after
him. The falls had hurt me, although they hadn't broken
anything; I was ready to quit if he was. He crouched against
the after bulkhead, bent into the yellow rubber as though at
some sort of work. I didn't realize he'd been digging for a
weapon. "I'm telling Newman to pack it in," I said.

"You are like hell," Sorel replied softly, turning a mad zoo
animal look upon me. The eyes said he had a good move
coming up, and he had. He brought out a Very pistol from the
survival gear, a toy-looking pistol loaded with a signal flare,
and poked its long snout into the stacked magazines of seeding
pyrotechnics. "Keep clear of this," he said in his low,
dangerous, crazy voice, "I'll give you a fire you can't put out if
you don't keep clear."

I feinted toward him; the trigger finger paled, tightening.

"Have it your way, Henry," I said.

"I intend to. Now both of you go forward. If anybody
interferes I'll burn us down."

Rory had unstrapped and stood in our rolling box braced
against the deck and the rail. She left ahead of me and took the
visiting scientist station behind Borg, who watched us for signs
of what had happened. We gave nothing back to him; I just
shook my head and tightroped back to my station, and
strapped in. To tell the truth it felt good to move aside.

Chung!

The seeders began operating, spewing the small, smoking
cylinders into the hurricane. I guessed Sorel only cleared the
mechanism with that one round. Then he said from Rory's
station, "Okay, Sam, let's follow a parallel track back to the
southwest and we'll do it again." He came on as calm and

professional; but the fight, the threats, the craziness hid in his voice.

"What's happening back there, Henry?" the pilot asked.

"Everything's fine, Sam."

"I felt that seeder all the way up here. You seeding this storm?"

"I accidentally fired one flare. Not to worry."

"Rory, you okay?" Sam asked.

She lifted her head off her folded arms, "I'm okay, Sam."

Newman still fretted. "You tied down, Henry?"

"I'm all right. Let's go back for another pass."

"Roger." The plane shuddered through a turn, moving like a troubled submarine in the dense currents of the storm.

Chung-chung-chung ...

"Goddamnit, Henry," Newman said, "you're seeding with that thing. I'm breaking off."

"Sam," Sorel said, the seeder continuing to run, "we're almost finished, let's fly one last pass back to the northeast ..."

"Negative, we're going home, Henry."

"We are like hell. Stay on the run or I'll burn the fucking tail off your ship."

"He can do it, skipper," Peterson said quickly. "He's ass-deep in those firecrackers back there. He can do it."

"He's got a Very pistol to ignite them," I said.

A short silence, then, "One more run, Henry," Newman said.

We bulled through the violent arc on our southwestward pass and turned back to the northeast for a third pass. Our red blip came back on line on my display, heading northeast along the faint red track the scope showed of our first two runs. The blue blip of Prospero One drifted through a butterfly pattern above us. The intruding amber blip floated into the display from the northeast, slower than before, down to a fairly fast maneuvering speed, but unquestionably on an interception heading. "Sam," I said, "traffic to the northeast."

"Roger."

Sorel came on. "What is it?"

"I think the administrator lost control of our situation," I told him. "We've got something fast coming in to intercept."

"We'll continue while we can," Sorel said; you could hear

the wear, as though he'd been running unlubricated all day
and was about to seize up.

We re-entered the seeding area. The machine spewed out its
burning silver sticks. And – something had begun to happen to
the storm. The red freeforms on my display seemed to bloom;
the amber corridors between them narrowed, were swallowed.
"Sam, those echoes are solid red on my scope." A
counterpoint barrage of hail drummed along the thin skin of
the airplane. You could see it shatter in the grey disks of the
props and fly back past our windows. Lightning glowed
everywhere around us. Waves of turbulence slapped and tore
at the plane, driving the vertical speed indicator to insane
oscillations, always lagging the event – three thousand feet per
minute down appeared as we hurtled upward, and the bottom
dropped out of our ascent before the needle quite registered
our rate of climb.

"Prospero aircraft at twenty-three thousand, this is Navy
moving up at twenty-three-five, two nautical at four o'clock."
The voice of the amber blip ghosted at us through all the
violence outside. I thought of the big photoprint on Charlie's
wall, where the intercepted aircaft suspended on the glowing
rectangular infrared display. Now Prospero Two, small and
birdlike, lay pinned to the Navy screen. And, watching us, two
men in G-suits and oxygen masks, green and black knights in
golden, bug-eyed helmets, sitting in chairs armed to rocket
them away from trouble; they watched, ready for anything.
Ready to stop us.

"Navy, this is Prospero Two. Say your intentions." Peterson
was former Navy and did the talking. Newman had the
airplane to push through the worst of Dolly.

"Prospero, my orders are to stop your mission. Peaceably, if
possible."

I knew the voice. "Gordineer," I said on the VHF, "this is
Warner."

"Hello, Warner. Sorry about this."

"Everybody okay in Key West?"

"Affirmative. On their way to the mainland now. Must leave
the small talk, old buddy. Can I have the aircraft
commander?"

"This is Newman, Navy. We'll break off as soon as we can."

"Prospero, is there a problem?"

"Navy, this is Dr Henry Sorel. We must complete one more run through the area. Then we will break off."

"Prospero, that's not acceptable. My instructions are that you will abort your mission immediately and leave the storm."

"We can't do that," Sorel said.

"Prospero, we're armed. Our instructions are that you *will* leave this hurricane or go down in it. Please break off *now*."

"Navy, this is Newman. We're breaking off."

"*I'll burn off the tail-cone*," Sorel yelled on the intercom.

"Somebody's going to regardless, Henry," Newman said.

The airplane grew heavy with our waiting, then. I don't know that we expected, but crazy behavior makes you look for more, so I think we all poised against the worst: in a moment the cabin air would stink with smoke from a white-hot fire in the seeding flares, a fire we could not put out …

But no smoke intruded on us. The intercom stayed quiet.

Sorel emerged from the seeding enclosure, pulled himself out and up like a British officer finishing an afternoon of hard interrogation. They'd wrinkled him up, and made him sag, and he was a bit ashamed of what he'd done in there; but now it was time to pick up the pieces and carry on. He'd ride back as the chief scientist. Sorel didn't look at Rory, or at me, and the crew mainly watched their consoles as he marched by, heading for his position behind Sam Newman. He trailed one hand lightly on the overhead rail; abstracted, he barely braced himself against the storm.

We had all forgotten Dolly.

As Sorel passed McBride's cloud physics station, Dolly gave a great shake that strained me against the straps. The airplane fell away, the altimeter unwinding impossibly. Sorel rose like a flying man, a dancer, and slammed against the overhead going about twenty miles an hour. Our earphones kept us from hearing his neck go, but the sight evoked the sound, like one of those killer stiff-arms in pro football when the head snaps horizontal and the helmet flies off; except that Sorel's head kept on going down to the shoulder and beyond, to a point of rotation from which the torn muscles of his neck could never retrieve it. He descended, his head dangling and flapping, an odd eccentric weight that merely swung from his flying body.

He settled suddenly to the deck, and rolled over, and lay still.

I yelled into my mike, "Sorel's hurt, head for the eye. Navy, Gordineer, listen, this is Warner. Sorel's hurt. We're getting into the eye. But don't get trigger-happy. The mission's over."

"Roger, Prospero Two. Prospero One, this is Navy, have you copied my transmissions?"

Gil Bradenton's voice floated in the storm. "Roger, Navy, keep it in your pants. We've broke off and are Miami-bound to the northeast."

I unstrapped and groped from handhold to handhold until I got to the long bag of nearly nothing that had been Henry Sorel. The heaving deck of the plane kicked the bag around, worried the limply wired head; Weld passed me a jacket, which I wedged between Sorel's head and the grey box the computers lived in. Dolly still kicked at us. I leaned over the curve of Sorel's chest and lay against him, hanging on with my hands and feet to keep from being thrown around. His face was not far from mine, and, incredibly, his eyes watched me, his lips moved. I wondered how any messages could work their way through the electrochemical mess the accident had left him. But he wanted to say something. I leaned closer.

"Cloud – physics ..." he breathed with enormous effort.

"We'll try. We'll try. Don't worry."

Sunlight streamed suddenly through the big windows. The deck stopped heaving. We were back in the eye.

I got off Sorel and Ed Mattson and Saperelli stuffed blankets and pillows from the two bunks after around the long, still form, crushed as a doll, all tangled and ready to die – and yet, not dying. Rory came forward and knelt beside Sorel, and touched his torso gently, familiarly, with her long, square hand. "You didn't do it," I said.

"Oh, I damn near did." She shook her head fiercely, then, indicating no more talk. Borg came over, fidgeting like an in-law in a relative's kitchen, wanting to help but knowing nothing of the lay of the place. McBride watched solemnly from the door of the cloud physics enclosure, which Sorel's body partially blocked, and he and Mattson and I jerry-rigged some cargo webbing around Sorel so the ride back through Dolly wouldn't torture him further. Rory knelt silently, motionless, the whole time, attached by her hand like a

mourning Siamese twin. I left her alone and went to talk to
Sam Newman.

"Say when, Jake," he said.

"Let's exit through the seeding area. We can take our data,
see what's changed. It won't hurt. Might help."

"You're as bad as Sorel. But we can do it. Shit, we'll all be
out there trying to work for Dogpatch Airlines tomorrow."

"Thanks. I'm going back to my station."

"Okay."

The big plane banked toward the eyewall as I went aft, I
knelt beside Rory. "Were going in, you'd best strap in."

She looked at me mournfully, as though something in her
had broken; and got up and walked to one of the passenger
seats and wrapped the belt around her. Then I strapped in at
my console. Sorel lay beyond the radar-scope, out of focus,
horrible to have to see.

Outside the Navy A-6 glided up to our port side,
maintaining its station a little aft of our wing, and maybe two
wing-lengths away. Gordineer had it dirtied up and nose-high
to fly along with us; it seemed to swing on unseen wires, the big
refueling probe jutting like a mandible out of the nose ahead
of the great eyes of the split windscreen. It was armed – God,
was it armed with six large missiles on pylons under its wings,
outboard of the external fuel tanks. I could see the two figures
in green and black, aliens in oxygen masks and golden
helmets, side by side. Beyond the grey interceptor the hollow
cylinder of the eye rose another twenty thousand feet above us,
and above that the sky ran dark blue out to eternity in sunlight.

I turned up the brightness levels and punched in the
medium-scale display that showed the eye and about fifty
nautical miles around it. The blue blip was gone, flying
somewhere off my close-up. I asked the computer for a wider
view. It blinked and the big picture appeared. Prospero One
crawled northeastward, clear of the storm, a third of the way to
Key West. We lingered in the eye, floating toward the wallcloud
with the amber blip of the Navy *Intruder*. Other amber traffic
moved like fireflies between Florida and the islands, Miami
and the world. The bright green outline of northwestern Cuba
arched into the display at the bottom. And there, about where
Havana would be, or south of there, at Los Baños, three amber

lights materialized, drifting quickly toward the storm.

"Navy, this is Warner. I've got three Cubans coming up."

"Roger." Hesitation, then, "Yeah, okay, we got them on our, uh, system."

"They're coming fast."

"Not to worry." As though invisible lines had been cast off, the *Intruder* drifted clear of us. "I believe they just want to fire a couple across your bow, Prospero. But we'll get in position anyway." He blasted away, burrowing into the eyewall on the far side.

Newman turned short of the eyewall, keeping us clear of the storm a moment longer, to orbit in the easy weather of the eye, "Where're those Cubans, Jake?"

I returned to my display. "They're about seventy-five nautical to the southeast, coming up fast."

"Roger."

The three amber blips floated toward our red one. I felt them out there, flying furiously, like nervous birds breaking cover. We'd pitched them higher and higher and higher through the day, and then something had triggered a show of force – the Navy plane. They were too far away to copy our plane-to-plane communications on VHF, so they misread the presence of the *Intruder* as evidence of a military ingredient in Prospero; and misread our mission as a tactical one, to steer a category five hurricane into Havana. Of course they'd scramble. But would they attack?

Navy moved across my radar on the far side of the storm, an amber corpuscle hurrying through the turbulent conduits of Dolly, an antibody going to eat the Cuban germs. Gordineer was putting his plane between us and the three Cubans, not quite giving them the finger the way he set up the *Intruder* as a target – as almost a target. Probably he was jamming the beJesus out of their radars too, giving them a transport image, or a squadron. As they neared the A-6 the three spread out in what looked to me like an attack formation. Then the central Cuban blip launched a missile. I watched the tiny stick of light crawl over my display toward the Navy plane, and past it. But now the *Intruder* turned to meet the attack, accelerating rapidly. A reciprocal light-stick drifted into the middle Cuban blip, which expanded briefly, then faded from my scope, dying as things do in arcade games. The *Intruder* accelerated to its left, and the second Cuban broke away; Gordineer pursued it, closed, launched another missile, another light-stick that drifted across the narrow interval on my display, and the Cuban blip faded. I looked for the third. It was gone. I adjusted the radars to scan downward and found only the clutter of the mountainous waves beneath the storm. He would be down there, a hundred feet of the wild ocean, vectoring through the storm toward us. An eternity of minutes south of us, the Navy *Intruder*'s echo turned back toward our position, moving fast, but not nearly fast enough. Gordineer had gone off to win his battle, and now we waited, an unarmed and ponderous target for the remaining Cuban.

I suddenly wanted to gather all the God-awful violence of Dolly more closely around us. She had been our enemy, and we hers; now she offered the only shelter against an interceptor hurrying to destroy us, flying somewhere down in the spurious radar returns from the sea.

"Sam," I said, "Navy got two, the third's on the deck I think, I can't pick him out. I think he'll come in on us, though. Navy's on his way back, but – the Cuban's probably between us."

Newman came back, "If that fucking Navy pilot had kids and played checkers he wouldn't have let that happen." He banked the plane toward the eyewall as he talked.

Dolly received us into her turbulent bosom, a haven now – and milder. She still raged as a category five hurricane, but maximum winds had dropped to a hundred sixty knots, and pressure was up above nine hundred twenty millibars. On my radar display I could see the crescent of old cells that defined the boundaries of the original eye; the newly formed eye had a diameter of about fifteen nautical miles. Perhaps we'd changed Dolly. Perhaps we saw natural variability. "Sam, we're still heading out through the seeding area, right?"

"Roger. Against my better judgement."

I unstrapped and climbed into the aisle, moving between handgrips like someone crossing a flood on a line. When I squatted down next to Sorel his eyes found and focused on me, a sign of life defying the saliva and tears and urine that had begun to soak him. His nose bore an ugly maroon swatch where I'd clipped him, damage I regretted doing now that so much more had been done. "Henry," I said into his ear, "the eye diameter is up to about fifteen miles, winds are one sixty, pressure's up. Westheimer was wrong. You – were right. We're going out through the seeding area on the way out. We'll get our data."

The blue eyes closed slowly, emphatically, blessing the news, and I guess the bearer of it. I climbed back to my station and tied myself in.

Shudders ran along the airframe as we fled across the hurricane. The wings paddled at the rough air. The intercom was quiet, while we waited for this ordeal by storm to end. Then we burst from the intermediate rainbands and found some canyons of clean air between the tall, wet towers; sunlight streaked down through the storm clouds and drew bright bands upon the sea. The Navy plane pursued us from the south. But ahead of us, suddenly, the Cuban blip reappeared on radar, climbing fast. It went past twenty-three thousand, which was still our altitude, and turned to intercept us. "Sam," I said, "the Cuban's back. I've got him at twenty-five thousand about thirty nautical at two o'clock."

"Roger." Newman pulled back the thrust and put the plane into a tight, spiralling dive back toward the towers around the eye. The ship strained as we pushed back into the storm and the power came up. Okay, he'd decided to push Prospero Two up against the limits, up to where you use the fatigue and stress data the manufacturer develops by slowly tearing a plane to pieces. We were indicating better than three hundred knots.

On the radar the Cuban blip closed rapidly. A stick of light left its amber blip and sailed toward our red one, floated past. The Cuban jet came past us, invisible in cloud, soon afterward, then made a long descending turn that put it in position to make the same approach again. "He's coming in from two o'clock level," I said.

"Okay." You could feel Newman's foot hit the right rudder and his hand yank the wheel to the right as he broke stride in a kind of heavy-airplane vertical reverse, and back into a dive, power back, heading for the sea.

We broke out at fifteen hundred and Newman turned back toward the storm center, the ocean rising toward us, hungry for us. He was contact, and trying to out-fighter the jet, a dot that broke out of distant cloud and background, closing with us in seconds, moving too fast to be seen clearly; but we heard the quick roar of the missile going past us as Newman rallied to another heading, and then the thunder of the fighter, all after the fact. It was a Stormbat, the Cuban insignia bold on fuselage and wing, radomes on the vertical stabilizers, and a big nose radome streamlined into the bottle shape of the fuselage.

Peterson muttered, "Hurricane research my ass."

I thought of Carney, wanting to know whether Stormbat was armed or rigged for hurricane research, and of Gordineer, unable quite to look me in the eye at Key West, and of the awful predictability of cracked men like Sorel. While we were running our hurricane models to predict what Dolly would do, Carney and his spooks had been running their models of us – their model of Sorel, built of his most private secrets, their model Cuba. They had let us fly Dolly *knowing* Sorel would want to seed her, knowing that he would *have* to seed her once the storm became a reincarnation of Camille; and our presence there, and the *Intruder*'s, might flush Stormbat into the hurricane. Gordineer wasn't sent to force us home, but to test his systems against the other side's; the hurricane was his laboratory too.

And, one knew, whatever happened to us now, whether we died or survived this day, nothing would be said officially, for everyone had lied. The Soviets had lied about Stormbat, and their secretly armed Cubans had attacked an unarmed American research plane, innocently probing a killer hurricane. Our country would lie about the reason the *Intruder* was armed and on the scene when Stormbat scrambled. The incident would vanish. All of our little machinations and pain and terror were just so much wriggling we did on strings that ran back to the clever fists of people like Carney. Yes, and we had lied too, lies upon lies, and now we had begun to pay for all the lying …

The Navy plane closed at altitude. The Cuban circled again, and got set up to come in from two o'clock. This time Newman climbed abruptly, and began a broad turn that threw the Cuban off his run initially. But it gave him our belly before we

got back into cloud. We felt the cannon rounds rip at the
fuselage and my radar display disappeared in a broken
rainbow. Burning smells spread fear in the cabin. Mattson, our
electronics hillbilly, punched circuit breakers on his consoles,
isolating the damage. We'd reinforced the floor to support the
computers and power units; maybe that had kept the
exploding shells out of the aisle, and kept us pressurized.

But we were blind, climbing on a compass heading through
the storm, running out of time to hide. I unstrapped and
groped to the mission scientist's station behind Newman. "My
radar's out," I told him when I had my headset plugged in.
"Thought I'd keep you company." My voice vibrated
involuntarily; changing stations had let the fear in. The Cuban
was going to kill us.

"I've still got my little nose radar," Newman said. "We're
not twenty-twenty, but we're not entirely blind. Can't see the
Cuban, though." After a short silence he asked, "Ever wonder
why we don't carry parachutes, Jake?"

"Not until recently."

"It builds morale."

"I'm glad to know that."

Newman said, "Look, I don't know where the Cuban is, or
Navy either. I'm gambling some, but I think we'll survive in
the eye, at least until Navy can chase this bandit off us."

No one said anything in reply.

We popped into the eye just over thirty thousand feet, and
Newman leveled out, skirting the eyewall closely, reluctant to
yield up our turbulent cover too quickly. Peterson scanned the
eye from the right-hand windows. "Looks clear to me," he
said, and began taking off his seat-straps.

"Where you going, Pete?" Newman wanted to know.

"Smoke," Peterson said, gesturing at a thin blue haze under
his side of the panel. He reached back for a portable
extinguisher, and knelt behind his chair, reaching around for a
better look. Nothing perturbed these men: if a jet stalked you,
avoid it; if you saw smoke during the fight, unstrap and fight
the fire. It was my first time under attack, though, and my legs
were shaking.

We had entered Stormbat's ambush. He must have had us
on his radar the whole time, watching us climb through the

storm, watching us circle in the eye, watching us relax a little. And he was there waiting for us. The jet burst out of the eyewall about three miles ahead of us, and about two thousand feet higher. There wasn't any sign of relative motion, we couldn't even see his smoke – he was on a collision course.

Newman kicked the airplane into a climbing right turn, then flipped it back to the left in a steep dive, trying to get back into the eyewall. Peterson, suddenly afraid, clambered back to his seat, holding on to anything he could find, and grabbed his seat-belt.

The attacking jet jogged with Newman's fake to the right, but not uncontrollably, so that he had our two o'clock position covered and could follow us down. I saw the twinkle of his cannon ...

The cockpit radar darkened as the shells tore at the radome, the wires, the delicate circuits. The people.

One round opened our cockpit. The window on Peterson's side shattered and the shell exploded agianst Bruska, fanning entrails and clothing across the left side of the cockpit, and my right leg. In the slow and graceful way of large events unfolding in a hundredth of a second, the flight deck came apart.

Peterson's seat-straps were still loose as our fuselage depressurized explosively, sucking charts and loose gear and some of the bedding we'd wedged around Sorel out into the slipstream. It took Peterson too. He screamed as the escaping air forced him through the ragged orifice of the shattered window, and tried to hang on, and was swept away into blue space.

A cannon round exploded against the bulkhead behind me, showering the aisle with metal and severing more wires. Sparks spat at the inert form of Sorel. Mattson kept shutting down systems to keep us from burning. The altimeter unwound crazily, fifteen thousand, thirteen thousand ...

Another round exploded through the right front windscreen, sending a blast of metal and Plexiglas and wiper into Newman's chest. "Jesus!" he yelped, shrill and frightened. His eyes bulged; his left hand clutched his severed torso closed. And his right, moving autonomically, the compleat pilot's hand, walked down to the autopilot and turned it on, set up a standard rate turn at twelve thousand feet, an endless circle to keep us in the eye. He forced himself out of his straps and wriggled free of the left seat, still holding his thorax shut with a grey hand. "Jake – get in." Blood flowed down his fingers when he spoke. "Get – in." For a moment we leaned together, there in the noise and gale of the flight deck; then I slid by him into his chair. He slumped behind me in the mission scientist's station. We were still plugged into the intercom. With this head on the pale metal console behind me he whispered, "Bradenton ..."

Again, we circle in the eye, held by the automatic pilot. I am nearly jellied, yielding up stamina with the release of tension now the first flying is done. I watch the wallcloud. The turbulent cylinders in the centers of hurricanes have always filled me with wonder;

now the wonder is colored by a drop of fear. I wonder how it will feel, riding the airplane – hurtling in an airplane under my tenuous command – into that wild annulus of wind and water.

Bradenton, silent for a time, returns. "Jake, we've been having a conference over here. The way I feel is you've got a damaged plane, and you don't really know how bad it really is. That number four engine worries us some. And you might have some damage that'll kill off your autopilot, too. So we can't get you too dependent.

"My own preference would be for you to go back right up at your service ceiling, which'd get you through the worst of it fastest and you'd be visual and could begin letting down on the far side. But the icing could turn you into a snowball. You've got an unpressurized, unheated airplane there, so going over high's just too cold for too long.

"Going back very low is out, too. Below cloudbase you'd be contact instead of IFR if you lost your autopilot, but the rain down there's so heavy I think it'd just fill your fuselage with water and kill your electrical system. And if something went wrong you'd be too close to the water.

"So here's our standard Mark Four compromise solution. You get everybody tied down and go back at about eight thousand. That's below the freezing level so you won't come out the far side looking like a Birds Eye package. But the rain is going to be pure bloody murder, and your cockpit's going to get wet. Also, you're going to be on instruments if the autopilot conks out. But you can't get five hundred hours in a plane without occasionally going IFR, so you more or less know how to handle that. Just keep the wings level, let the wind blow you up and down, and try to hold your heading. After about a thousand years you'll find yourself in the clear again." He is silent for a moment. "Like I said, it's a compromise. Okay?"

"Okay."

"Good. We're working up a path of least resistance for you from our radars, so stand by. Go ahead and take her off autopilot and do a gradual descending turn until you're level at eight thousand. But have everybody get strapped in real good, too."

"Roger." On the intercom, I say, "We're going back through at eight thousand. Everybody get strapped in. Watch the – watch the wounded."

I adjust my seat and shoulder straps. Borg does the same at his station. In his eyes I see reflected a thought of mine: that along with our large, real problems of survival on this day, there is melodrama; the grade B movie that cranks up when people view themselves against dramatic adversities.

Now, feeling delinquent without specific guidance from Bradenton, I disengage the autopilot. Again the plane suspends from my grip upon the wheel. I reduce power slightly and drop one wing into a shallow, descending bank, keeping us away from the wallcloud, whose curved sides still pluck at us, or seem to. The shallow dive restores my sense of this airplane's power, it's grand contempt for hurricanes.

Saperelli says, "Everybody's strapped in, Jake. Newman, and, uh, Dr Sorel, everybody."

"Thanks, Gino." I look back at Sorel's body in the aisle. Rory squats near him; she wears a body harness, which ties her on a three-foot length of webbing to a cargo ring, so she can move without being battered by the storm.

I tell Bradenton. "Level at eight."

"Okay, Jake," he replied, "put on some power and trim the plane to fly at two twenty." I comply. "Now, go on and make one last turn to get centered in the eye." I begin the maneuver, tightening the turn toward the imaginary middle of the white cylinder. "When you get to the center, level her out and take up a three zero zero heading, and set the autopilot, but keep the altitude hold *off*. The autopilot'll give you the best ride and you don't care what your altitude is – let Dolly blow you around. Just keep the ship horizontal.

"Okay, now, get your ship crabbed around so she'll be headed upwind at the eyewall – go on, skew her around there ..."

I nod, act on his orders, but silently, not trusting my voice in a reply. Just past the midpoint I engage the autopilot, feel its (his?) hand close upon the controls, which I still hold. The white cliff of the wallcloud covers our northern horizon, approaches as swiftly as a crash. Although I've flown this penetration from the eye as a passenger a hundred times, today it frightens; my heart expects the collision of cloud and airplane to kill us. My neck braces like a tackle's; involuntarily, at the last instant, my eyes squeeze shut.

Then Dolly accepts us, the airplane swerving in the sudden, ferocious turbulence behind the white wall. I feel the mechanical pilot's cool commands beneath my sweating palms. The world of indigo cloud splits around glowing bolts of lightning, and the gale blowing through the cockpit brings torrential rain and graupel and snow, so that slush begins to rim the cockpit, drift against the dark form of Bruska, the grim statue made by Rory and Sorel just aft of the flight deck door. I sting with cold, my fingers do not willingly unbend. *Blup, blup,* the curds and crusts of nearly frozen water slap against the bulkhead.

And we hear another sound, a new voice added to the roaring wind and the turbines: it is the terrible wail of Dolly herself, the wild-throated song of the storm.

"Jesus Christ," I whisper, half curse, half prayer. Dolly shakes us like the hand of God, the altimeter and vertical speed needles rotate madly, impossibly. And yet, I can feel here, as one cannot as a passenger, the steadiness of this airplane, unbending, stronger than the hurricane ...

I withdraw from what is fearful outside, watch the little facsimile airplane fly the illuminated blue world of the artificial horizon, the airpseed, the altimeter – the digital clock, whose bright fluid numbers cheerfully unravel our ten-minute eternity second by second, numbers dissolving into numbers, counting us down, counting us out of hurricane Dolly.

There – the light increases.

Sunlight gleams beyond the thick rime gathered on the windscreen, and, looking back, I see the rough white cover weighing on the wings. A quick break in the clouds, a moment's calm, then back into another tower of the storm, then out again. Cumulus spires rise as from great fires on the sea; we clip them; then we are clear, flying an infinite curve of indigo sky and nearly open sea below the long curving streets of rainbands that feed the lower levels of the storm. "Gil, we're out," I say.

Prospero One closes, seems to skid toward us from its point of exit from the hurricane, perhaps two miles off to our right. As though he has flown within earshot, Bradenton breaks his silence. "How was it, Jake?"

"Strange." The wrong word. It will be a week, a year, before I can answer his question.

"Yeah, well – your airplane okay?"

"Flight deck's wet, but, yeah, we're okay."

"Soon's your knees settle down, we'll try some flying."

Ah, he knew – I touch my trembling thighs, will them to be still. "I'm okay," I say.

"Okay, take it off autopilot."

"Roger." I disengage the mechanical hands, returning the airplane to mine.

"Now make a standard right turn to a heading of zero one seven."

"Roger." We bank into the turn, the remote magnetic indicator spins toward the new heading. I level the wings and come up on zero one seven, feeling good at the precision.

"So," Bradenton says. "We're level at eight thousand, headed right for St Pete and MacDill. Be there in about an hour. We best try an approach."

I shake my head, but say, "Okay."

"Bring it back to about two hundred."

I back off on the power and raise the nose a bit more. The airspeed drops to two hundred knots. "Now – remember when you put on flaps you've got more lift initially so you'll climb some unless you get the nose down."

"Okay."

"Put on ten degrees of flaps."

I comply. The airplane rises. "Nose down!" Bradenton barks. I push on the wheel and reach for the trim; the plane stabilizes, nose slightly down but holding altitude, at a hundred eighty-five knots. "Go to approach, flaps twenty degrees." I add more flaps. We slow quickly, the airspeed diving to one sixty. "Pitch and power, Jake, pitch and power. If you want to sink leave it the way it is. If you want level flight you need more power to drag those flaps along."

I add power. The airspeed ascends to one seventy, and more. I pitch the nose up to compensate. The airspeed comes back to one seventy and holds there. "Holding one seventy," I say, inclined to smile at being able to control the ship this well.

"Now put on full flaps," Bradenton says.

"Roger." Confidently I move the switch all the way to the stop. The airplane brakes, the bottom drops out of our airspeed. I push the nose down to work around the approaching stall, and add power; then as the airspeed comes up I raise the nose so that we are flying nose high but maintaining altitude at a hundred fifty knots. The ship is stable again, but I feel it pushing me, making my mind rush along, urging me to make that critical mistake: a maverick quality in this machine *wants* me to lose control.

"Nice save," Bradenton says. "Now look on the panel, just to the right of your control wheel. You'll see the gear control. Standard gear up and locked, gear down and locked deal, just like a retractable single except you're moving bigger wheels and more of them. Got that switch?"

"Yep."

"Okay, clean her up and we'll shoot some landings."

I ease the flaps back into the wings, lower the nose, get the ship back to two hundred twenty knots.

"Good," he says. "Put on ten degrees of flaps and maintain one ninety." I comply. "Now twenty. You're landing, so let it pitch down some, but not too much – and let the airspeed decay on down to one seventy. Okay. Now drop the gear." I press the switch to the GEAR DOWN detent. Electric motors and hydraulics rumble in the middle fuselage and wings; we hear nothing for the roar in the cockpit but the vibrations travel through the hull, the wheel. The airspeed descends past one fifty. I push the nose down a couple of degrees. The airspeed trembles back to one hundred fifty. "Okay, turn ninety degrees to your left, maintain your airpseed and attitude, keep it shallow – you're getting down near the stall here." I ease the plane around and turn past the ninety-degree point, then coax it level. "Full flaps." I move the flap switch down the last notch. The airplane shudders and seems to fall.

Before I can add power Bradenton says, "You're on final. Let the airspeed go down to one thirty. But remember, you *stall* at one ten. Hold that one thirty now, pitch and power, pitch and power. Watch the vertical speed. You want to come down about five hundred feet a minute, maybe a little more than that. Need quite a bit of power to drag all those wheels and flaps along such a flat slope. But that's how you'll do it, Jake. Just like a night landing in an overloaded Cessna. You'll fly that mother right onto the runway at MacDill."

We continue our descent to seven thousand feet, where Bradenton yells, "*Abort, Jake, take it around, get that power on, gear up, clean it up!* Keep the nose flat." I force the big machine through a frightening simulation of a go-round, the airplane laboring near the stall which always stalks you close to runways. By the time I have the situation controlled, the aircraft trimmed, I am exhausted, my flight suit soaked with perspiration so that the wind roaring through our shattered cockpit leaves me chilled. I feel a moment's hatred of Bradenton; through my fatigue a vague conviction grows: his enthusiasms will kill us. Satan.

Now Satan speaks. "Jake, we're done practicing. Let's get back on that zero one seven heading now." I bank the airplane back to the northeast, while Bradenton talks. "This heading'll get us about thirty nautical from MacDill, and offshore; we'll give you another slight heading change then that'll bring you into alignment with the big runway at MacDill. I've told the bluecoats your problem. They're much better equipped for this kind of stuff than a civilian field, and they've got a ground-controlled approach, which is a pretty neat way to land. Miami Center's keeping the traffic they control out of our way and they'll try to get the light VFR stuff out as well.

"I think you've got a good shot at this landing. If something comes apart on you, just put on power and go around. It works the same way at five hundred feet that it does at seven thousand. What I'd like you to do now is turn on the autopilot and take a ten-minute break. Stretch. Get clearheaded. I think you're going to do just fine."

"Thanks, Gil." I engage the autopilot, relieved to feel its phantom hand clutch the controls once more. When the airplane does not slide away from level flight in this mode, I

turn loose, get up, stretch, try to still the shaking of my hands,
the errant nerve that twitches behind my knees. Borg catches
my eye. I shake my head and touch his shoulder, gestures
intended to mean: I hope I don't kill you today. I gesture
vaguely toward the others: I hope I don't kill you, and you,
and you ...

McBride, I imagine, soaks in crimson blankets in one cot.
Newman utters whale sounds and dreams morphine dreams
upon the other. Rory sits in the galley, still wearing the
harness, her head on folded arms, her eyes open. I wave.

She doesn't move her head, but tries to form a smile. I want
to knead her shoulder muscles gently. She shuts her eyes.

I pour half a cup of coffee from the themos, sip at it, then
hand the cup, half-full, to Borg. He nods, recognizing the size
of simple ceremonies done at crucial times. I strap myself back
into the pilot's seat, and ride along, waiting to hear the bull has
come into the arena.

Everything outside is sunlight, white cumulus, turquoise
ocean. It lulls, so that I feel myself come suddenly awake when
Bradenton calls. "You back in position, Jake?"

"Roger." My mouth is dry. In airplanes and in ships one
must not watch for coastlines, cities, destinations, that are
destined to appear only in the fullness of time. I know this, and
yet I ache toward the eastern horizon, willing the low,
grey-green coast of Florida into view. The horizon stays blue.

"Good. Just leave it on autopilot. We're going to come up
on the two-twenty radial from MacDill omni about thirty
southwest of the runway. Don't try to navigate. I'll tell you
when we're there and you can make that turn. Surface wind's
from the northeast, more or less, so you'll be on a long final
for runway four, on a heading of zero four zero.

"We'll follow you down about a thousand feet off to your
right. Don't pay us any mind at all. We'll imitate you to make
sure your angle of attack isn't going to bite you down near the
stall, stuff like that."

"Fine."

"When we get to the two-twenty radial and turn toward
MacDill, the bluecoat GCA will come on and bring you in."

"Okay."

"You aren't landing instruments, so you're going to have a

whole bunch of visual cues to do something other than what the man is telling you. I want you to ignore what you see outside. Just fly down the slope the way he tells you. He'll bring you right down to the runway in good shape. You just fly the plane on, the way you'd land your plane at night. If the approach falls apart, you know how to put on power and go around. We've done that. It's behind us." A silence. Bradenton rests, I think. Then, "So, okay, he's got you down on the concrete. There's lots of concrete at Macdill. You'll have about two miles of it on runway four, which is the way they're landing today. And its five hundred feet wide. Shee-it, you can land two, three times at MacDill." I laugh; he fills my world with talk, drives out the fear, the discomfort, the fatigue.

"Gil?" I say.

"Yep?"

"I get the impression you've done this before."

He imitates Gable. "Frankly, my dear, you are not the first." He laughs on the air for me, a gift.

I reciprocate, conscious that, as he must reassure me, I must reassure him. He is flying two airplanes. I admire his stamina. Now he says, "Okay, the GCA controller will get you on that expanse of concrete, Jake. You'll be going pretty fast, a hundred and ten knots, maybe a little less, when your main gear touches. Maybe you'll bounce. Just hold the wings level with aileron and hold your landing attitude with the wheel and keep it straight with the pedals. There's no crosswind so the wheel'll be centered. Don't drop a wing or anything. Keep her straight. Get the power levers back to flight idle. Then she'll just settle back on that main gear. Okay?"

"Okay."

"When the main gear is *on* and you're rolling, put down that nose wheel. It isn't like a Skylane nosewheel, you're not going to pop it off or anything. Get it down and get on the toe brakes, which are the same kind of brakes your airplane at home has, only bigger. Now. I don't want you to try reversing the pitch, and you shouldn't have to – it's a hell of a long runway. But you do need to steer. Look over on your side console, forward end. Little wheel there, looks like the wheel on a toy car. Once you're down and braking you hang on to the control wheel with your right hand, but start steering the

nosewheel with that little wheel on your left. It's easy to use –
you just kind of drive along with it, okay?"

"Okay."

"When you've stopped don't worry about shutting it down.
The Air Force'll get somebody aboard to shut down your
airplane. Any questions?"

"I don't think so. Maybe some will come to me after the
landing."

He laughs. "Right on."

Bradenton makes it sound simple. But I sit with so much
airplane around and behind me that I have a feel for the
degree to which we are a projectile. I've had landings turn to
shit on me in an airplane weighing three thousand pounds,
going seventy-five miles an hour – I clench my eyes against the
spectre of all that can go wrong in one weighing fifty times
that, going twice that speed – the loss of directional control
near the ground, the high-speed ground loop that rips away
our wings and immerses us in burning JP-4, the approach stall
near the runway threshold, the aborted landing and departure
stall on the go-round. Sometimes aircraft love returning to
earth, to rest; and sometimes they hate the surface, you feel it
in their way of landing. So I ask in a whisper, "Which is it
today, old friend? Which is it today?"

Behind me a squad of men, living, dead and in-between,
ride this in with me. And Rory. They must wonder how I am
today, too. I go on the intercom. "This is Warner," I say to all
the people I prefer not to kill. "We're heading for MacDill. I
want you to know that Gil Bradenton's got me pretty
comfortable in this airplane. I think we're going to be okay."

"Come on, Jake," whines Chesney, "we know it'll be okay."

"Doing great, Jake," Mattson puts in.

They talk it up, boost the home team, on the intercom. It has
an awkward sound, though; we all understand they are
soldiering.

"Prospero One, this is Jake," I tell the other plane.

"Yeah, Jake?" Bradenton answers.

"Gil, I may get delayed after the, uh, landing. My son's at
Bella's. My secretary's. Let me give you her number." I fish the
crumpled paper she gave me from my pocket; it is rimmed
with a bloody rust. Then I read Bradenton the number. I want

to give him messages for my son, and for Lennie – even for Lennie. But I resist.

"If you're delayed I'll call her when we get in, Jake," he says.

"Thanks, Gil."

"Don't worry."

Ah, he adopts my message to the world. Don't worry. Don't worry, Charlie. I'm doing the best I can. I think of my son, and of my broad and endless love for him; I think of the pale form sinking through cylinders of bubbles in the turquoise sea, of his "Dad"s and "Daddy"s, and of his fucked-up little life. I must not fuck it up more with a fatal crash.

Rory enters the cockpit, leans past Borg to touch my shoulder with a hand, then touches Borg, sharing whatever remains in the wand. A ripple, nearly a shudder, of gratitude shakes me. My heart swings toward her, I want to chat, tell her I love her, stroke and receive counterstrokes. Except – the poor bastards who must ride to earth with me have no one to chat with now; they must descend, they may die with brainfuls of unspoken words to loved ones, to their own pale, serious sons and daughters, their unestranged waves. Rory unfolds the jumpseat behind and to the right of Borg and straps in. Ah, God, what a long way to MacDill.

Bradenton speaks. "Okay, Jake, best take her off the autopilot and get accustomed again." He tries to conceal an audible fatigue.

"Roger," I say, and turn off the machine that flies us. Once more, the tons of airplane suspend from my hand. The airplane flies along as though it senses no difference. Clever airplane. Brush me off against some bridge.

I yearn toward the Florida coast, to have the matter done with. But, yearning eastward, I am shocked to see the dark green line begin to fill that horizon, the flat shadow of land and its mantle of low clouds. We fly to this grave.

"Hold it at about two hundred," Bradenton says.

"Roger." I bring the power back, the nose stays where it is, the airspeed trembles back to two hundred knots. We are level at seven thousand feet. The engine instruments flicker identically.

"Jake, we're coming up on the two two zero radial from MacDill. Go on to a heading of zero four zero, now." I bank the ship. The RMI spins the new heading to the arrow and I level the wings. "We're about thirty nautical southwest of MacDill. Bring back your power some and let's start down at eight hundred feet a minute. Bring back your power, trim her."

I comply, and, after an initial oscillation of airspeed and rate of descent, get the ship stabilized. The land emerges from the haze and water in the air. I see the thin arch of the Skyway Bridge across the gleaming blue-white mouth of Tampa Bay. St Petersburg Beach runs off to my left front, low-slung, curving like a mandible southward from the larger peninsula, where St Pete and Clearwater lie, old and expensive, pretty and green. We pass the small keys that point northward to the island beach, cross the southern roots of the Skyway Bridge. Pinellas Point wheels below us, the flat southern edge of St Pete's peninsula.

"Field's dead ahead, Jake," Bradenton says. "And that town off to your right front, well that's the city of Bradenton, Florida, where we'll have our ticker-tape parade later in the day. Go ahead and level out at sixteen hundred feet on this heading."

I adjust the controls, but lag the tolerances; we are level at fourteen hundred.

"That's okay," Bradenton says. "Go on over to the tower frequency now — two nine four point seven. I'll be on there with you."

Turning the frequency selector isolates me almost unbearably. But Bradenton waits on the new channel.

"You on, Jake?"

"Yep."

The field takes form in the horizonless flow of bay and sky. The northeast runway lies foreshortened, white, expansive, sticking out into the Bay on a peninsula of fill, the instrument landing system equipment on masts and islands planted offshore, rising like the rigs of sunken ships from the gleaming water. About ten miles across the water. Two shorter runways form a rough isosceles triangle among the hangars and beige buildings and barracks and red checkered water-towers. Slack-winged bombers row the distant apron.

"Jake, put on ten degrees of flap."

"Roger." The flaps slide out of the wings a little. We slow.

"I'm right over here if you need anything. Here's the GCA coming on."

"Prospero Two, this is MacDill GCA, how do you read, over?" The professional young voice, tinged with some north Texas or Oklahoma, surprises. A boy brings us in. Except – he talks in B-52s and F-4s and all manner of more formidable aircraft than this. Trust the clear, young voices.

"Loud and clear, MacDill."

"Prospero Two, I have you nine nautical on final for runway zero four, eleven thousand four hundred and twenty feet long, five hundred feet wide. Altimeter nine eight nine, visibility one five in haze, ceiling two five scattered, winds zero four five at one zero. Over."

"Roger, MacDill." I alternate removing my hands from the wheel, to wipe them on my shirtfront. The earth crowds my flying. Pleasure craft, people in them, nun buoys, the bright wings of small aircraft, streets, structures, even birds near the water are crisply visible. My mind rushes along now, driven by what it perceives as our excessive speed.

Bradenton comes on. "Pull it back to one eight, Jake." I take off power; we sag. "Twenty degrees of flap."

"Roger."

"Gear down."

The landing-gear shaped lever glides down beneath my hand. The ship trembles as the great wheels thrust into the wind. I correct for pitch.

"Prospero Two, MacDill. I have you on final for zero four, seven nautical from the threshold. Over."

"Roger."

"Prospero Two, say your airspeed. Over."

"One five zero."

"Prospero, descend to one thousand two hundred, over."

"Roger." I come back on the power slightly and we drop toward the new level.

Bradenton intrudes. "Go ahead and put on full flaps, Jake."

"Roger." I drop the flaps and we slow enough to make me jump; then, recovering, I add power to bring the nose up. The airspeed decays to just above one hundred thirty knots. "Airspeed one three zero," I say, wanting MacDill back.

"Prospero," the young voice of MacDill says, "you're descending too fast. Maintain five hundred feet per minute."

I add power until the rate of descent comes back to less than three hundred feet per minute, and trim the airplane there.

"Very good, Prospero, you're intercepting the slope now. You're a little right, steer left to zero four zero."

"Roger." My airplane is the one in the artificial horizon; I ignore the monster that encloses me. Reluctantly I raise my head and look into the future. The field hurries toward us, vividly close. But going visual makes me skew the plane slightly. I feel a touch of panic in my movements to make it come right. The surface flows by, too close, too close, and we are going too fast, and – and there is something else, too, barely perceptible, some vibration, some buried noise of failure

"Prospero Two, steady as you go. Do not acknowledge further transmissions unless you are unable to comply. If you don't hear me for any five-second interval, climb to one thousand feet on this heading and ..." The GCA voice stops its hypnotic song. *"Prospero, you're on fire!"*

"Jake," Bradenton yells, *"pull number four!"*

But the sudden yellow-white bloom of flame to my right has already drawn me away from them, filled me with fear, robbed me of all action – I seem to dither, to be unable to act quickly; I cannot look away from the bright pulsing freeform that was our number four engine.

"Pull number four, Jake!"

Moving like a diver, I reach through the nightmare to the candy-striped handles along the top of the engine-instrument panel, and pull the one at far right, where a warning light blazes urgently. The big flat blades of the damaged engine feather into the slipstream, and cease their drumming. The fire itself dwindles, almost throttled as fuel, oil, and air are automatically withheld. But now the airplane's healthy pair of engines try to fly around the slower wing, and we begin a rolling skid to the right.

"Left rudder, *left* rudder!" Bradenton chants. I push the rudder pedal and the airplane cocks back to straight flight. My leg trembles visibly, straining against the rudder. But we have gone astray, the runway flashes by a hundred feet below, well

to our left. And I am now very far behind my airplane, barely
in control, convinced there is nothing one can do …

"*Jake, you're still on fire!*" But I am mesmerized by the
nearness and inevitability of our crash. Bradenton's voice is
distant, even irrelevant, in my headphones.

"HIT THE HRD, JAKE. YOU'RE BURNING! HIT THE FUCKING
HRD!'

And, yes, the bright flower blooms once more in number
four – a fountain of flame hot and big enough to rouse me. I
hit the HRD button for number four engine and the flower
withers, eaten by chemical within.

"Okay, I think you're okay. Now go around. Take her
around, Goddamnit!" He mutters at me like a disappointed
instructor.

I jam the power levers forward, forgetting we are flying on
only three engines. The increased power makes the plane roll
into a sudden yawing right turn that I correct by adding full
left rudder, but not before the turn eats away our altitude.

"*Gear up*," shouts Bradenton.

I bring the wheels up. We shudder along near the stall,
yawing crazily not fifty feet above the field, as I overcontrol
nervously against the plane's mad wish to roll to the right.
Beyond the base, pastel houses and glass shopping centers
whip toward us, people running, pointing – they whirl dizzily
past a couple of stories below. We are descending,
imperceptibly, still close to the stall, but accelerating. While I
am flying the plane, I am flying it into the hollow sockets of the
death's head that stared at me all afternoon, I yield us up …

A green cloud of tree tops explodes as we plunge through
the thin upper branches. Beyond this gentle barrier, a line of
high-tension wires fills the windscreen. The cracked nose grabs
the highest cable, rips it loose with a blinding blue flash. My
fingers are jolted by some increment of high-voltage current,
as sometimes happens when the plane takes a lightning strike.
But the sight of the approaching wires, the larger fear of
hanging in a tangle of sparking snakes, burning and burning,
trips my numbed reflexes. I have already started the climb as
we clip the wire, as our world is turned blue-white for an
instant, and then into a sharper climb yet, watching the
airspeed, flying the airplane, moving, finally, as quickly as one

must move in a cockpit ...

Incredibly, at two hundred feet. Prospero One comes into view a few hundred feet off our right wingtip.

"Still with you, old buddy," Bradenton says almost cheerfully. "Fire's out. You okay?"

"I'm – okay." My hands shake and I am half blind with perspiration; my stomach carries the nausea one feels from a groin injury. "Yeah, I'm okay."

"Bring your flaps up to twenty degrees, Jake. Power on number one engine back to flight idle, keep your power up on the two inboard props. It'll be a little easier on your left leg."

I nod, tired of my echo, and pull back the power lever nearest me. The airplane stops pushing against my rudder pedal, stops trying to fly round itself, and steadies, the incipient turn almost erased from its contols. "Thanks, Gil," I tell lilui.

"*De nada.* Let's climb on back up to two thousand, Flaps back to ten degrees. I've told the Air Force our intentions."

Level at two thousand, the airplane calm, I explore. My jitters have begun to abate, my head is clear; it is as though, having now died in a crash that somehow occurred incompletely, I am beyond death. In that sense I feel reliable. But I also know that, when tested in this crash, my reflex had been to fly my people into the death's head, to surrender them.

I explore. The intercom is quiet. One senses general despair. "Everybody okay?" I ask the silence. The reply is a reluctant chorus of I'm okays. "Now that we've had our crash," I tell them, "I guess we can go on and land."

"Nice crash, Jake," Saperelli sings.

"Best crash in a long time," adds Weld.

"Which engine we going to lose this time, Jake?"

"Number three, of course."

Mattson says, "Losing that number four engine delayed us twenty minutes, Jake. We lose the other three, we'll be up here all day."

Laughter.

The living live, speak and, I think, begin to forgive me my flawed impulse to give them over to death.

Soon we are banking into a long final approach, out over the ocean, the bridge sliding toward us, and the runway at MacDill shifting its axis until we are aligned. "Prospero Two, nice save there," comes the calm voice of the GCA. "I have you eight nautical miles final for runway zero four," and, as though we had not done this before, he tells me the runway length, altimeter setting, surface weather. I put out flaps, then undercarriage, and reduce power on the two inboard engines. But I am wary as a burned child, only half my mind on the plane, the other half trying to peer through time for the next surprise ...

"Prospero Two, steady as you go," the GCA voice says, again repeating all that had gone before. But this time he finishes his sentence without telling us any bad news. It has the effect of cancelling out the lost engine, and swings my attention sharply back to where it belongs. "Resume five hundred feet per minute descent. Range four miles. You're going above the glide path, you're twenty-five, forty feet high ..." I increase the rate of descent slightly. "Good. Coming down to glide path, fifteen, ten, on the glide path. Resume normal rate of descent. Range three miles. You're holding the glide path very well. Going below now, ten, fifteen, twenty-five feet ..." I add power. "Coming back now, fifteen, ten, back on the glide path. Heading zero four zero has you lined up with centerline. Range two miles. On glide path. Going five feet low." I pull back. "Holding five feet low." I pull back a little more; the airspeed decays toward one forty, thirty knots above the stall. "On glide path. Over the end of the runway, on centerline. On glide path approaching touchdown." The world tumbles past in the edges of my vision, suggesting angles, speeds, contradictions I cannot ignore. I look up, suddenly afraid of diving into the runway, see us near the concrete and pull back instinctively to flare. "Touchdown in three seconds."

"*Get it level, Jake,*" yells Bradenton.

The nose gear is almost back to the right attitude when our main gear strikes the pavement. We're hot, and carom.

"Keep it level, hold your landing attitude," Bradenton repeats.

The big ship falters in the bounce. I try to keep the wings level, the nose in a landing attitude, which feels low to me; an unnatural act, to land an airplane with its nose there. The main gear hits again, our bounce is less ruinous. But I have done all

I can do. The omni station sits near the far end of the runway, a small white conical structure to my left front, a thin forest of ILS apparatus beyond it. It approaches swiftly, and I am helpless as a priest observing God. The runway whirls past my window, a blur of tire-streaked concrete. But – the main gear is on. I stay on the rudder pedals to keep the hurtling plane on the broad, hard surface, hoping that when the ground loop signals I'll be ready with the brakes, and push the control wheel forward, forcing the nosewheel to the ground. We slow. I stand on the brakes, move the power levers back to flight idle. We slow. The omni shack approaches less relentlessly on our left. The blur of the concrete has detail. We slow. We slow. Ah, God, we're down.

Prospero One streaks over us. Low and off to our right, getting its wheels and wings cleaned up to go around and land behind us, I push forward on the power levers and use the toy-sized nose-steering wheel to make a tight turn off the runway, taxi well clear and stop with the levers back in flight idle. Crash trucks and ambulances, aflame with flashing light, crowd crying around us. I hear Saperelli open the fuselage hatch, and soon an overalled Air Force captain reaches past me and begins to shut down Prospero Two. Beyond his hairless, muscled arms I see the other plane's landing lights flash, as it turns final. My vision blurs. for a time I must look away from the Air Force captain, and Borg, and Rory, and others crowding the flight deck with their help. I touch the grey metal of the window with affection and regret, and tell my airplane, "Thank you."

Dusk turns the eastern sky indigo grey by the time we escape MacDill, the sun riding red and oblate in the haze near the horizon to the west, flashing through the windows at us as Prospero One turns to the southeast, toward Miami. Paul Wright flies as pilot; Gil

Bradenton, exhausted as I am, has the right-hand seat. We almost embraced on the ground, Bradenton and I, feeling the excitement of boys sharing blood; but, deeply Anglo and grown, we resisted, kidding one another. "You ever consider a career in aviation, Jake?"

"Only until today."

With laughter we steer around affection.

The Air Force has taken our wounded, our lame, Sam Newman to have his chest sewn up and new blood poured into his grey, leaking body, Sorel to be fitted with tubes and launched in a vat of formaldehyde, or dextrose, or something, like a hydroponic plant. One wonders why he clutches at a life that must now merely unfold outside him, like a film; but clutch he does, guided by the grand selfishness behind obsession. His eyes watched us like a petrified father's as the bluecoats littered him out of Prospero Two. Probably they watch the doctors and nurses assess his damage, the headshakers who in their hearts must wish Sorel would close those glaring sapphires and sleep forever.

We carry most of our dead. Bruska and McBride sleep in plastic body bags in the galley of Prospero One. Peterson – ah, Peterson, he roams the earth eternally. If we had been in outer space he would be hurtling still. Bruska. McBride. Peterson. Say the names a final time.

Aside from such ghosts, I sit alone in the forward pair of airliner seats we use for non-technical visitors, no head on my shoulder, no sweet odors of Rory's dark hair. At MacDill she had looked at me across the broken form of Sorel, acknowledging with shining eyes that she must stay yoked to her damaged mentor. As they moved him away, she crossed to me and said, "He doesn't have anyone, Jake."

"Ah. He has you." My voice comes out of an aching hollow within, but carries an angry, not a melancholy sound.

"It isn't a matter of loving or needing or wanting. I've just done too many selfish things." Then she said goodbye, and followed Sorel's stretcher to one of the vehicles that exploded with light around our crippled airplane.

I shake my head, driving memory away ...

And think of my other love. I called Bella from MacDill, summarized our flight in general terms, asked her to bring Charlie to the field to meet us. I think of him waiting on a streaked, rain-gleaming ramp. My heart contracts, responding to this young phantom I must love, and, yes, cleaving to what is permanent and important in my own life.

We have also left some of those we hate at MacDill. In our first hour on the ground there, the grey Navy bomber landed, popped its drag chute, then taxied toward the apron where Prospero Two had been towed; a crewman opened the hatch and ran up a dark blue flag bearing two stars. Carney had come to pay his respects. He stepped out of the bomb-bay first, followed by Ted Grose, and then by Jonas, as though, having begun all this killing and destruction with a meeting, we must now reconvene the same meeting to end it. Carney surveyed the situation quickly, one of those people who pulls everything in at a glance, like any spy, and came over. But he had also read me, registered my hatred, and so did not extend his hand in false friendliness, "Resourceful bit of flying," he told me. I gave no reply; these people must do what they do without anything more from me. "Cubans responded with, er, more vigor than expected. Sorry you had to carry the load. Could have been much worse, of course. However – it has essentially, uh, dried up the so-called Stormbat Crisis, and that was the purpose of the – experiment. So, on the whole – a successful action."

He turned away before I could, gave a faint salute and marched off toward a gathering of MacDill officials. He would spread silence and security upon the incident. If he had his way, soon our ordeal would not have happened. But he was too late. There had been too many calls to too many families. Some of Carney's state secrets had already been rendered into neighborhood gossip.

Ted Grose watched me from a distance. I shook my head at him, and he joined a cluster of lab people. But the opaque Jonas followed, chattering about my bringing the airplane back, about our death-filled day, about Cubans and Stormbats and budgetary constraints, a cloud of language so unintelligently empty, so unconnected to our hard realities, that I whirled upon this seersucker-suited man and told him to go away in a voice that scared. Then I was left alone by these minions of the national interest, to walk beneath my airplane ...

Prospero One whines softly. No rush of air. No ruined panels, no burning smell. No blood.

I think of Dolly. After talking to Bella, I'd called Chatham, who told me the Air Force flight that flew the storm behind us had found maximum winds of about a hundred fifty knots, central pressure of 930 millibars. The eye had widened to about eighteen nautical miles. Still a serious storm, but only marginally in the same category as the old Dolly – or Camille.

"There's some other, uh, interesting news," he went on. "Dolly seems to be staying just about on the centerline of the Florida Straits, centered about forty nautical south of Key West. They've got their problems, but at least they're not going underwater. We look for her to head on out into the Atlantic and turn north-east, crossing Great Abaco this time tomorrow. So they've got their hardships still ahead of them out there, but south Florida and Cuba made out nicely ..."

"Cuba," I responded, finding it hard to speak.

"Uh, I talked to Ted Grose, Jake. Everybody's just going to tough it out, on both sides, until it goes down to zero." Then, "You know, I wish I'd stepped in at the beginning."

"Jesus, Chat, none of what happened is your fault. You couldn't have stopped it anyway."

And, remembering this now, I think: whereas, I could have. I get up and walk forward, stopping at the scientist station Borg occupies. It is as though he's been teleported from one plane to the other, as though nothing happened in the hours between his being here and being there. Except one shoe is caked with blood. I am bound to him as I am to Bradenton. After the landing, we also evaded the need to embrace a friend. Now I tell him what I remember of Chatham's conversation.

Borg smiles. "Not the same storm we flew," he says.

"No one knows. That kind of fluctuation is within the natural variability of intense hurricanes."

"But rare?"

"Yes, rare."

"Why –" he said, imitating Boris Karloff, "it's as though someone *mawdified* it."

"Isn't it?" I shift my weight to leave, but change my mind, lean toward Borg. "A serious point to be made here is that the computer model didn't understand the storm as well as Henry Sorel."

"That's like saying Ahab knew his whales."

"Maybe it is. He did."

"You think it was right for him to seed the storm, given the costs?"

"No, God no. I just want to be sure you know that he knew what he was doing, scientifically. He should have been given a legitimate opportunity to run a Prospero experiment."

"You're saying that all the death and damage and fear and other shit today derives from the whims of government budget people."

"Has anyone ever told you you tend to oversimplify?"

"Not since your lady said my hypothesis was shit." He laughs, and I laugh too.

I look up the aisle at Carla Hendrix, who fidgets with the keyboard of her mission scientist station. Himmell hovered near her for the early part of the flight, but she kept to her work, leaving him idle, forcing him back to his seeding station, where he rides now, bewildered perhaps but probably not disconsolate. He was still boy enough not to be able to see the world as hard-hearted. She had deemed, it strikes me now, to avoid him at MacDill, too. I think, Maybe everyone is starting over. She catches my eye with her golden look, and we are held by this contact for a time, neutrally, with no unnatural loads between us; the mission has rinsed away extraneous material.

Bradenton says on the loudspeaker, "We're coming up on Miami, let's strap in." He no longer makes the effort to conceal his fatigue.

I return to my airliner seat and strap in. Carla follows, and asks if she can join me. I nod, happy not to be alone, resolved not to use this lady selfishly. I tell her about our hurricane. She does not respond immediately, then says. "Maybe we did some good."

"Maybe." I watch her. She wants to say something else. After another silence she does.

"I think they'll give the lab to you."

"I don't think I want it." I cannot read her. I try to look behind her pretty eyes, see her thoughts; but she has gone opaque on me. "I don't know," I add.

"What do you want?" she asks.

"I don't know." Although, what I truly want is to lay my tired, heartsick self against her, again like a drowning man hugging a rock in the sea, and cleave and cleave. "I don't know."

"If you want a lap to lie on ..."

"Ah, babe." I look at this lovely, generous girl with misted eyes. "Ah, babe." I want to say, You've had enough pain from me; and I really, really, really don't want to give you more. But I cannot force these fragments into sounds. We let things rest, then, our only signal a faint one that we will give and take some comfort. Hearing even that slight signal now, we move closer together.

Prospero One enters cloud, the skirts of our distant hurricane spinning over the southern tip of Florida; Miami is a plain of light interrupted by black scud and rain. The airplane skips through modest turbulence. The tower brings us in from the north-west, the airport appearing for a moment through the low clouds before we make the turn to an eastward final, dropping toward the light-streaked earth, into a greater darkness than the sky. We touch down, roll, and turn onto a taxiway, then trundle toward our hangar.

Grey sheets of rain sweep the wings, lightning glows around the field. Strobes and beacons taxi past us in the darkness, great insects tired of flying, or preparing to fly. Figures populate the broad arch of our hangar door, small silhouettes almost eaten away by the powerful lights within. Bella holds the slender young man's hand at one end of the group. Murchison, transfixed, merely watches us taxi up. An ambulance crouches nearby, flashless, gleaming red and cream and in the hangar lights and rain, and close to it, as though afraid of being left alone once more, the pale-haired girl McBride had married stands, bereft and streaked, her untouched face gone hollow-eyed with loss. She will ride away with the two body bags, and bury one of them. It is just as well she's there, for no one waits for Bruska; sand already fills in around his absence. I shake my thoughts away from this, and look at Charlie. He has never looked more noble, or so strong. "Look there," I say to Carla. She does, and smiles for me, wanting to appreciate this son.

Saperelli, making territory of this airplane, pops the hatch and the ground crew move the ladder in place beneath the fuselage. I hurry through it, clatter down the metal steps in the rain, run across the inch of water that floods the ramp tonight. Charlie runs to meet me. We collide in an unthinking hug. After a moment, I release him and we walk like friends into the humid, lighted cavern of the hangar. "Hi, Charlie," I murmur. "I'm glad to see you, boy."

"Hi, Daddy."

Bella comes over. "You all right, Jake?" she asks.

"Fine, I'm fine. Bella – thanks."

"We had a good time, didn't we?" she asks Charlie, as she flees my gratitude.

My boy grins. "Sure did," he says. Then, "You flew the other plane back, Dad?"

"Yep." I try to sound proud of it for him, ignoring the ghosts that live in the event. "I thought of you flying Charlie Whiskey. That's how we got back, with my thinking of you, boy." His grin broadens. My affection makes me want to cry.

Carla approaches tentatively. I introduce them. They meet warily, and Charlie turns almost immediately away, asking me, "Dad, where's Sam?"

"He's hurt," I reply, but without my mind really on Sam. Seeing my son with Carla, my mind, in a peculiar reflex goes to Lennie, alone somewhere in the city, robbed of her lover, a lost woman, whose disappointment could still touch me. I think how she will miss Charlie as he begins to spend more time with me, and wonder if that will help her expand her life, or simply add more inertia to that which nails her to the stucco and dark veneers of Pyrenees Village.

"Can we see Sam?" Charlie wants to know.

"Sure we'll go up as soon as we can, maybe Saturday."

Murchison pushes in on us, moves the others out of mind. "What happened, Jake?" he asks. "I understand you've had a bad day, but I really need to know." His face creases with blended relief and pain: he has finally had the casualties he feared; men in his charge did not return, body bags crowd the galley of one of his aircraft. The other squats on a distant ramp, too sick to fly.

I shake my head. "Murch, I've had it. Talk to Bradenton. I'll come out tomorrow sometime and we can talk." Tomorrow, I think, is Friday. Only Friday.

"Okay. Okay." Murchison wanders sorrowfully away into the rain and minor flooding on the ramp, takes up a station by the ladder, waiting for Bradenton to descend. The body bags are passed hand over hand down the ladder and carried through the rain to the ambulance, inserted through the rear door. McBride's widow trails the bags. She does not preside, but participates, one of the casualties. The door shuts, the ambulance spins away through the night, businesslike but unurgent without its noise and flashing lights.

Bradenton emerges, trots down the steep ladder, and is taken by Murchison, who walks the pilot under the wing to get out of the rain. I see the big man importuning Bradenton, Bradenton shaking his head; then more urging, a shrug – the two go into Murchison's office along the far wall of the hangar.

Borg is next. He strolls across the wet ramp with his bloody shoe and Nikon bag and damp long hair, caring nothing for the rain, as if to say, Where I have been today rain is unimportant. He comes over to me in the hangar, and we spend a moment looking into one another's eyes, searching for visible thoughts back behind the clear animation of the iris. Then he says. "That was some drill."

"Yes, it was."

"Wasn't a bad philosophical quest, either."

"I felt that. I'm glad you were along."

"Me too. But now you wonder what I'm going to write."

"I wonder, but I don't worry about it." I send out feelers within: Do I really worry down there somewhere? The answer comes back: No.

"It's a problem for me, choosing between more quest and a couple thousand word of easily forgotten prose." He pulls out his notebook and flips through to something he wants. Then he says, "You know how reporters always have a quote at their

fingertips, like the last two acts of *King Lear*? Well, I can't do
that. But I did write this down when I was getting up for the
Prospero story. Listen:

> But this rough magic
> I here abjure ...
> I'll break my staff,
> Bury it certain fathoms in the earth,
> And deeper than did ever plummet sound
> I'll drown my book.

"Know what that is?"

I shake my head. But Carla says, "That's Prospero saying
goodbye."

"That's what it is. And Sorel. And, for all I know, Steve
Borg. Let's get drunk some evening, man."

"I wouldn't mind," I reply, and take his proffered hand.
The contact is inadequate; nothing is enough, we only try, or
try too little. "So long."

"So long." He waves to us all. Carla draws in closer,
Charlie's hand steals into one of mine. We watch Borg cross
the rainswept ramp and vanish in the darkness beyond
Prospero One.